WITNESS FOR THE PERSECUTION

WITNESS FOR THE PERSECUTION

E.J. Copperman

SEVERN HOUSE

First world edition published in Great Britain and the USA in 2022
by Severn House, an imprint of Canongate Books Ltd,
14 High Street, Edinburgh EH1 1TE.

Trade paperback edition first published in Great Britain and the USA in 2022
by Severn House, an imprint of Canongate Books Ltd.

severnhouse.com

British Library Cataloguing-in-Publication Data
A CIP catalogue record for this title is available from the British Library.

ISBN-13: 978-0-7278-5076-8 (cased)
ISBN-13: 978-1-4483-0811-8 (trade paper)
ISBN-13: 978-1-4483-0810-1 (e-book)

All Severn House titles are printed on acid-free paper.

Typeset by Palimpsest Book Production Ltd.,
Falkirk, Stirlingshire, Scotland.
Printed and bound in Great Britain by
TJ Books, Padstow, Cornwall.

To the people who made the works that helped get us through
these past couple of years:
Call My Agent!
The Great British Bake Off (Great British Baking Show
on my side of the pond)
Somebody Feed Phil
The Repair Shop
Ted Lasso
You can't possibly know how much good you've done. Bravo.

PART ONE
Here

ONE

The thing about a red carpet is that it smells like a regular carpet. You think it should be different, in some way better, than an average living-room wall-to-wall, but the truth is that whoever is supposedly honoring actors, directors and assorted celebrities is less interested in the honors and more in the *perception* of them. So they go out to a rental house and get a rollable expanse of cheap rug that will stretch from the curb to the door.

This was an especially redolent one, I thought. I hadn't been on many in my life – none until six months before – but I was noticing the scent of fresh polyester (you'd think in this eco-friendly a town they'd have used natural fibers, or better, nothing) more than I had before.

It was hardly the only thing assaulting my senses. Being a 'plus one' here affords a person the chance to take in the experience more than the star or wannabe-star attracting attention from the 'press' in the area, the fans lining the streets for a glimpse and the relentless, nova-bright lights.

I looked over at Patrick McNabb to my right, holding my hand and leading – I'm sure Patrick would say 'leading' and not 'dragging', which is more what it felt like – me toward the interview area, where we would stop and Patrick would speak about what a privilege it had been for him to work on *Desert Siege*, in which my boyfriend (although he hadn't been that when the movie was shot) played a two-fisted research sociologist who stumbles across neo-Nazis in the Arizona desert and has to stop them from . . . doing something I had never understood despite having seen the movie twice. Maybe at the screening tonight, which would constitute Viewing #3, I'd pick up the subtle nuances I'd missed the first two times.

'McNabb!' 'Patrick!' 'Hey, Pat!' The photographers lining the runway were doing their collective best to get Patrick looking in their direction, ideally in the midst of a remarkably unflattering facial expression. As the 'arm candy' (although I felt I was more like 'arm brussels sprouts') I could be assured my 'look', which had taken two solid hours to achieve despite my best efforts to sabotage it, would appear to be an attempt to look as much like a raccoon as possible if it ever appeared in print or pixel.

Patrick was practiced enough to ignore their shouts. His eyes were fixed on the woman standing about twenty yards from us. The one holding a microphone.

The one with the light in front of her and the TV camera trained at her upper body, which was impressive. But I'm sure they managed to get her face in the shot as well, just for balance.

'We'll get this done and then we can go inside and relax,' he said in my ear as his grip on my right hand tightened. I'd seen him at these things before. Patrick's idea of *relax* and mine were clearly two different things. But I nodded dutifully. Because this whole evening was going to be about duty. I was a dutiful girlfriend, and nobody was going to deny that.

We walked toward the woman, whose name I'm sure I was supposed to know, and her already incandescent smile brightened to blinding when she noticed Patrick approaching. Patrick is a handsome man and a commanding presence, but my guess was she knew she was going to get a good interview and, if she could, get exposure outside the Los Angeles area. Everyone comes to LA to get noticed and then wants to get noticed everywhere except in LA.

I'd been here a little under two years and I'd been paying puzzled attention.

Just as Patrick reached the TV woman and let go of my hand (which was a relief to my fingers), I heard someone behind me shout, 'Hey Sandy!'

It's my natural inclination when hearing my name shouted to assume either that I have done something terribly wrong or, as in this case, that someone else named Sandy was nearby and surely the person calling out meant them. So I kept walking, just to Patrick's left but out of camera range, because there was surely no one watching whatever infotainment show this was who would know or care who the hell I was.

The women watching would resent me for being with Patrick and the men would likely be more interested in the reporter's upper body, which had been getting so much well-deserved attention.

'Sandy!' the call came again and instinctively I turned. The man calling out was holding a sheaf of papers and approaching me faster than I thought was appropriate in such a public place. I have been lunged at before, more often than I cared to think about, by people with the intent of doing me harm. I flinched a little.

Behind me I heard Patrick saying, '. . . such a layered, complex character. It was a privilege . . .'

Before I could think of a way to escape without damaging Patrick's moment the man, wiping sweat from his brow (welcome to Southern California), extended the sheaf of what I could tell now were legal documents. 'Sandy!' he shouted again.

Patrick turned to look over his shoulder at me. His expression was either annoyed or concerned but I didn't get a long enough look to determine which before the sweating man reached me and said, 'What about the Langhorne case?'

The Langhorne case? What did that have to do with *Desert Siege*? 'The Langhorne case!' the moist little guy said again. 'You're behind!'

Now Patrick was next to me. 'What about 'er behind?' His accent always reverted to Cockney when he was angry. I thought it was charming but Patrick believed it to be coarse and did his best to conceal it when he had control of himself, which was almost all the time.

'You're behind on the case!' This guy was so melodramatic he could have been an actor on the British soap opera in which Patrick told me he'd made his first big break seven years earlier. This man would not play one of the romantic leads. He'd be the doctor nobody wanted to get at the hospital, or a delivery guy who never let go of his bike.

'A little, but I can get on it tomorrow,' I said. My voice was getting lost in the tumult around me. 'Why are you here?'

'The Langhorne case!' he hollered again.

'Let her *go*!' Patrick demanded, despite the man not touching me at all. I'd never seen Patrick look like this before, except when he was acting and about to 'hit' someone.

'Patrick,' I said. 'This man is talking to me about a case.'

'The Langhorne case!' What was the point, really?

'Get away from her or I'll kill you,' Patrick said quietly but with malice in his voice.

'Patrick!' I said.

But it was too late. Patrick leapt at the little perspiring man and had him on the red carpet in seconds. Photographers swarmed around them while I tried desperately to pull my suddenly volatile boyfriend away, already calculating the irreparable damage done to his career and, in my lawyer's mind, estimating what charges the police might bring when they inevitably arrived.

And man, did that carpet smell bad.

'Sandy,' Patrick said, snapping his fingers in front of my face, 'it's me, Patrick. You're completely ignoring your sandwich.'

I shook myself back to reality. 'I'm sorry,' I said. 'I was just daydreaming for a second.'

Patrick smiled that irresistible little grin that the camera adored and I knew was him hiding his concern. 'More like having a daymare,' he said. 'What were you thinking about?'

Could I say I'd been living a nightmare scenario of his movie premiere in my head? Patrick knew it was part of his job, but he labored under the delusion that I found all the glitter intoxicating like my best friend (and Patrick's executive assistant) Angie does. I find it pretty distasteful, to tell the truth. Or couldn't you tell?

'Just something from work,' I said. 'The Langhorne case.'

Now Patrick's smile, with a touch of regret in it, was sincere. 'Sandy, my love. If you don't want to go to the premiere, you can just say that. It's months until the thing and you're already in a state about it.'

'It's not that I don't want to go,' I answered. 'It's more in the area that you knew what I was thinking about that scares me.'

'I'm an actor, darling. I observe.'

I chose not to think too hard about that.

We were sitting in Patrick's kitchen, an expanse in which my entire apartment could fit, having what he called 'a casual lunch'. The fact that it had been served by a staff of two sort of contradicted that description, but there was no arguing with Patrick. Ever. There just wasn't much point to it. I'd learned through hundreds of attempts.

'Don't think that I don't want to be with you,' I told Patrick. 'I just always feel so out of place at those things, and I'm afraid of embarrassing you and ending your career.'

Patrick's laugh is one of the things I love about him. It's unforced and delighted, like a child's laugh but with so much more insight behind it. So when he came within inches of roaring now, it only bothered me a little bit.

'Oh Sandy,' he said when he could catch his breath, 'you truly do make me see things differently. Why don't you m—'

Patrick had asked me to marry him seven times since the historic first attempt on the floor of the Glendale courthouse. It had gotten to be such a habit that I'd had to impose a strict ban on proposals. I raised a finger to the ceiling and he caught himself. 'Move in with me.'

Now that was a new one! 'Move in here?' I said. It wasn't like I didn't know this was Patrick's house and that was what he'd meant. I was buying myself time because some knee-jerk impulse in my brain (if brains have knees) was telling me to say no.

'I think there's probably enough room,' Patrick said with the desired twinkle in his eye. Patrick does a hell of a twinkle.

'There's enough room for the 101st Airborne Division,' I said. 'The room isn't the point.'

Patrick let out a long breath and tossed his (yes, cloth) napkin on to the table. 'What is the point, Sandy?' he asked.

Could I go back to the daydream about the suffocating red carpet? 'Look, it's not that I hate the idea.'

'Oh, that's very encouraging.' Patrick was rarely moody and almost never petulant, but hey, I have a way with men. 'Your not-loathing the idea of living with me really makes my day.'

I stood and walked over to him and took his face in my hands. 'I'm sorry,' I said. 'That wasn't how I meant it to sound. But it's a big decision and we shouldn't just rush into it because

I did or didn't want to go to your premiere.' Before I moved to LA I wouldn't have known what a red-carpet premiere was, let alone dreamed of attending one.

When I'd first met Patrick, I didn't know he was a very famous television and occasional film actor. I wasn't much into popular culture like Angie is. I knew Patrick as the first client I'd met at Seaton, Taylor, Evans and Bach (now Seaton, Taylor, Evans and Wentworth and good riddance to Bach), a family law firm with which I'd recently accepted a job so I could get away from the criminal law I was practicing as an assistant county prosecutor in New Jersey. Then Patrick was charged with murder, I became his lawyer, and the whole not-practicing-criminal-law thing pretty much flew out the window.

Having now spent some time in Patrick's orbit, I knew some more entertainment industry terms that I never would have been familiar with before. I still didn't know how anything worked or what a 'best boy' was, but I did know about red carpets and how they smell.

'I told you,' Patrick said. 'You don't have to go to the premiere if you don't want to. I thought you'd find it fun.'

'I know.' I nodded to prove that I knew. It's a futile gesture, but I'm really good at those. 'Hesitating about moving in here is not about the red carpet.'

'Then what's it about?' Patrick asked.

I hugged him because I didn't know the answer and my cell phone rescued me by ringing. I dug it out of the front pocket of my jeans. You'll never catch me butt-dialing someone. I thigh-dial them.

The Caller ID showed Holiday Wentworth was on the line. Since Holly is my boss, I figured it was probably a good idea to take the call. And I could put off continuing this conversation with Patrick.

'What's up, Holly?' I asked, trying to sound like it must be an emergency, when I knew it was probably Holly calling to ask about the Langhorne case, which was actually a pretty simple child-custody matter that was probably never going to see the inside of a courtroom. I just had to find a way to make my client, a well-known talent agent, not act like a jerk.

Not that he was acting.

'I need you to come in.' Holly sounded like it might actually be an emergency. What some people think are emergencies in a family law firm are . . . well, I could tell you stories from New Jersey that would curl your hair. Seriously, if you're thinking of getting a perm, call me up and ask about the small-time weed dealer (before New Jersey legalized) and the melon baller.

'It's Saturday,' I told Holly. 'What's so urgent?'

'We have a client who's been accused of murder,' Holly said.

And I swear the first thought I had was, *Great! Now I don't have to argue with Patrick!*

TWO

'We created the criminal law division specifically for you,' Holly reminded me.

'And you'll recall that I resisted the idea from the beginning,' I reminded her back.

We were walking through one of the interminable corridors at Seaton, Taylor, heading for one of the consultation rooms. I'd been working here for nearly two years and would still have benefitted greatly from a map of the offices.

At least the carpet wasn't red.

'You successfully defended two murder trials,' she said, as if I didn't know that. 'We started getting phone calls about more criminal cases and you and Jon were the only attorneys we had with any experience in that area.' Soon she'd no doubt start reading my CV aloud to me just so she could hit the highlights. I love Holly, but she's such a *boss*. 'We weren't going to pass up the opportunity. Besides, I think you actually like these cases.'

Seriously, if we didn't reach this conference room soon I'd need to stop in at a local bed-and-breakfast for the night. 'I like the cases where I get to defend people in their right to peaceful protest, or a woman protecting her children from an abusive partner,' I countered. 'Murder trials have too much on the line and they make my stomach clench. Can't Jon do it?' Jon Irvin, the only other attorney working in the (part-time) criminal justice section of Seaton, Taylor, had no prosecutorial experience, which I considered a plus. We were working on the other side.

'The client asked specifically for you,' Holly said as we stopped at a door. I caught my breath; this was the longest I'd walked in heels since my senior prom. 'He'd been referred.'

'By whom?' I didn't have enough former clients in LA to be referred.

Holly shrugged. 'He didn't say.' She reached for the doorknob.

'Didn't or wouldn't?' But it was too late. Holly had opened the door and we were stepping inside.

This was one of our small conference rooms, which made sense for a group that was going to consist of the client, me and Holly. I did my best not to look like I'd rather be pretty much anywhere else – except answering Patrick about moving in with him – and approached the man, who stood when he saw us enter.

'Sandy Moss, meet Robert Reeves,' Holly said.

Reeves wasn't especially tall, but it was clear from the way he stood that he thought he was. His shoulders were back, his gut was pulled in, and he looked for all the world like a man trying to be better than he really was, which was in its own way sad.

'Mr Reeves,' I said. I nodded a greeting toward him. I haven't actually gotten back to the handshake thing yet, but that's just me. Before he could offer one I sat down at the table and Reeves did the same. Holly stood next to the chair to my left.

'Suppose I leave you in Sandy's hands, Robert,' she said. 'She's really much more experienced at this sort of thing than anyone else here at the firm.'

Holly hadn't mentioned that she wouldn't be staying for the conference, which was sneaky on her part because she knew I'd insist that she stay so she'd be there when I politely declined the case based on my overextended workload. I chalked that up to being outplayed and decided I'd expense out some lunches on the company card just to show her. Maybe with Patrick and Angie.

The fact that such things were not considered breaches of the practice's rules was no comfort at all. Nobody ever checked. It was amazing we were still a functioning business.

I looked up at her and gave her a look Reeves couldn't see. She smiled pleasantly because he *could* see her and left the room.

Holly had given me the thin file we'd gotten on Reeves's arrest when I'd arrived at the office, and I'd been able to give it a perfunctory glance while we were hiking it down the Lack of Freedom Trail to this conference room. Apparently Reeves worked on a film set (of course) and, in the midst of filming, a stunt performer had died. What made Reeves responsible and why this was not seen simply as a tragic accident, I had not yet been able to grasp. I opened the file and laid it out in front of me then looked up at Reeves.

'So, Mr Reeves, please keep in mind that I'm new to your case so you might have to explain some things to me that you've already told to the police and to . . . you're awaiting trial, so I assume you had an attorney before you contacted us who worked with you through your arraignment.'

Reeves, sitting straight up in his chair with an aura of authority (which was clearly assumed, although I had no idea why), nodded his agreement, but his mouth twisted into a sneer that I hoped was aimed at his previous lawyer and not me. 'Yes,' he said. 'Herbert Bronson. And all he did for me was suggest that I take a plea deal. He thought I was guilty.'

Uh-oh.

'You've been charged with first-degree murder, Mr Reeves,' I said. Of course he knew that but hang on, I was making a point. 'That implies premeditation. Did you have any reason to want Mr . . .' I checked the file in front of me. 'Mr Drake dead?'

'Absolutely not,' Reeves answered, at the same time he was not suggesting that I call him Bob, Rob, Robbie, Bobby or even Robert (with the French pronunciation). 'I barely knew the man. He was a stunt guy on my set.'

His set.

'What was your job on the set?' I asked.

Reeves's eyes bulged a little bit at my blatant impertinence, but he regained his composure quickly. 'I am the *director*,' he answered.

That explained a lot. I'd been in Los Angeles and, more importantly, with Patrick long enough now that I'd met a few directors. They tend to have fairly healthy egos (sometimes bigger than those of their actors, which is impressive) when they direct film. Television directors lean toward the unassuming sorts, knowing their jobs are temporary and hoping they'll be rehired for another episode later in the season. Reeves was clearly accustomed to a pretty high level of deference. And I wasn't supplying it, because first of all I had no idea who he was and second, I don't think directors are better than other people. Some of them are fine artists, but so are some short-order cooks.

'OK, so you were directing a scene and, as far as I can tell, a stunt performer fell from a crane and was killed, is that right?' Best to get past Reeves's issue with my having never heard of him, which was something I'd gotten used to since moving to California. I hadn't heard of Patrick when I met him, either, but in the almost two years since then he'd mostly gotten over that fact.

'Yes.' Either Reeves was auditioning for his testimony in court, or he was still mad at me for being ignorant of his amazing-ness.

I looked through more of the file, which was astonishingly thin given that another defense attorney had been through it, the police report was included (bearing a name familiar to me) and an arraignment and release (cash bail no longer exists in California) had already taken place. I'd have to give all of this a long look as soon as the meeting was over. 'That doesn't sound like a case of first-degree murder to me,' I said.

'Exactly!' Reeves leaned forward and placed his hands flat on the table in front of him. He appeared to be acting as if I was on an award-nominating committee. Which I feel it's important to emphasize I am not. 'That's what I've been saying this whole time! It was an accident!'

I didn't point out that what I'd been about to say was, 'It sounds like negligent homicide.' That probably would have dampened my client's mood. 'So why did the police and the district attorney think charges should be brought?' The question was more for myself than Reeves; for all I knew he possessed a law degree and had obnoxious-ed his way into having the charge escalated, but I doubted it. The part about the law degree, anyway.

'You'd have to ask them,' he said, shaking his head. 'I didn't have anything to do with it.'

'Well, let me play devil's advocate for a moment,' I said, looking back at him. 'Obviously there's some basis or the DA and the cops wouldn't have arrested you. When did this happen?'

'Nine months ago,' Reeves answered. 'The film is going to open in a few months and this was when we were shooting it. I got out of jail the morning after they arrested me, and Bronson has been hacking around at it since then. The imbecile.'

'All right. So here's me making the prosecution's case, OK? This isn't what I think; it's what they're going to say. So let's see how you'll answer.' I paused, waiting to see Reeves's reaction.

He just looked at me, arms folded. He didn't speak, but if he had I'm sure it would have been, 'Bring it on.'

So I brought it on. 'As the director of this large production, isn't it your responsibility to see that a dangerous stunt like this is carried out safely? Why did James Drake fall and die?'

'Because the stunt coordinator was incompetent. *He's* the one who should have been arrested.'

One thing I had noticed on the film and television sets Patrick had invited me to was that stunt coordinators were pretty much never women. But that was another observation I choked back in order to keep the business of a man who had been charged with murder in what I could only assume was an odd game where I had to figure out why.

'What did the stunt coordinator – and what's his name? – do that created the situation where Mr Drake died?' I asked.

'Burke Henderson, the stunt coordinator, did not see properly to the cables that were holding up the unfortunate Mr Drake, and so they snapped and he fell to his death.' Reeves huffed and settled back in his chair. He folded his arms. He wanted to come across as indignant and couldn't muster up more than petulant.

'Mr Reeves, I'm going to need to do some research on your case before I can advise you on your next steps,' I said, closing the file just to give him a sign that our meeting was about to end. There was way too much I didn't know yet that I could find out quickly on my own. 'I just came into your case a few minutes ago and I have to do my work. Let's say we meet again in about two weeks and then we can plot a strategy once I have all the information I need.'

Reeves looked stunned; he blinked like an actress whose false eyelashes were glued on badly. 'Two weeks?' he said. 'I don't think we can afford two weeks.'

'Why not?' They tell you in law school never to ask a question to which you don't know the answer, but that's only supposed to matter in the courtroom. Still I had the feeling I'd just taken a step into something that might require me to throw out my shoes altogether.

'Won't you have to prepare a whole case and ask for witnesses and all that?' His haughty demeanor was cracking, which meant Reeves was starting to panic.

'Yes I will, but I assure you I've done this before.'

'But the trial is scheduled to start six weeks from tomorrow,' he said.

OK, but . . . *wait, what?* 'Six weeks.' I tried not to make it a question. 'Well, the first thing I'll do is file for an adjournment.' I'd had bad luck with that on Patrick's trial, but that was an aberration. Any judge other than Franklin would have allowed it, and even that wasn't his fault. It's a long story. It involves a guy I was sort of dating. Suffice it to say.

'What does that mean?' Clearly Reeves had never directed a courtroom drama.

'It means we'll get an extension of time before the trial can start,' I said. 'The judge will understand that you changed attorneys recently and he or she will give me time to prepare. Which judge heard your preliminary hearing?'

'Judge Hoffman,' he said. 'But the judge who's hearing the trial is named Franklin.'

Well, that figured.

THREE

'It wasn't Franklin's fault,' Angie said.

We were eating at our apartment for a change. I had been spending a lot of time at Patrick's house, but now I wanted to be with my roommate, my best friend, my companion, the woman who had moved herself 3,000 miles just to watch out for me. You don't see that kind of loyalty and devotion in the vast majority of people, and I felt it was more than due time that I showed Angie some appreciation.

OK, so I wanted to give myself time to think before I continued the conversation with Patrick. So sue me.

'I know Judge Franklin never saw the request for an adjournment on Patrick's trial,' I told her. I put my feet up on the coffee table and lost myself in the sofa cushion. Sweatpants and an old T-shirt felt good. 'But I didn't find that out until much later and I'd already decided I resented him.'

'What I'm saying is that there's no reason to carry that over to this guy's trial.' Angie was doing pushups and planks on the floor because she's Angie and wants to be both strong and sexy. I can't personally attest to the latter, but I've seen men look at her and I know she can lift heavy objects and throw a very effective punch. I've seen it. You don't want to. 'In the end, the judge was completely fair.'

I hate it when she's right.

The doorbell rang and there was a guy with the pad thai we'd ordered and which, frankly, I'd kind of forgotten about. But it gave me a good way to get out of the conversation because I knew I was going to lose.

'Patrick wants me to move in with him,' I told Angie when we'd settled in and started eating (turned out I did want the Thai food after all). I watched her face carefully as I told her to gauge her reaction. Angie has always thought that Patrick and I were destined for each other and does nothing but advocate on his behalf.

So it startled me a bit to see her frown when I said that. 'Are you gonna do it?' she asked, revealing nothing in her voice.

'Why? Do you think I shouldn't?' Any argument Angie offered would be helpful. I felt deep in my gut that I should tell Patrick it was too soon (it wasn't) or that I wasn't sure I loved him (that wasn't going to fly), so an alternate excuse would be useful.

Why didn't I want to move in with Patrick? That was something I'd need to think about later for sure. Because on paper it was absolutely the right move. My mother called twice a week to see if Patrick and I were getting married 'yet'. Patrick would probably have agreed with her. I was the stick in the mud. Why?

Later.

'Well for one thing, that would leave me without a place to live, unless I'm coming as your valet.' Angie had a point. She couldn't afford the rent in this place on her own even though Patrick paid her nicely. I don't know if you've heard, but Los Angeles (or in our case, Burbank) was not an inexpensive place to call home.

'There's enough rooms. You could probably have your own wing.' For one demented second, the idea of bringing Angie along to live in Patrick's ginormous house felt logical.

'Great,' she said, dropping her fork (we weren't using chopsticks because who are we impressing?). 'I can be installed as the permanent fifth wheel at Patrick's house. It's not like I don't see him all day everyday anyway.' There had been a time when spending five minutes with Patrick McNabb was essentially Angie's idea of heaven. She still loved him and was still in awe to an extent, but as his assistant she had normalized him. He was now Patrick, the guy she worked for who dated her roommate.

Probably her moving in with us was a bad idea.

'I was joking,' I said.

'Sure you were.'

Neither of us ate anything for a full minute. 'What do you think I should do, Ang? I mean, Patrick's never been anything but wonderful to me, whenever he wasn't driving me crazy and even sometimes when he was. How come I'm not jumping at the chance to live with him?'

Angie is my conscience. She's my level. She tells me the truth when no one else is willing or able to find it. 'I dunno,' she said.

So that was a huge help.

'Come on,' I said. 'The last thing I need right now is for you to hold back because you're afraid to hurt my feelings.'

Angie's lips moved left into something approaching a sneer. 'I'm not afraid of hurting your feelings. I'm afraid you're going to snitch on me to my boss.'

Snitch on her? 'Do you know something about Patrick that I need to know?' Was he seeing someone else on the side? Would I be hurt or relieved? *Hurt.*

'Nothing you don't know. You said it yourself, Sand. Patrick is all about the pursuit. He goes after a woman he wants to fall in love with him, and then once she does, well, he still likes her well enough but he's not as passionate about her as he used to be. It was true when he got married and it was true with that nutjob he was going to marry last year before you talked him out of it.'

'Yeah and look how well that worked out.' Patrick's most recent fiancée was currently awaiting trial on charges of attempted murder, conspiracy, and a few things the Los Angeles County District Attorney's office had thrown in for a laugh.

'I'm just saying.' Angie stood up and repackaged her food for storage in the fridge, just as I was about to do. Neither of us felt like eating anymore. 'You're skittish because you're afraid that once he knows he has you, he won't want you anymore.'

Like I said. I hate it when she's right.

FOUR

Detective Lieutenant K.C. Trench was the most composed man I had ever met. Despite having seen a broad array of horrors as a homicide detective in a city of four million people, he was as stoic as Mr Spock and three times as logical. So it was no surprise when I knocked on his office door and the response was simply, 'Yes.'

Somehow it had also not shocked me to find Trench's name as the arresting officer and lead investigator in the James Drake murder, which the police report (which I had read over the weekend) had been clear to note was in fact a homicide and not an accident. Since I knew Trench relatively well and had met Reeves once, I was inclined to put more weight in Trench's version of the events than in my client's. Or was that wrong?

'Ms Moss,' he said simply when I walked in. It was like he'd been expecting me, but not that he'd been especially thrilled with the prospect. Trench and I have a mutual admiration. I consider him to be an exceptionally good and fair police detective and he thinks I'm something of a nuisance but a decent lawyer. So perhaps 'mutual admiration' was a bit of a stretch.

'Lieutenant, I have worked on three homicide cases since I moved here and you have been involved in all three,' I said. Best to disarm him with attitude, something which comes genetically to a Jersey girl. 'Do you get all the murder cases in Los Angeles?'

'Just the ones on which you are the defense attorney,' he countered. 'The rest of the time I occupy myself with handing out jaywalking tickets and rescuing kittens from tree limbs. Which of my cases has brought you here today?' He gestured vaguely that I should sit down, which I took to be a sign of reluctance because Trench never does anything vaguely when he cares about it.

I sat down.

'The charges against Robert Reeves in the death of James Drake.'

Trench did not have to refer to notes or even consult his computer screen, which was out of my view but was probably activating a screen saver displaying crime-scene photographs of his past cases. Trench, in my mind, did not exist outside a murder investigation. Maybe not in his mind, either. 'The director who murdered his stunt performer,' he said.

'Allegedly murdered his stunt performer,' I corrected.

Trench waved a hand casually, palm toward himself. 'Allegedly, of course.'

'So exactly how is this a homicide and not an extremely unfortunate accident?' I asked. 'The stunt was set up and the cables broke. My client believes that he did everything possible to keep the performer safe. Why do you think that's not true?'

If Trench were the type to allow himself a rueful smile, this would have been the moment. One of the things I like about him is that he is not that type. 'Ms Moss, how many of your clients tell you they are innocent of the charges brought against them?'

'All of them,' I admitted.

'And how many of them are convicted?' he continued.

I had a hole card to play. 'In Los Angeles murder cases, none.'

'None so far.'

I tipped my head in his direction. 'So far,' I agreed. 'And yes, Lieutenant, I did notice that you haven't answered my question.'

'So far.'

Why was Trench being cagey? 'Are you confident in your facts?' I asked him. 'Are you concerned that maybe you arrested the wrong guy?'

'Ms Moss, in this case I believe your streak of wins is in serious danger. The *facts* are as follows: Your client devised an unnecessarily dangerous stunt for this man to perform. He overlooked several ways in which it could have been made infinitely safer, including the possibility that it might have been done digitally and therefore would pose no threat to the victim at all. He had access to the cables holding Mr Drake at the very point where they were severed, including times when no one was on the set but him. We have witnesses who tell us the accused had mentioned despising the victim before he was killed. There are no other people of whom all those facts are true. So you tell me: Why do you think, other than listening to the word of a man facing a lifetime in prison, that your client did *not* murder James Drake?'

At that moment I was very glad I had personally filed a request for an adjournment with Judge Franklin that very morning. I was going to need as much time as I could get.

'Because my client had no motive. He barely knew James Drake and didn't have any reason to want to see him dead.' Beat that, Trench. 'You and I both know he's a big jerk, but that doesn't make him guilty of murder.'

In a bad movie, Trench would have picked up a paper clip from his desk and unbent it to show that he was a man of great complexity and possibly sinister intent. In real life, however, his desk was so neat that a paper clip would by comparison have looked like someone had dumped toxic waste on Trench's blotter and caused an emergency call to people in hazmat suits. He just sat there and looked at me.

'Perhaps you'd best have another conference with your client,' he suggested in that soft, consistently modulated voice. 'Mr Reeves appears to have left a few details out of the story he told you.'

'Like what?' I asked. Sometimes with men you have to set them up in order to get the information you need. (Although, to be fair, they'd probably use the same trick on their male friends when they have some enjoyable information to share.)

'Like the fact that James Drake was having an affair with Robert Reeves's new wife,' Trench answered. 'That provides a decent amount of motive, wouldn't you say?'

The key here was to avoid looking like I'd just been blind-sided and stunned. 'My client says that was just a rumor and that his marriage is completely happy,' I said. I was sure that's what Reeves *would* have said if I had realized that was a question I should have been asking.

'It is a rumor that was substantiated by three other witnesses, including Reeves's new wife,' Trench said. He was polite enough not to point out that he knew I had been lying.

The best defense, despite the popular football saying, is often to pivot and change the subject. 'The incident report filed at the time doesn't list the implement you think Reeves used to sever the cables,' I said. 'Didn't you have it at the time? Why am I not seeing it listed in any of the paperwork I have?'

Any slight sense of smug enjoyment Trench had been exhibiting was immediately gone. He straightened up even more in his seat, making me wonder if the last electric chair used to execute prisoners had been installed in Trench's office. But I knew California had never used the electric chair. So it was simply a sign that perhaps the lieutenant was . . . what? Embarrassed? Had the LAPD screwed up this investigation?

'The cables were severed and we aren't sure how that was done yet,' he said. Trench was avoiding eye contact. 'As of yet the precise implement, which was used to cut through the cables almost to the point that they were severed before the stunt performer was hoisted up, has not yet been recovered.'

I rewound the conversation in my mind. 'But you said my client had access to the implement.'

'He did. As the director he had access to every piece of equipment on the set.'

'My client is a man of many . . .' What was a polite way of saying 'lies'? '. . . layers.' That wasn't really the same thing.

'You are arguing this case with considerably less passion than the previous two, Ms Moss. Is it possible you're not as certain about your client's innocence this time?'

'You're being cagey, Lieutenant, and you're not a cagey guy. It bothers you that you can't produce, or even completely identify, the thing that you say caused James Drake's death, and yet you're hanging the charges on the idea that only Robert Reeves could have sawn through those cables. You know perfectly well how flimsy that reasoning is.'

Trench did make eye contact now. 'As an *attorney*, Ms Moss, you are certainly aware that the police do not bring charges. The district attorney does. And this district attorney took the evidence to a grand jury, which brought an indictment. I suggest you take any criticisms you have of the process to that office and not mine.'

'James Drake has been dead for more than six months,' I said. 'There doesn't seem to be a really great chance that you guys will stumble on the weapon now. The set was struck a long time ago. You can be pretty sure it's not there anymore.'

'Thank you for pointing that out to me, Ms Moss. Now if you don't mind, I have other cases to investigate.'

'So you were lying about the kittens in trees?'

'Goodbye, Ms Moss.' Trench literally showed me the door, but that was unnecessary. I already knew where it was.

FIVE

Calls to the numbers I had for Robert Reeves went straight to voicemail and were not returned for the rest of the day. When I finally got his assistant, a young woman (naturally) named Penny, on the phone, she informed me that, 'Mr Reeves is in a meeting about his next project and can't be called out.' I suggested that his next project might be postponed until Mr Reeves was released from his lifetime sentence in jail and she didn't miss a beat, saying she'd be sure he got back to me as soon as he possibly could.

'You won't hear from him if it's up to him,' Patrick told me that night. 'I've worked with Reeves and, even among directors, he's the most arrogant man I've ever met.'

I was in the office of Patrick's production company, Dunwoody Inc. (named for Patrick of course, since that was his name before he and various managers, agents and studio executives decided 'McNabb' was the ticket to success. And now he had great success, so who am I to argue?), which was closer to a private apartment than a real place of business. There was an office and a reception area, and Patrick had a corner of the place, located on the studio lot that his television series *Torn* was currently calling home, which served as his business office. But if you exited that room through the wrong door (or the right one, depending on one's perspective), you'd find yourself in a very well-appointed apartment including a working kitchen, a home theater, a bedroom – because Patrick would often sleep here during the series production schedule – and a dining room, where we were currently having a glass of wine in anticipation of pizza. All good things in life come from pizza.

Angie, having officially completed her day as Patrick's executive assistant, was having a beer and sitting across from me. She liked to beam at Patrick and me since she was living under the delusion that she was the reason we were together now. She, and if you're reading this, Angie, I apologize, wasn't.

'When did you work with Reeves?' I asked him. This was the first time I'd seen Patrick in person since taking the Reeves case, which for the official record I had tried to pawn off on Jon Irvin but the client absolutely refused to accept anyone but me as his attorney.

'You really don't pay attention to the movies, do you?' he said, smiling and shaking his head at my oddity.

'She doesn't know her Spielberg from her Michael Bay,' Angie volunteered. My best friend, ladies and gentlemen.

Patrick stood up because we had finished the bottle of wine and the next one was in a fridge across the room. 'Robert Reeves directed *Desert Siege*, love,' he said to me. 'So that means I was working with him nine or ten months ago.'

Nine months . . . wait. 'So hang on. You were working with Robert Reeves nine months ago? The movie that James Drake died on was the one I don't want to go to the premiere of?'

'See? She can do math,' Angie said. She might not have been on her first beer.

I shook that off. 'So you were on the set when the stuntman fell off the crane into a ravine and died?' I said to Patrick.

He uncorked the new bottle and poured me some, despite my having not asked. Still, I wanted the wine, so why should I argue? 'No, no,' Patrick said. 'I wasn't even on set that week, I don't think. I had finished my location work on the movie

in Tunisia for the most part, and did only indoor scenes on
an actual soundstage after that. I was probably back on the
set of *Torn* by then.'

'But you know Robert Reeves. Did you know James Drake?'

Patrick sat down and relaxed into his chair. He thought
we were just discussing an interesting coincidence, while I
was finding what might easily be a reason to remove myself
from the case entirely. This was a brewing conflict of interest
if the man I was dating was the star of the movie being filmed
when the murder – if that's what it was – happened.

'Jimmy? Oh yeah, I knew Jimmy. A tragedy that he died,
truly. He was a big rough-and-tumble kind of guy, but very
sensitive when you got to know him.' Swell. I could ask the
man who wanted me to move in with him to be a character
witness for the victim at a murder trial in which I was
representing the man accused of the crime, who had been
his director on that very movie. This day was getting better
and better.

I put down my wine glass and wished I'd stopped at one
glass. I needed to think clearly. 'I have to get myself off this
case,' I said. I hadn't meant to say it, but that was the second
glass of wine talking.

'Why?' Angie asked. 'If this Reeves guy didn't do it, don't
you want to defend him?' Angie lives in the world of filmed
entertainment, where lawyers take cases because they have
a sacred duty to defend the innocent and uncover the truth.
Patrick, who used to play a lawyer on television and now
was playing a private detective with multiple personality
disorder, tends to see things the same way. They both have
jobs they do for money, but they think I work for a higher
purpose.

'That's not the point. I'm dating the star of the movie
where it happened. He knows the defendant. He knew the
victim. That's a clear conflict of interest, and I need to alert
the judge that I have to withdraw from the case. I'm not even
sure if Jon can take it, given how closely we work together.'
Scenarios ranging from the judge scolding me to my
spending time in jail for contempt were racing through
my brain and I wasn't enjoying any of them.

'I don't see why,' Patrick chimed in. He was his usual relaxed, jovial self. Usually I really loved that about him. Not now. I felt like he should have realized how I felt and supported me. After all, he used to play a lawyer on TV. (Yeah, I'm a hypocrite.) 'I'm not a witness to the crime. The police didn't even question me because they knew I hadn't been there for days.'

'Really? Lieutenant Trench didn't talk to you after the, I'm gonna call it, accident?' That was very un-Trench-like.

Angie rolled her eyes. 'Lieutenant Trench,' she said, and put her head down on the table. Next to three empty beer bottles.

What were my options? First, I had to talk to Holly Wentworth. She'd need to know about this. After all, Reeves was a very well-paying client who had insisted on me and only me to defend him in court, and . . .

No.

'Patrick,' I said carefully, 'have you spoken to Robert Reeves since all this happened? At all?'

'I'm sure I called him after I heard what had happened,' he answered. 'You know, how awful and all that. I called Jimmy's mum, I remember that. Awfully nice woman. She was devastated, of course.' He stared off into the middle distance, which I knew was one of his acting go-tos. He probably couldn't remember the conversation at all and felt bad about that.

'And you haven't spoken to Reeves recently?' I braced myself because somehow I knew what was coming.

Patrick looked away and that was all I needed to see.

'You gave him my phone number, didn't you?' I said. I heard my voice rising in pitch and volume. 'Somehow you found out he didn't like the attorney he was working with, and you parachuted in and suggested he give your girlfriend a call, right?'

Patrick actually looked a little sheepish. 'I thought I was doing you a favor, bringing in a new client.'

'I have *got* to get off this case!' I reached for my phone to call Holly just as it rang.

Sure enough, the caller was Robert Reeves.

'Seriously, you can't interrupt me when I'm in serious

negotiations for a new project,' he began. Some people start with, 'hello', but this was Hollywood.

'Mr Reeves, I'm trying to keep you out of jail and I have very little time and a large number of questions. I will feel free to call you whenever I see fit and I will expect you to answer me every single time because you know that I'm your best defense' (literally) 'against a life sentence. Are we clear on that?'

Patrick, grinning, mimed applause. Angie kept her head on the table but, lady that she is, did not snore. I turned away from both of them because I had to be Professional Sandy right now and they weren't helping.

Even Reeves, who seemed to be an ego in pants – if that's not redundant – appeared impressed. 'Very well. What do you need from me?' Who says *very well*?

'I need to know why you didn't tell me that your wife was having an affair with James Drake at the time he was killed,' I said.

'That's just a rumor. My marriage is very happy.' Can I call them? This was not my first such case. I used to be a prosecutor and now I'm seeing things from the other side. But even in my family law cases, which are mostly divorces, I heard this kind of thing a *lot*.

'Then can you explain why your wife has admitted to the affair?' I was skating the line between providing a vigorous defense and hoping to get fired and, frankly, I would have been happy with either outcome. One more than the other, truth be told.

There was a moment of silence, possibly in honor of the truth, after which Reeves said, 'No she hasn't.'

'Mr Reeves,' I said as Patrick watched and Angie's nostrils flared a bit, 'I have represented clients who were guilty of the charges they faced.'

'I'm not . . .'

'Hear me out. I did not have a problem defending those clients because everyone is entitled to a defense. That's how the legal system works.' I considered my next words carefully. 'I defended those clients and I have represented many who were not guilty. I understand the way our courts are set up and I play my part as I should.' Patrick especially liked the reference to playing a part; I think he still truly believes he and I have the same job.

'But there's one thing I won't do and one type of person who I will not defend, and that is a client who lies to me,' I went on. 'Now. One *last* time: Why didn't you tell me your wife was having an affair with James Drake?'

Angie looked up.

I could hear a noise on the other end of the call and it sounded like . . . yes, that was what I'd sounded like before I left Middlesex County and my ex-boyfriend! It was tooth-grinding. Reeves was either extremely nervous or very angry with me.

He spoke very carefully. 'My wife has been having some health issues . . . mental health issues, and doesn't always have a firm grasp on reality. She did not have a physical relationship with Drake. But she imagines things.'

Sure. 'Then we will need a complete evaluation of her by a recognized psychiatrist and it will have to be certified before we go to trial, which I am hoping will be more than three months from now,' I said. 'If you and your wife don't agree to that condition, I will withdraw from the case. Are we clear?'

I don't know how, but you can hear teeth clench even when the person speaking is not in your view. 'Yes.'

'We need to have a long conference to go over every aspect of this case and your role in it,' I continued. 'What time can you make it tomorrow?'

'Tomorrow! I can't—'

'I'm sure your next lawyer can be much more accommod-ating of your schedule,' I said.

'Fine.' Barely audible. 'I can see you tomorrow at ten in the morning.'

'Make it nine, at my office,' I said, and hung up before he could protest.

I felt like I'd been holding my breath for three whole minutes. Patrick stood up and reached for my hand. 'You are amazing,' he said tenderly.

'If you ever recommend one of your movie friends to me

again, yours will be the next murder and I'll be defending myself!' I shouted. Patrick looked baffled.

'Um . . . all right,' he said.

'You two should *definitely* move in together,' Angie said.

SIX

I spent the night at my apartment doing research. I can't do research at Patrick's house; it's too nice. My place is just downscale enough (by comparison) that it doesn't distract me from the task at hand. Another reason I shouldn't move in with Patrick. I'd never get anything done.

Making excuses? Me? Perish the thought.

There had been press coverage of the incident right after it happened and more when Reeves had been arrested and charged. I tend to miss all those things because first of all I insist on reading actual newspapers and not online sources whenever possible, and second because I don't read the entertainment news. Patrick reads that religiously, I believe out of a central insecurity in his personality that's convinced he'll be washed up and forgotten by the middle of next week, all the time. I see no reason to follow it. I do google Patrick's name every now and again, but we were not together when he was filming *Desert Siege* and I wasn't paying the same level of attention to his career (or, I was afraid to say, his personal life) as I do now.

From what I was able to piece together from the press coverage, the police report, and the discovery supplied by the district attorney's office, it seemed that a nine-one-one call had been made from the set by Catherine Briggs, the assistant director (who no doubt wanted to be a director director), who had been present when the stunt was being rehearsed. The cameras had not been turned on so there was no video record of James Drake falling to his death, which I considered a major plus for the defense. Once jurors saw the man plummeting and screaming, they'd convict their own mothers of the crime.

Paramedics arrived at the scene, which was actually in a closed-off area of Griffith Park, within ten minutes, but no one believed there was anything that could have been done for Drake. He had been hoisted fifty feet in the air, suspended from steel cables that were to have been strategically hidden so they didn't appear on camera, and fell into a ditch of another twenty feet. There were photographs of the remains in the police report, but I spent as little time as possible examining them. I'd hire a forensic expert to testify if necessary.

Robert Reeves, who of course had been supervising the rehearsal, had been 'uncooperative' when the police arrived. His assistant Penny Kanter told Trench – get ready – that Reeves was 'concentrating on his vision of the piece as a whole', and couldn't think about the individual pieces, like a man dying.

That was going to play really well with a jury.

I figured the next day's conference with my client would be, if you'll pardon the expression, a trial. Reeves was not exactly cooperative, not exactly respectful, and not exactly believable, a difficult mixture at best. His superior attitude would be something of a deficit with any jurors, should we actually get to trial, and the evidence against him was piling up to the point that the prosecutor who lived in my head was advising me to take a plea deal if one was available. Best to get in touch with the assistant DA handling the case, Justin Renfro, first thing in the morning and see what might be offered. At least I could present it to my client at the meeting and watch him look down his nose at me in person.

There are people who think my job is cushy. They watch too many lawyer shows on television. But don't tell Patrick I said that.

I slept, let's say, periodically that night, and woke up the next morning less refreshed than badly preserved. My hair looked like it had been stored overnight in an accordion and my face was wan and drawn. If I'd run into me in the street, I'd have assumed I'd had a date the night before. With Dracula.

One low-fat corn muffin and a gallon or so of coffee later

I was pulling my ancient Hyundai into the municipal parking lot at the office of the District Attorney of Los Angeles County, an imposing building with *Hall of Justice* carved into its side. I'd been there before so I didn't bother to look for justice there. What I was coming for today was a deal.

Justin Renfro worked upstairs in an office that looked like every other municipal office in the world (except maybe in France; do they have nicer offices there?), with government-issued furniture and a paint job that had (impressively) been recently refreshed, but was still as bland a color as exists on Earth. If there hadn't been palm trees visible through the window (if you looked down far enough), I could have closed my eyes and imagined I was back in New Jersey, where we don't have palm trees but there's little danger of your town combusting spontaneously. There are trade-offs in everything we do.

Justin Renfro turned out to be a man of less than average height, curly brown hair and a waist that suggested he did a *lot* of sit-ups before work every morning.

'I want to be clear,' I told Renfro. 'I have not discussed any possible plea offers with my client. I'm not certain he's even open to the proposition. But I thought I'd come and ask you what might be possible so I'd know what I could tell him when we meet later today.'

Renfro smiled, a friendly smile. We could have been colleagues, his smile was saying. He knew my side of the argument, it suggested. Certainly we could reach an equitable agreement.

'I'm glad you said that,' he told me. 'You haven't asked your client about a deal yet. That's good. Because we're not offering a deal.'

That couldn't be right. A prosecutor would at least *discuss* a plea bargain with a defendant, unless he had an absolute slam-dunk of a case, and Renfro did not possess one of those here. Yes, there was circumstantial evidence piling up against Robert Reeves, but he had no witnesses I was aware of and no murder weapon (whatever had cut through the metal cords), so it was going to take some serious convincing to get a conviction here. Why wouldn't he at least allow the possibility of getting this case off his agenda?

'I beg your pardon?' I said. 'You won't even discuss the idea of a possible offer?'

The smile dimmed not one watt. 'No.'

'Mr Renfro,' I began.

'Justin,' he corrected.

'Justin. I've spent more time as a prosecutor than I have as a defense attorney, and I have to say I'm baffled by your stance. You can't possibly believe that you have an open-and-shut case against Robert Reeves. There are plenty of holes in the charges and you can count on me exploiting each and every one of them in court. I'm here as a courtesy and a matter of policy. Candidly, why isn't your office more interested in a plea deal here?'

'May I call you Sandra?' he asked.

'It's Sandy. Feel free.'

'OK, Sandy. We're not offering a plea deal because we want your client to stand trial in front of a jury of people who don't like the elite members of the movie business. In Los Angeles it's not hard to find jurors like that. We could mail in our evidence and get a conviction.'

I shook my head to indicate I was baffled. 'You've got nothing.'

'You've been on this case, what? About a day?'

'Wow. Have you been bugging my office?'

Renfro's grin grew a little. 'No. Don't worry. Yesterday we got the paperwork indicating that Herb Bronson had withdrawn from the case. Today you showed up. I wasn't a math major but that's not hard to calculate.'

Dammit! Now I liked the guy. 'So what has my time on the case got to do with you not being reasonable about a plea?' I asked.

'You just haven't had time to really dig in on it yet,' he said. 'All you've seen is the police report and all you've heard is your client's story, which is at best thin. I'm telling you we have enough physical evidence to convict Reeves in a day and that's what we intend to do.'

'Fine. Blow me away. Tell me something that will have me despairing of my ability to defend this guy.' I probably shouldn't have said that.

'I have witnesses, I have motive, I have a prior statement of hostility and a threat of violence. If I had actual video of your client cutting the cables himself, it would be only slightly easier to convict him.'

OK, that was bad. But I could defend against it in court because apparently Renfro's witness hadn't actually seen Robert Reeves sawing away viciously at the cables and cackling to himself. So I wasn't devastated. Yet.

'So you have one witness who saw my client somewhere near the crane but probably not attacking the cables with a chain saw. I'm not losing sleep. And the other one?' I asked.

Renfro couldn't resist the impulse to grin. 'The other one heard Robert Reeves say that he was going to kill James Drake because of the affair with Reeves's wife.'

I stood up and nodded toward Renfro. 'Nice meeting you, Justin,' I said. 'Thanks for reassuring me.'

He raised an eyebrow. 'Reassuring you? I just told you about two damning witnesses against your client.'

'I'll see you in court. I assume more discovery will be on its way.' I let myself smile just a little.

Renfro, seemingly stunned, nodded. 'I'll email it over. Bronson should have had it already. Nice to meet you, Sandy.' He thought about sticking out his hand but had noticed that wasn't my preference and tilted his head in my direction.

The instant I was outside his office door, I called Holiday Wentworth. She asked what was going on with the murder case. I told her Patrick had worked with the defendant and Holly was disappointingly uninterested, particularly when I told her I had no intention of calling him as a witness.

'Tell me what you need going forward,' she said and that left me no choice.

'The DA has two witnesses who are going to lose me this case,' I said. 'I need Nate Garrigan.'

SEVEN

'So we meet again,' Nate Garrigan said. I couldn't see him but I knew Nate well enough to hear the sardonic glint in his eye.

'It's our third case together, Nate. You're not the cavalry coming over the hill. I'm asking you to investigate for me, not rescue me from a high tower.'

I was in my office, finally. It was a nicer office than the one I'd been assigned when I first arrived at Seaton, Taylor, largely because I'd scored with a few cases, some of which involved no violence at all. Well, not physical violence. Now I was head of the criminal justice division and I got a window. Not a big window, but a window. People in law firms value such things. This whole private practice thing had taken some getting used to, but I was starting to get a taste for it.

'You need to know what really happened with this Reeves guy and you want me to find out, right?' Nate was savoring his moment. I liked the guy with his ex-cop gruffness and blunt charm, but he wanted to always have the upper hand and sometimes there's just no hand.

'Without any major melodrama, if you can make that happen,' I told him.

'I'm the very picture of discretion. Just one thing—'

'Patrick's not involved this time,' I said, cutting him off.

'How did you know I was going to ask?' It's not that Nate and Patrick don't get along. Well, yes it is, but it's not because they dislike each other; it's because Patrick often thinks he's being helpful when in fact he's setting you back a couple of eons with his enthusiasm.

'I'm psychic. The thing is, he might end up being a witness in this trial, although I think it's unlikely. He was working on the movie where this stuntman was killed.'

A sound came through the phone. At first blush it seemed

to be a beluga whale dying of old age, but it turned out to be Nate groaning. 'How is that not involved?' he asked.

'It's not involved because he wasn't there when it happened. He won't have anything to do with the investigation. As a possible witness – although again, he hasn't been subpoenaed and isn't even mentioned in the police report – he knows he can't have any involvement in my work because that could compromise my case and he definitely doesn't want to do that.'

'My god, you're dating him,' Nate said. 'I saw it coming but it was like a train wreck that you just can't get out of the way of.'

'Don't end sentences on prepositions,' I said, and hung up.

I had worked with Nate enough to know that once I sent him the information I had (which I did immediately after disconnecting the phone), he wouldn't need me to tell him what to investigate. He'd know I needed expert witnesses on the kinds of cables used to 'fly' actors and what sort of implements would be both available on a film set and capable of cutting through those cables. He'd know I needed to find witnesses who might have seen Robert Reeves *not* being on the set when the cables were cut, preferably some who would have seen a person other than my client involved in the task, although that was almost certainly asking for too much. And Nate would know that if he found people who had motives other than James Drake *shtupping* Reeves's wife, that would be a big help. Character witnesses, given Reeves's normal disposition, would probably be few and far between, but that didn't mean nonexistent. Nate would look for them too.

I had about an hour to review the added discovery that Renfro, as good as his word, had sent over. His witness list included Burke Henderson, the stunt coordinator Reeves had said was incompetent and a cause of Drake's death, and Penny Kanter, Reeves's assistant. That last one was curious. Did Penny know something that was going to damn her boss? I could imagine what working for Reeves was like, and the possibility didn't sound entirely implausible.

There was also the head of a studio's computer effects department, which I thought was odd. The scene in which Jim

Drake died was not computer generated, so the use of CGI or computer-generated imagery would not have been necessary. One of the tasks ahead of me was figuring out why CGI might be relevant to the case against Robert Reeves.

Another was figuring out whether or not I thought my client had actually arranged for a stuntman in his employ to die horribly.

He arrived at my office with some fanfare, preceded by his assistant, Penny Kanter, who announced his coming as if he were a head of state at a fancy-dress ball in 1887. Janine McKenzie, our receptionist, looked a little panicky at the fuss when Penny shouted out, 'Robert Reeves is here!' Maybe Penny expected us to throw rose petals in her boss's path or something. At least she hadn't said that Robert Reeves had arrived, because the alliteration might have been just a tad over the top.

Reeves himself, head held just a little too high and chest puffed out just a little too much, looked like a cartoon rooster on a cardboard bucket of fried chicken. He strode into the reception area, no doubt awaiting a sash declaring him Client of the Year, and looked a little miffed at receiving none. I was watching from my office, which is adjacent to the reception area, and immediately called Janine to tell her that Reeves should wait a minute before being admitted. Let him sit and read magazines like everyone else. We even stock *Variety*.

I couldn't hear his reaction because the glass in my office door's window is quite thick, but I could see Reeves's eyes widen and his nostrils flare. Which should tell you something because I was at least twenty feet away. A nostril really has to work hard to be seen flaring from that distance.

I waited until the second he sat down to buzz Janine and tell her to let my client in. Snarky? Maybe. But there was a point to be made and I was just the lawyer to make it.

Reeves seemed to be sniffing the air as he entered my office, wondering if it was safe to breathe in this space. 'Ms Moss,' he said before I could make a sound, 'I don't like being kept waiting.'

'Neither does anyone else, Robert. Sit down, won't you?' I looked over at Penny, who was attempting to enter behind her boss. 'Can you wait outside, please?' I said to her. 'I need for this conference to be confidential.'

Penny did what came instinctively to her, which was to look at her boss for direction. He was a director, after all. His eyebrows rose to the point that I thought they might hover over his forehead and he said, 'Anything you say to me you can say in front of Penny.'

Usually this sort of contest would have required the presence of at least part of another man but I wasn't giving in. 'Fine,' I said. 'Then both of you can wait outside until you want to come in here and talk to your attorney, Robert. I'm sure Janine will be able to schedule you an appointment sometime next week.' I sat down and opened a file on my computer. Reeves and Penny couldn't see the screen so I opened a game called MacBrickout, which is somewhat simple but oddly addictive.

Before I could start the game I heard Reeves sigh. 'Fine,' he said, dragging it out to an indeterminate number of syllables. 'Penny, please wait in the reception area. I'll let you know when you can come back in here.'

'No, *I'll* let you know,' I said. 'And the answer is that you can come back in here when I have questions I need to ask *you.*'

Penny glanced again in Reeves's direction, saw his face, and left the office without another word. I closed the blinds on the floor-to-ceiling glass wall next to the door.

Reeves fixed his gaze on me. 'Was that display necessary?' he asked.

'As a matter of fact, it was. I need you to understand – *really* understand – that you're here seeking legal representation and that I'm the person who can provide it. You're in a very serious situation here, Robert, but you've been acting like it's a parking ticket. If you don't take my advice, answer my questions and do what I tell you to do, you can spend a large percentage of what's left of your life in a very unpleasant environment with bars on the doors and windows. Do you get that?'

His mouth curled. 'And because of that you have to act rudely to my assistant?'

'No. I didn't have to act rudely to your assistant, and in

fact, I didn't. I require that our conferences be private and confidential. You may rest assured that I will record every session so you won't have to worry about accuracy, but I don't want anyone, not even your most trusted assistant, to hear what's said in this room. It's too easy for that information to show up in court being used against you. So I'll ask again. Do you get what I'm telling you?'

He waved a hand. 'Sure, sure. I get it. You think Penny will turn state's evidence on me and send me to jail. But here's the thing: I didn't kill Jim Drake, no matter what lies you've heard about him and my wife Tracy. So Penny wouldn't hear anything in here that could prove damaging because there's no such thing to be heard.'

I knew he was completely wrong about that and could have continued the debate for the foreseeable future, but there is no point with some people, and Reeves was most of them. 'Let's get a few facts straight. I'm going to question you in the same way Assistant District Attorney Renfro will question you in court should we be foolish enough to let you testify, which we won't. Is that clear?'

'Not really.'

'Great. First, were you the director of the film *Desert Siege*, on whose set this murder took place?'

'You know I was.' Reeves was a busy man and didn't have time for this nonsense.

'But the jury needs to hear it. Answer the question and answer it in as few words as possible. Don't embellish, don't explain and don't justify. Just answer. Were you the director on *Desert Siege* when James Drake was killed?'

'Yes, I was and am the director of *Desert Siege*.'

'Just say yes. Let's try this again. Were you the director on the day James Drake died doing a stunt for *Desert Siege*?'

'It was a perfectly safe—'

I cut him off. 'Were you the director of *Desert Siege*?'

Teeth so clenched you couldn't fit the remnants of a word through them. 'Yes.'

'That's it. That's good. Keep doing that. Now. Were you present the day that James Drake died?'

Now there was just a touch of trembling from pent-up

frustration in his head and neck, but the word came through as though spat. 'Yes.'

'Excellent.' It's good to praise the subject when they do what you want. I'm told the same works well with dogs. 'Now, tell the court, how close were you to the crane that held Mr Drake in the air before he fell to his death?'

Reeves seemed legitimately confused. 'How close?' he asked.

I nodded. 'Yes. From your position, how much distance was there between you and the crane?'

'Probably about thirty feet,' he said. 'I was over in video village.'

'What is video village, Mr Reeves?'

He gave me a look that indicated I had been dropped on my head as an infant. 'You don't know what video village is?'

'You're on the witness stand, Mr Reeves. What is video village?'

This was clearly a more comfortable Robert Reeves. Showing off how much he knew about making movies was his happy zone. 'Video village is an area of the set where the director, the cinematographer and a few other crucial crew members gather around a monitor to watch video footage taken at exactly the same time that the main camera is rolling.'

'What is the purpose of that when the camera filming the scene is already in use?' I asked. Yeah, I was playing prosecutor – my old role – but I didn't want Reeves to know that I had only the vaguest idea of what he was talking about. I was very sheltered before I moved to California.

'If there are mistakes or issues that the camera picks up, we can do it again right away,' Reeves lectured. 'We don't have to wait for dailies like Orson Welles did.' He allowed himself a smug grin to think of himself in the same breath as the director of *Citizen Kane*.

But Patrick had told me about the concept of taking video when filming and I knew it had been invented by Jerry Lewis. Patrick is a collector of movie memorabilia and has one of Lewis's monitors stashed away in a corner of his home. I have a fear that one night when I'm visiting, the spirit of Jerry Lewis will escape from that monitor and yell, 'Hey Lady!' at me at an inopportune time. If there's such a thing as an opportune time for that.

'So you were at least thirty feet from the crane, but I thought the camera wasn't rolling for the rehearsal. Isn't that right?'

Reeves was back into tight-lipped witness mode. 'Yes.'

'Then why were you in video village?' Hey, use the term if it makes you sound like an insider. Loosens the witness up.

'The video camera was pointed at the crane but we weren't recording,' he said. 'I wanted to see it on the monitor but preferred not to have a recording of the rehearsal to protect my talent.'

I looked at him for a moment, wondering how his directorial ability would leave him if a tape was made of a stunt rehearsal. 'Your talent?' I asked.

'Yes, both the stunt performers and the people running the crane. I knew it was a challenging stunt and I wanted to be sure it looked good.' Not that it was safe, mind you. That it looked good.

It was time to end the fake questioning. 'OK. That was good for today,' I said. 'But there are things I need to know to prepare your defense. You need to be honest about your wife's association with James Drake.'

Reeves's face stoned over and he looked at me like a constipated bald eagle. 'I have told you. My wife has some mental health issues and—'

'Yeah, and she doesn't remember that she didn't have an affair with Drake. I get that's your story and I will make an appointment for your wife with a psychiatrist we've used before. But I need to meet her before that happens.'

'I don't think that will be necessary,' Reeves said with an air of haughtiness that Charles Laughton himself couldn't have mustered.

'Mr Reeves, don't make me remind you that you don't get to decide what is and is not necessary. I'm the one keeping your ass out of jail and I will in fact drop this case like the hot potato it is if you ever treat me like I'm not. Clear?'

The lockjaw expression came back and the word was practically squeezed out of his core. 'Clear.'

'Great. So you're going to see to it that your wife, Tracy,

is here tomorrow at eleven a.m. and you will *not*, under any circumstances, be sitting in during our conference. Is that clear as well?'

'Yes.' Dark stare. He would have been very happy if an anvil had dropped from the ceiling at that moment and landed on my head.

'Good. Now tell me who you think had some beef against James Drake and wanted him dead.'

There was absolutely no hesitation in his reply at all. 'Burke Henderson, the stunt coordinator,' he said.

That was the second time he'd mentioned Henderson in our only two conversations. Either he really believed the guy was responsible or he really wanted me to believe it. Or both, I guess. 'Why?' I asked.

'I hired Drake to do the stunt and Henderson wanted it,' Reeves said.

'That's enough to kill him?' It didn't make sense.

'It was enough because Drake really *was* having an affair with *Henderson's* wife,' Reeves said.

Smiling.

EIGHT

'What is it you want me to determine?'

Dr Sidney Chao, a psychiatrist with twenty-three years' experience in the field and six as a witness in (mostly divorce) trials, didn't care for Zoom calls, but he was an hour away from my office without traffic, which is never the condition in Los Angeles, and he didn't care for traffic even more. So we'd agreed to meet on our screens and let the fake backgrounds be damned. I was in my actual office and he was clearly in his home, which was a lot nicer than mine. I had realized long before that I could never be considered a candidate to consult on one of the cable news networks because I don't have enough bookshelves in my apartment. Blame the landlord.

'I don't want to prejudice your findings, Sidney. You know that.' Dr Chao and I had worked together on a number of cases, dealing with everything from a husband's state of mind when he'd decided to have an affair with a cocktail waitress, to the toll a divorce had taken on a twelve-year-old girl who wanted desperately to emancipate herself from her parents. This was the first time I'd consulted with him on a criminal case. 'But the client is insisting here that his wife, who admitted to having an affair with the victim of the crime, is having delusions and never did any such thing. It would be helpful to know your opinion on her grasp of reality. Is that the technical term?'

'No. I believe what you're looking at is whether or not she's nutsy coo-coo.' Sidney is not without a sense of humor, something he luckily keeps to himself when he's on the witness stand. Jurors hate a funny expert witness.

'That would be helpful too,' I admitted. 'Does it bother you to be consulting on a murder case?' Some people don't want that kind of responsibility.

'No,' Sidney answered. 'I offer an educated opinion and I don't pretend it's anything else. It's the jury that decides if it proves innocence or guilt.'

'So how will you make a determination?' Not all shrinks work the same. Sidney is careful and thoughtful in his work and he's very good at explaining himself, which makes him a wonderful expert witness.

'There are a number of tests I can choose from, but mostly it'll be a series of questions that will determine her ability to distinguish between fictional and real situations. I'll make the questions more personal as we proceed so that eventually she'll be answering strictly about things that have and have not happened to her.'

I know very little about human psychology, which is why I'm a lawyer. So that sounded fairly reasonable. 'How will you know if she's lying?' I asked.

'I carry a bullshit detector with me to every session,' Sidney said.

'I don't suppose you could tell me where you bought that,' I said. 'It would shorten trials and improve the country's back-logged justice system beyond anyone's wildest expectations.'

'Sorry,' Sidney answered. 'The company went out of business right after I was born.'

'You're a real shrink, Sidney.'

'Please. We prefer the full term, *headshrinker*.'

'Stop it. The technical jargon is overwhelming me.'

'How much time do I have to make a report, Sandy?' he asked.

'Believe it or not, the trial is scheduled to begin in six weeks, but I've applied for an adjournment, so I'm pretty sure we'll have a few more months to prepare. Guess four months as a minimum and we'll work forward.' I looked around at my office and realized I didn't have much in the way of bookshelves here either. Was I anti-book? I shuddered to think of it. The problem probably was that in the digital age we use physical books less than we ever did and all the information we need is at our fingertips (literally) all the time. It would be weird to decorate my office with novels by Hank Phillippi Ryan and short stories by Annie Proulx. But they might class up the place, now that I thought about it.

'That should be enough. When do I get to meet this woman for the first time?' Sidney never looked around the room he was in. He lived there. He knew what it looked like. He was a logical man.

'I'm meeting with her for the first time tomorrow and then I'll tell her when she can meet with you. What works for your schedule?' I asked. I liked doing the take-charge persona that intimidated Robert Reeves enough to back down and let me interview his wife alone.

'How's next Tuesday, around three?' Sidney was clearly consulting a calendar elsewhere on his screen.

'I'll make it work,' I said. 'Thanks, Sidney.'

'Don't thank me. Just pay up on time.'

I hit the End Meeting For All button and turned my attention once again to the police report that had been the basis of the charges against my client. It seemed a little circumstantial and thin to charge Reeves, even if his wife was sleeping with the victim, based on the physical evidence cited in Trench's report. And that was very unlike Trench.

But there wasn't anything in the report now that hadn't been there before. The crane's cables were cut but the method wasn't clear and no implement had been discovered. The suspect's wife had reportedly been having an affair with the victim. The suspect, as director of the film, had unlimited access to the set. Fine. So it (barely) covered the bases of access, motive and ability. But – extramarital activity aside – there were dozens of other people who could have done it. I could ask Trench why he'd focused so exclusively on Robert Reeves but he'd just be Trench and say something inscrutable. *I'm the police, Ms Moss. I know about these things.* Except pithier.

I'd given Nate Garrigan a look at the report and had yet to hear back. I was stalled.

So I called Patrick because sometimes it's better to talk to your boyfriend than the non-existent books on your non-existent shelves.

Patrick was between shots on *Torn*, which is the case most of the time. Patrick says film acting (or in this case, television acting) is 'mostly waiting, doing one thing, and then waiting again.' He understands why it has to be that way – although I'm not really clear on it – and doesn't complain about it. But the rigors of not doing all that much in a row make it easier to get in touch when necessary, or in this case simply wanted.

He told me virtually nothing about how his day was going, largely because he knew I would understand about half of it (which is an improvement over when we met) and think the other half was odd. I respect Patrick's work but only because I see how much preparation he puts into it. Still feels like a game of pretend to me.

Then Patrick made the mistake of asking how I was doing and got the full libretto of the Robert Reeves opera. I did leave out anything that would be considered evidential because Patrick was still a potential witness in the case and had to be kept in the dark on the details of the crime. It was more about the machinery of the court, and even then I left out the names. If Renfro ever got to question Patrick, I didn't want any of my personal impressions to color his answers.

It's exhausting being ethical.

'I think you need a night out,' he said when I was finished.

'I'm getting done by six tonight. Where do you want to go for dinner?'

'Someplace easy,' I said.

'Done. And Sandy. Don't let them get you. You'll get your adjournment and you'll build a case that'll get Reeves exonerated.'

I wanted to say that was what I was afraid of, but again, don't prejudice the witness. 'Thanks, Patrick.' He really was dear when he wanted to be, which was most of the time.

'No charge, love.'

Before the conversation could get too adorable, I saw an email appear on my screen from the office of the courts. 'I'll see you later,' I said to Patrick, and hung up.

I reached for the mouse to open the email and immediately my phone rang, with Nate Garrigan calling. I clicked on the email and answered the call at the same moment. 'What's up?' I said to Nate. I can be as abrupt as the next woman, assuming the next woman is somewhat uncomfortable being abrupt.

The first paragraph of the email informed me that the adjournment I had requested had indeed been granted by Judge Franklin. So I breathed a little easier.

'Why did you send your crazy roommate here to follow me around?' Nate demanded. Apparently he thought I knew what he was talking about. Silly Nate.

I re-listened to his question in my head. 'Angie's there?'

Hang on. The rest of the notice from the court said that the new date for the trial was . . . in *nine weeks*? Franklin had given me another three whole weeks to prepare a capital defense in a murder case I'd first heard about two days before? Was he nuts?

'Yeah, Angie's here. Apparently your lunatic boyfriend thought she should be riding shotgun on my investigation and she won't leave until he tells her to go home.' Nate has a natural sense of outrage that colors virtually everything he says. But he did sound unusually steamed about this one. You'd think, given the choice between having Patrick dog his steps and Angie doing the same, he'd go for Angie. But I was finding out how little I knew about the people I'd met in Los Angeles in the past two years.

'Why?' I said, trying to do the math about nine weeks. That was sixty-three days. I had, at this moment, enough evidence to perhaps, if I was extremely cunning and lucky, reduce Robert Reeves's sentence to twenty years with no chance of parole. That was probably not good enough at the prices we were charging.

'How could I know? Actors are crazy.'

It was at that moment that I decided to take up yoga. 'Put Angie on,' I said.

The next voice I heard was familiar from Westfield High School. 'What is this guy's *problem*?' Angie said. 'It's not like he never met me before.'

'He never thought of you as an assistant investigator, and neither did I. What are you doing there?'

In sixty-three days, I'd maybe be able to get a psychiatric evaluation of Tracy Reeves from Sidney Chao. Sidney was good and he'd understand deadline pressure. Nate had worked under a tighter deadline in Patrick's case and we'd won, although much of the most relevant evidence was turned up after the trial had already started. I'd never be able to visit the scene of the murder because it no longer existed, although Griffith Park was still there. I could find maybe three or four expert witnesses, but would I be able to talk to everyone who was on the set that day? Sixty-three days sounds like a lot. Trust me, it isn't.

'Patrick was worried that you had to get this big murder case together and he'd kind of been the reason,' Angie said. 'He couldn't come with Nate himself because he's shooting, you know, so he sent me. It's only part-time.'

A part-time investigator's . . . what? Assistant? While being the executive assistant for a famous television actor and head of a production company. It was amazing Angie had time to squeeze in being my best friend.

'What are you supposed to do?' I asked. I had to get to Judge Franklin and speak to him personally. The last time there had been sabotage; this time there had clearly been a misunderstanding.

'I'm supposed to help Nate find out the stuff he wants to find out,' Angie said. That was specific.

'Uh-huh. And here's the thing: As Robert Reeves's attorney, I'm telling you that you can't report back to Patrick on anything Nate finds out.'

I could picture the blank expression on Angie's face. 'Huh?'

'You heard me. Patrick's a potential witness and he's not allowed to know anything about what we find in any investigation. He gets to testify on what he knows and nothing else. Got it? So you can stay there with Nate all you like but you can't tell Patrick any of it. And I'll bet Nate isn't that crazy about having you tag along anyway.'

In the background I could hear Nate saying, 'You got that right.'

'Don't worry about Nate,' Angie told me. 'He'll be my best friend by the end of the day.'

I pretended to pout. 'I thought I was your best friend.'

'You're my BFF. He'll just be my BF.'

'I'm not going to be anybody's B anything,' Nate grumbled.

'Seriously, Ang,' I said. 'You can't tell a word of it to Patrick. There's no point in you staying.'

'I get that. But he sent me here and I'm kinda into it, so we'll see how it goes. It's only a couple of half-days a week.' The Angie in my mind's eye was already grinning over at Nate to flirt with him. It's her go-to tactic when a bare-knuckle brawl isn't appropriate.

'No it isn't,' Nate said, but his voice was already less steady than before. Angie can flirt with the best of them.

'Put Nate on,' I told Angie. It was, now that I recalled, his phone to begin with.

'She's crazy,' he groused at me.

'Yeah, but she's smart and observant and she's fun for you to look at, so you'll put up with it but she's off limits to you,' I said. 'Now. What have you found out in your thorough investigation?'

'She's young enough to be my daughter,' Nate said. 'Don't be disgusting.' He meant it, too.

'The case, Nate.'

'Yeah. I'm looking for an expert on the crane, the company that rented it to them and the kind of cable that got cut. We need someone to tell us what would have done enough damage to snap when the guy was attached to it but not be obvious before, when the stunt coordinator was checking it for safety.'

Yeah. The stunt coordinator. 'You mean Burke Henderson,' I said.

'I know that.'

'Reeves says Burke is incompetent and that Drake was actually having an affair with *Burke's* wife, not his own.'

'Well, aside from Burke being gay that makes tons of sense.' Nate wanted me to know that he'd already looked into the possibility. 'He could be bisexual, I guess, but I don't know of any other women who could testify to that. No, the word that I have is from three different people from the film company and they all say it was Reeves's wife Stacy who was bopping the stunt guy.'

Damn. That meant – 'Stacy?'

'Yeah. Stacy Reeves.'

'Nate, Reeves's wife is named Tracy. Patricia, to be exact.'

'You've met her?'

'No, but I'm going to tomorrow. Reeves says she's got mental health issues. You think she uses two names? Like multiple personality disorder?' That would figure. It's an extremely rare disorder, despite what shows like Patrick's *Torn* would have you believe.

'No,' Nate answered. 'I've traced Stacy back to her childhood in Kenosha, Wisconsin. Nobody made her up recently. Maybe Tracy is the alternative personality, but you know, that doesn't happen too often.'

'I know.' Tell that to the producers of Patrick's TV show.

There was a long pause. 'Sandy,' Nate said slowly, 'there's a real possibility that Robert Reeves has two wives.'

'Ooh!' I heard Angie say.

NINE

'You call this easy?' I asked Patrick.

The restaurant we were sitting in, which operated under the completely unpretentious name of Voilà! (including the exclamation point), would have been easily at home in a Jane Austen novel, except that it would have been someone's dining room. The chandeliers were enormous, the rugs were Persian, the music was a string quartet and the people were dressed for, at least, a formal Zoom meeting. The characters in the Jane Austen novel would have been complaining about how poor they were and never would have considered selling the sterling silver dinner set and renting a cozy little apartment in Essex.

'It's extremely easy,' Patrick told me. 'You just ask them for food and they bring it.'

'Yeah. They do that at Nathan's, too, but this isn't like that.'

'You're supposed to relax tonight,' he told me. 'You've been working very hard.'

He had no idea, largely because of the volumes of information I had not told him. When Patrick asked me about the case I gave him the minimum of answers and left out every name I possibly could. He was getting suspicious but hadn't said anything yet. That wouldn't last long, I knew.

'I'm going to have to work even harder,' I said. 'The trial starts in nine weeks.'

After the close of business today, which had been three hours previous, I officially had sixty-two days to prepare for Robert Reeves's murder trial. And I was so deeply in the dark that I didn't even know how many wives my client had.

'I thought you were going to talk to Judge Franklin about more time,' Patrick said.

'I am. We'll see.' I'd made an appointment with the judge for the next morning before court opened but I was, based on my previous experience with the man, less than euphoric about

my chances. Something else I wasn't telling Patrick, given
that he might have to appear before the judge in question, and
Patrick's wildly protective nature regarding me.

'So you'll get more time.' Patrick studied me, no doubt
expecting a response and wondering why he wasn't getting
one. 'So. You've been ducking me about moving in. And I'm
being open-minded about it. What's making you hesitate?'
Patrick is, after years of being a television deity, not used to
people pausing between the time he asks for something and
the time he gets it.

'Nothing about you,' I assured him. 'It's my own stuff. I'm
resistant to change.'

'You moved here all the way from New Jersey,' Patrick
reminded me.

True. 'I worry about sharing my space with someone,' I
tried.

'You'd have six times as much space than you already share
with Angie. Come on, Sandy. Tell me what's really bothering
you. It's me, isn't it?'

Of course it is. 'Of course not,' I said. 'I don't have any
doubts about you.'

Patrick did his half-smile, where he grins only on the left
side of his mouth. 'Everyone has doubts about me, love,' he
said. '*I* have doubts about me.'

I was trying to think of the proper words to say that I was
afraid he'd dump me on the side of the road the second I
stopped running away from him – but in a nice way – when
a thickset man in a dark sport coat approached our table.
'Excuse me,' he said in a hoarse voice, 'but are you Sandra
Moss the attorney?'

Now, that was unusual. When Patrick and I went out to
dinner (or anywhere else), people who approached us would
be interested in talking to Patrick, the TV star. I was basically
wallpaper. But in a place like this it was odd to be approached
at all. It was so chic here that King Kong could have walked
in and everyone in the room would have pretended not to
recognize him.

'Yes I am,' I answered. 'Have we met?'

Patrick's eyes narrowed a bit. There was something about

this guy he didn't like, but it could easily have been that he wasn't the one being recognized.

'No,' the man said. 'But I've been asked to tell you that you should drop the Robert Reeves case.'

That sent a jolt through me, but Patrick was quicker to react and started to stand. The man made a gesture with his right hand, inside his sports jacket. 'There's a gun in my pocket,' he told Patrick. 'You want to sit back down and then nobody will have to get hurt. We're all just good friends.'

Patrick sat back down. And smiled his actor smile.

'Who wants me to drop the case?' I said, trying to keep my voice as normal as possible.

'I don't think we want to mention names,' the man said. His voice sounded like he'd been gargling with battery acid. But his face was as bland and nondescript as any passerby in the street. 'The message has been delivered and that's all I was asked to do.' He turned and headed toward the exit. 'Enjoy your dinner.'

He was gone before either of us exhaled.

'Did you see a gun?' Lieutenant Trench asked.

In the evening, Trench's office was even more intimidating than during the day. He didn't bother to put shades on his window and it never would have occurred to him that high-wattage lighting would be a nice touch. This was the office he'd been given, and it would no doubt look exactly the same on the day he finally retired to go off and solve crimes on a freelance basis in an active adult community. Trench would make his mark on the world in a noticeable way, just through the many criminals he would put behind bars.

Patrick had insisted on coming to see Trench after the Plain Man with the gun had left Voilà!, which luckily had been after we'd eaten dinner. I didn't want to contact Trench at all with such an incident, seeing as it had never actually escalated to the level of a threat. The man had referred to people 'getting hurt', but had not specified which people, how or why.

I'm a lawyer. We think like this.

'The man *said* he had a gun,' Patrick told him.

'That doesn't answer the question I asked, and you are not

the person of whom I asked the question.' That's Trench being irritated, and he still has perfect grammar. I'm scared of Trench. 'McNabb, if you are going to interject, I will ask you to wait outside my office. There's a vending machine.'

Patrick held up his hands in a gesture of surrender. 'You'll hear no more from me.'

'Until you're asked.' Trench turned toward me again. 'Ms Moss. Did you see a gun?'

'No.' Now I was the witness, and if there's one thing I know, it's how to keep answers short on the witness stand.

'So you can't be certain the man threatened you with a gun, can you?' Trench asked. He twisted where he stood – Trench sits down only as an occasional nod toward gravity – and gave Patrick a look. Patrick did not speak.

'That's a gray area,' I told the lieutenant. Before he could raise an eyebrow (one of his favorite tactics), I added, 'He threatened us verbally by saying there was a gun in his jacket pocket. I can't attest specifically to the presence of the actual gun.'

If Trench were to allow himself a smile it would have been at that moment. 'Clever,' he said. 'A clever attorney.' I expected to hear the next statement attest to his hatred for clever attorneys but did not. 'Did you feel physically threatened?' That's a legit question. Sometimes the threat is in the manner in which it was delivered, not in the fact of a weapon being brandished. Charges can be brought if it's found that a person has a reasonable fear of a physical threat.

'Yes,' I said. 'I was afraid that he did have a gun and that he might shoot Patrick.'

Patrick looked up. 'That he'd shoot *me*?'

'You were the one he pointed his pocket at.'

'That's sweet.'

'Is there a reason you two brought this adorable scene to my office?' Trench asked. 'I'm a homicide detective and not a couples therapist.'

'I'm an attorney on a murder case that you investigated, Lieutenant,' I told him. 'A man came to our table at dinner, which means he'd been following us. He was very clear that he or someone he works for wanted me to drop that case. He wouldn't say who he was working for or why whoever it was wants me to stop defending Robert Reeves. I figured that had some impact on your work so I'd tell you about it. Also I'd like people to stop pointing guns at me.'

Trench sat down. He doesn't lean back in his chair. That would be an admission that he could, conceivably, relax. He sat straight up and kept his gaze on my face, from which it had only strayed when Patrick was speaking. 'Since I have known you, Ms Moss, people pointing guns at you has appeared to be a natural part of your existence. I would think you'd miss it if it stopped happening completely.'

'You'd be mistaken,' I said. I was doing my Trench impression, which consists essentially of trying to sound like paper.

The real Trench nodded and leaned forward a bit. 'To that end. I can't offer much more than sending a unit out to drive by your apartment a few times a day, and even then it would be just as a drive-by. If I recall from the times I've seen the building you live in, it has five floors, you live on the fourth and your apartment does not face the street. So it would be at best unlikely that an officer driving by would notice anything unusual.'

'That's reassuring,' I said, not mentioning that I stayed at Patrick's house more often than not these days because . . . don't ask me. I don't know why I didn't want Trench to know that. It was bad enough he knew more about my building than I did.

'We're the LAPD, Ms Moss. Not a private security company. As I recall, you have employed one of those in the past.'

Patrick nodded and pointed as if to say that was a great idea. 'And we shall do so again, I believe,' he said.

'I don't believe that,' I answered.

Trench stood, mostly to indicate that our meeting was over and Patrick and I should leave. Also because standing is more formal than sitting, which to Trench means it's better. 'Either way, I would advise you to be careful. I don't believe there is an imminent threat, but I assume you have no intention of giving up the case against Robert Reeves.'

I shook my head. 'I am handling the case *for* Mr Reeves,' I corrected him. 'And no, I'm not going to drop it because some guy told me to in the middle of my pasta primavera. At least in New Jersey they have the manners not to strong-arm you until you've paid the check and tipped the waiter.'

'My apologies for the manners of Southern California criminals,' Trench said. 'But because this is a case of mine, closed though it is, I will monitor your activities and know if someone is serious about stopping you from doing your job.' To Trench, doing your job is about what there is to life. 'Now if you don't mind, it's getting late in the day and I am heading home.'

'To see Mrs Trench?' I asked. I had no idea at all whether the lieutenant even had a personal life.

'My mother lives in Milwaukee, Ms Moss.' Interesting fact. And he'd told me nothing.

Once we made it out of the inner sanctum, Patrick hooked his arm through mine and started walking more purposefully than was his custom. He'd taken the threat seriously and now I had to rein in his natural inclination to – you know – be Patrick about it.

'I'm not going back to having a bodyguard,' I told him even as we practically sprinted for the elevator.

I saw Patrick process my words and my decisive tone. He nodded. 'OK, then,' he said. 'We'll do the next best thing.'

I knew even as he said it.

TEN

'You're not coming with me to work,' I said to Angie. We were getting dressed the next morning and shouting to each other through the corridor separating our bedrooms. The couple in the next apartment, Roy and Howard, were probably listening and having a laugh.

'I work for Patrick McNabb,' Angie said back. 'If you think his instructions to me are interfering with your life, you need to take it up with him.'

'I took it up with him for an hour and a half last night,' I told her. 'Why do you think I came back here at one in the morning?'

Angie leaned out of her room wearing what she believes to be professional attire: a black T-shirt so tight it was a wonder she could still process oxygen through her body, a pair of equally snug blue jeans and a 'working' jacket, bright royal blue. If she were the kooky best friend in an eighties romcom she might have gotten away with it.

'Please. Your love life is not part of my job profile,' she said.

'Angela. You're dressing for a shift at a really classy Seaside Heights arcade. I work at a law firm. If you're coming with me you need to frump it up a little.'

Angie, understanding that I'd just given up the argument about her coming to work as my bodyguard, grinned. 'You want to come look in my closet for something appropriate, *Sandra*?'

'No. I want you to stay here or go work for Patrick. Or bother Nate. How can you do all three of those things at once?'

She ducked back inside her own bedroom but her voice came through loud and clear. Loud, I think, because she wanted Roy and Howard to hear her exit line.

'I'm multitalented.'

We went to the office in my Hyundai and not the new Lamborghini that Patrick had loaned to Angie 'for professional activities', because I would have been terrified to ride in such a vehicle and, besides, I was hoping to duck Angie at some point in the day. Having my own car would make that so much easier.

She was, however, wearing muted colors that allowed for blood to circulate all through her body. That was the concession she'd made to being at my office.

First, though, we had a judge to meet. Or I did, anyway. And this meeting would be critical to the case that the Plain Man didn't want me to defend. I'd given it a good deal of thought, considering whether I wanted to take his subtle advice. For one thing, I wasn't the least convinced that Robert Reeves hadn't actually killed James Drake. As I've said, that in itself wouldn't necessarily be enough to have me withdraw, but there were other circumstances. One was that the man I was currently considering moving in with was a figure in the case. Another was that I preferred to cower and run when threatened rather than offer resistance. It hadn't been my strategy in every possible instance, but it had served me well when employed.

There was also the fact that I didn't like Robert Reeves. I'll grant you that was kind of secondary, but don't tell me there's a lawyer on the planet who isn't affected by the temper and personality of the client. Sometimes they just (unconsciously) do a less-than-stellar job on the case. Other times they do it on purpose. In rare instances it doesn't actually have an impact on the defense or prosecution either way. But it's always there in the back of your mind.

'So am I going to get to meet the jerk later today?' Angie has an uncanny ability to read on my face what I'm thinking.

'He's my client. You can't refer to him as "the jerk", and frankly, I'd be much happier if you *didn't* meet him later because that would mean you weren't following me around all day like an attack dog trained to protect me.'

'Nice way to talk about the woman who's here to save your life.' She was kidding. I'm almost certain.

Maybe I could pivot. 'I don't suppose there's any way I can talk you into staying out of the meeting with Judge Franklin,' I said. 'Judges don't enjoy having extra participants in private sidebar meetings. You can just stay in the car.'

I caught a glimpse of Angie rolling her eyes, something I had seen many times in my life but never had it cross over from annoying to endearing. 'I'm not here to protect your *car,*' she snarled. 'I don't know why this old bucket of bolts would need protection anyway.'

'It was already shot up once.'

'And I wasn't there, was I?'

Somehow she thought that proved something. So much for pivoting.

We drove in silence for a while and I got back to musing on the reasons to withdraw from the case. But the only thing that I kept coming back to was that if I left because of the vague threat from the Plain Man, Trench would know, and the thought of him thinking I was a coward – even if he had suggested dropping Reeves was the logical thing to do

– was too much. Because now I had an imaginary Trench in my head, along with the imaginary Angie who had been there for years. If the two met it was possible the universe would come to an end.

But what it mostly came down to was that if I withdrew from the case, *I* would think I was a coward and that wasn't acceptable. I wouldn't ask the judge to excuse me from the defense. But I certainly was going to make as convincing a case for an adjournment as I possibly could, and there I was on considerably more solid ground. Nine weeks to prepare a major murder trial in Los Angeles under the spotlight that every entertainment and crime reporter in the world would be bringing to the courtroom? I'd have to make sure Franklin saw that in his mind's eye. He was fastidious about his court and absolutely hated the idea of it being clogged with untidy people.

I parked the car in the courthouse's garage and, after another round of not getting Angie to stay with the Hyundai, took the elevator up to the judge's chambers with my best friend in tow.

Angie stretched her arms into the air in the elevator just to get loose after the car ride. There was a glint of something shiny in the area of her belt, which had been covered by the mauve jacket she was wearing to show off how professional she was.

'What's that?' I asked.

'What's what?'

'That.'

I pointed at her waist and she gave me a look like I had suggested she'd never been in possession of a midsection before. Then she shook her head in understanding. 'Oh you mean *this*,' she said, and – I swear to you – pulled a very shiny pistol from her belt. 'I got it yesterday after the waiting period was over. Patrick thought I should carry one and then, once I became your bodyguard, we figured I should have it with me all the time.'

My eyes must have been the size of hubcaps. 'Are you out of your *mind*?' I said. 'Taking a loaded gun into a judge's chambers? How'd you get it through the metal detectors in the lobby?'

'I showed it to the guard and gave him my permit to carry,' she said. 'I had written permission from the judge. He knows I'll be there.'

'Nice of you to tell me,' I grumbled.

Judge Franklin, who had seen Angie before during Patrick's trial but might not have remembered, did indeed welcome both of us into his chambers and asked that she put her gun into her purse and zip it up before we began our meeting. Angie complied but the looks she was shooting around the room indicated she expected an attack from any area at any moment. I reminded myself to stay away from my trigger-happy roommate as much as possible while she was protecting.

I already had a headache.

'I granted you the adjournment, Ms Moss,' Franklin began. 'I'm not sure I understand why this conference is necessary.'

'Yes you did, Your Honor. And I appreciate that. But I believe the extra three weeks is simply not enough time to prepare my case adequately. I've only been Mr Reeves's defense attorney for a few days. Nine weeks is, I'm sure you'll agree, much less time than one would normally expect to get a defense like this together.'

Franklin looked over at Angie. I'm used to men looking at Angie when she's with me; she has the kind of look that attracts their eyes, among other body parts. But I didn't think the judge was lusting after my roommate. He was trying to avoid looking me in the eye, and that wasn't good.

'It's going to be a high-profile, highly covered murder trial, Your Honor.' I went on to avoid his dismissing me on the spot. 'You know what that's like. Every move and every word will be dissected and analyzed. You'll be second-guessed on television and so will I. But the real reason I need the extra time is that I don't definitively know what happened on that movie set the day James Drake died, and I need to have more information in order to provide a suitable defense.'

The judge closed his eyes for a moment and I worried momentarily that he was feeling ill. Franklin is not a young man. But then he exhaled and looked back over at me.

'I want to help you, Ms Moss, truly I do,' he said and I knew I was sunk. 'But the fact of the matter is that the three

weeks I gave you is the most time I could possibly justify. Mr
Reeves had an attorney representing him until this week and
he had been working with that attorney for six months.
And I'm sorry to say it, but the courts are so completely
backed up now that we're still adjudicating cases that are
pre-pandemic. If I postponed the Drake murder again, I'd have
to do it for more than a year.'

'We wouldn't object to that amount of time, Your Honor,'
I said.

'No, but the prosecution would and they'd be right,'
Franklin answered. 'They've built a case and they believe
they can convict your client. That's not a reason to deny your
adjournment, but I haven't done that. I've literally given you
all the time I can possibly offer, and I'm sorry but you'll
have to be satisfied with that.'

There was no point arguing. Franklin truly believed he
was doing the best he could do for me, and wasn't being
unreasonable from his viewpoint. Not even from mine. I
stood and Angie followed, no doubt weighted down by the
firearm in her purse. I chose not to think about that, but I
chose it too late. I had already thought about it.

'I do appreciate your courtesy, Your Honor,' I said. 'Thanks
for seeing us.'

'I'm sorry I can't do more, Ms Moss. But if it makes you
feel any better, Lieutenant Trench has informed me of your
situation, and there will be added security in and around the
courthouse during the trial.'

Yeah, that made me feel tons better. 'Um . . . thank you,
Your Honor.' What did you want me to say, 'Big help that is,
Walt, you ineffectual old coot?' That wouldn't have served
me well in court. And he'd cited me for contempt before.

'Don't worry, Judge,' Angie said. 'I'll be behind her the
whole time, packing heat.' She patted her purse.

'I have no doubt,' Franklin answered. He was visibly
impressed.

Nine weeks.

Once we were out of the judge's earshot, I called Nate.
'Whatever you're doing,' I told him, 'start doing it faster.'

ELEVEN

Herbert Bronson was not expecting us, so our arrival, fifteen minutes out of Judge Franklin's chambers, caused a bit of a stir in his offices. Herbert Bronson had offices. He had two receptionists, six partners, fourteen associates, and a coffee machine that made me wonder if I should drop off a résumé at the front desk and hope there was an opening.

'Mr Bronson is in conference with a client,' the receptionist, who informed us that her name was Brandee (I'm guessing on the spelling), said. 'He can't be disturbed.'

The waiting area was roughly the size of a football field and not completely full, so only thirty or so people heard when I raised the volume in my voice to say, 'Well, I'm representing a client in a murder case that Mr Bronson couldn't handle and he didn't give me much time to prepare, so I'll just wait for him to free up his schedule.' Angie and I walked to a space right near the desk as a few heads turned. 'Are these seats taken?'

'We can just scoonch over,' Angie suggested as we chose seats right next to a very well-dressed couple in the front row. 'We can make new friends.' She looked at the woman in the next comfortably upholstered chair. 'Can you pass me a copy of *Us*?'

Brandee was already on the phone. She was talking fast. After a very short conversation she called out, 'Ms Moss?'

I was on my feet immediately. 'Has a slot opened up?'

We were in Bronson's office in less than a minute, and given the distance we had to walk that was saying something. He turned out to be a tall man, well-proportioned if you like scarecrows, with a full head of expensively coiffed hair, mostly brown but with fashionable gray around the temples and anywhere near the part. He was well dressed. Patrick dresses casually but very well. Bronson dressed well but formally, which made sense since this was a law office.

'Robert Reeves is guilty as hell but he wouldn't accept a deal for manslaughter and ten years, which probably would have ended up being three years behind bars,' he said before I could even tell him why I was there. He'd been reading the legal news.

'Renfro didn't offer any deal,' I pointed out.

'No, but show me the DA who wouldn't have jumped at that offer if Reeves had allowed me to put it on the table.'

'Robert Reeves insists that he is completely innocent of the charges, that he barely knew James Drake and that he was nowhere near the crane when the cables snapped. But then, you probably know that,' I countered.

Bronson shook his head, not to disagree but to express his bewilderment with Reeves and my insolence at showing up in his office unannounced. I could only empathize with one of those.

'Yes I do. And I'm here to tell you I've looked through every shred of evidence the police have and every possible witness who could testify and Reeves is the only person who had a motive and opportunity,' he said. 'The only way to defend him, if I may offer the advice, is to plea him down and hope nobody shivs him in jail just for being him.'

Angie, even in what was for her conservative attire, could command a man's attention. She rotated her shoulders back in a 'working-out-the-kinks' movement and suddenly Bronson was noticing her. 'Is that why he fired you?' she asked. Angie appreciates subtlety but doesn't see where it might apply to her own behavior.

Bronson redirected his attention to Angie's eyes and his own narrowed a bit. 'For the record, who is this?' he asked me without actually diverting his gaze.

'Record or no record, that is my security officer,' I said. I had made up the title on the spot but thought it sounded official and worthy of respect. 'There are people who want me to drop this case and they aren't being especially delicate about it. So I need to take some extra measures.' I indicated Angie, but nobody was looking at me.

'Reeves says his wife is crazy and never had an affair with the guy who fell off the crane,' Angie went on. I got what she was doing; she was trying to get a rise out of Bronson to see if he would drop his pompous façade under direct attack. The problem was, I suspected that under the pompous façade was a pompous interior.

'That's nonsense,' he said. 'And why are you the one asking the questions?' His tone took a softer quality when talking to Angie. Like he had a chance.

'She's the nice one,' Angie said in a dismissive tone. 'I'm the security officer.' She said that with more pride than was appropriate considering I'd just invented the term. 'I'm the blunt one. So. What about Reeves's wife?'

Bronson pursed his lips like something tasted sour. 'He has a habit of marrying women who are . . . unstable. But everyone I spoke to who might have been a witness and was on that set agreed it was common knowledge that Drake and Tracy were, let's say, involved.'

That's not how I would 'let's say' it, but I didn't appear to be part of the conversation anymore so I just sat back to watch my bodyguard (I'd just demoted her again) pursue her line of questioning.

'So everybody knew about it but it was just gossip,' Angie said. 'Is that even admissible in court?'

'As hearsay, no,' I jumped in, just to remind everyone that I was an attorney and the one representing Robert Reeves. 'If no one actually *saw* something going on between those two, I don't see how it can be admitted as a possible motive for my client to have killed James Drake.'

'Tracy Reeves will testify to it and she should know,' Bronson said, finally looking back at me again. 'You must have seen her name on the prosecution's witness list.'

'A wife can't be compelled to testify against her husband,' I said. I *had* noticed her name and intended to call Renfro about it later today or tomorrow.

'She's not being compelled,' Bronson said. 'She volunteered. There was no subpoena. You've met with Tracy?'

'She's my next appointment after you,' I told him.

'You didn't have an appointment with me.'

'And yet, here I am.'

Bronson's pomposity was at full strength. He shoved his shoulders back and straightened in his chair to achieve maximum height. If he'd put on a few pounds he could have been a GI Joe doll. Sorry. Action figure.

'When you meet her you'll find a woman who's been married to a man she doesn't especially like for less than a year and who had affairs – yes, more than one – just because she wanted to humiliate him. When Robert Reeves killed Jim Drake, he was doing exactly what his wife wanted him to do.'

'We'll see,' I said. 'Just so I know what I'm not going to do, how would you have defended Reeves in court?'

Either Bronson didn't notice the insult or he just couldn't come up with a snappy reply fast enough. 'I would have had him plead down,' he said with great force.

'And that's why he fired you,' Angie pointed out.

As we were standing up to leave and Bronson (who had a picture of his wife and three children on his desk) was trying to figure out a way to ask Angie for her phone number, I checked my phone for messages: One from Patrick (typical), one from Nate (not urgent but important), one from Jon Irvin with no explanation, and one from my mother (definitely to be put off until later).

Bronson apparently decided on the sanctity of marriage and watched us (mostly Angie) leave. But before we made it to the very tall oak door he said, 'People are threatening you to get you off the Reeves case?'

That was a weird question after all this. 'Yes,' I said. I reached for the doorknob.

'I wonder why they didn't threaten me,' he said quietly as we left.

TWELVE

I checked in with all the men vying for my attention (I excluded my mother) as I drove back to the office. Jon asked if I wanted a second chair on Reeves. I guessed he was feeling bad about having turned down the case when I'd offered it to him.

'Of course I want you to do that,' I told him, 'but don't you have a caseload of your own?'

'Yeah, but they're all divorces. Our criminal justice division is basically the Reeves defense.'

It was true. 'Maybe we should learn more about marketing ourselves,' I said.

'Billboards? TV ads? Pop-ups on Instagram? "Bring your crime to Sandy and Jon?" I don't know if that's the way we want to go. I'm bored with carving up the community property. Let me work with you on the guy who fell into a gorge.'

'That's so charming.'

'I'm a charming guy.'

'You know, the last time we worked together you got shot.' I mean, he'd recovered, but it had taken a while and I still cringed at the thought.

'Yeah, and in all my years as a lawyer, that was the only time. Go figure. Come on, Sandy. I need to get back on the horse.' Jon was a good lawyer and a friend. I didn't want to see either of them get shot again, and I'd been threatened once on this case already.

'If you get killed I'll never forgive you,' I said.

'Imagine how I'd feel. I think my chances are pretty good,' Jon said. 'I've learned how to duck since then.'

'You don't have to do this out of guilt,' I said, and meant it.

'Send me what you have and I'll be up to speed in an hour.' How is it you can tell when a person on the other end of the phone is smiling?

Nate Garrigan answered on the second ring. His text message had said it wasn't urgent but his speed in picking up spoke otherwise. I had the Bluetooth on in the car so his voice sort of boomed throughout. 'You out getting a latte?' Because people who aren't from New Jersey think that constitutes sarcasm. Colorful.

'Oddly, when someone leaves me a message that says it's not urgent, I tend not to dive for the phone,' I said. 'Forgive me for not sending a SWAT team to your house. This is nine-one-one. What is your emergency, sir?' *That's* sarcasm. You're welcome.

'Gee, Moss. Maybe you don't want to hear about the

evidence I've turned up.' Nate, despite being a crusty old cop, has a flair for the dramatic that he must have learned from watching reruns of *Law & Order*. Or maybe he was born with it.

I sighed audibly for effect. 'OK, fine. What'd you find out? Garrigan.' If we were going to call each other by our last names, I was not going to be left out.

'Hi, Nate!' Angie, from the passenger seat, was determined to be if not the center, at least the center-right of attention.

'You have me on speaker? And *she's* there?' Nate was operating in a world where women were . . . well, let's not dwell on what Nate thought women were. Or, to be more precise, what he *pretended* he thought women were. Nate is actually very respectful but he wouldn't want me to tell you that. So hi, Nate!

'Deal with it,' I said.

I could hear the scowl. 'Fine. I have video footage of the guy falling off the crane and the five minutes that led up to it.'

OK. That was a development. 'But the camera wasn't running,' I said. 'Everybody has been very clear about that part. The camera wasn't running.'

'No, it wasn't. Not the main camera. This was a five-camera shot and even the other four weren't turned on.'

There's a flair for the dramatic and then there's just being annoying. 'Cut to the chase, Nate. What do you have?'

'There was somebody on the set taking video on their phone,' he said.

I sat there wondering whether that was good news or bad news, and if it was bad news for Reeves, was that necessarily bad news? I spent years as a prosecutor and there's still part of me that wants to lock up the bad guys. If Reeves had really caused the 'accident' that killed James Drake, did I *want* him to be acquitted?

Life would be so much easier if I had no morals.

'Sandy?' I guess Nate was now happy using my first name to demonstrate what great pals we were. 'Did you hear me? Someone on the set got the whole thing on their phone.'

I coughed. Angie was blinking. So was my right turn signal.

Probably best to make the turn. 'I heard you,' I told Nate. 'Who was it?'

'Who was it got the video?'

'No, who was it that stole the cookie from the cookie jar. Of course, who got the video!' Don't play with me when I'm not in the mood. Patrick has learned this. It hasn't stopped him, but it has slowed him down.

'I've been asked not to mention a name,' Nate said. 'The person doesn't want to testify.'

Well, that wasn't going to be much help. If I couldn't question the videographer about how the footage was taken and whether it had been edited or digitally manipulated, I wasn't sure Franklin would even admit the video into evidence. 'I'm not loving this yet, Nate,' I said. 'Does the footage at least show that our client didn't kill James Drake?'

It was Nate's turn to hesitate and fake-cough. 'Um . . . I'm not a hundred percent sure yet,' he said finally.

'Say what?' That was Angie. Let it be stated on the record.

'Nate, tell me you've seen the video.' That was me. I mean, I'm sure you could tell, but clarity is half the battle. Or something.

Nate's voice took on a steelier quality. 'Not. Yet,' he said.

'Are you sure it exists?' I mean, people will do pretty much anything to get attached to a big sexy murder case. I don't know why, but they will.

'I'll have it within twenty-four hours,' Nate insisted.

'How'd you find out about it?'

He sounded offended. 'I'm an investigator, Moss.' We were back to that. 'I find out stuff.'

'Yeah, that's gonna sound great in front of a jury. How did you find out about the video footage of the murder?' At the end of the day, I had to remind him, I was Nate's employer.

'Just tell her,' Angie suggested. 'She'll get all legal on you.'

Nate sighed, which sounded like an elephant having gall bladder surgery with very little anesthetic. 'I got it from the friend of a friend and no, I'm not providing a name until we're sure you're going to use it in court. Suffice it to say my friend had reason to be very beholden to me.'

I made an executive decision not to ask what Nate might

have done for this 'friend', which might have ranged from a night of passion to a contract hit. I guessed it was more in the area of calling an old cop acquaintance to get a traffic ticket fixed, but there's no knowing for sure with Nate.

'OK,' I said. 'Call me the minute you get the footage and don't look at it until I'm there, understand? I have to be absolutely sure there hasn't been any doctoring done to that video.'

'You think I would . . .'

'No,' I told Nate. 'I don't think you would. But I have no idea who your *friend* is or what he, she or it might be capable of. Don't watch one second of that video until I'm in the room with you, *capiche*?' No matter who you are, in New Jersey you pick up the odd Italian word. Most of them, very odd.

Then I hung up on him just to avoid any possible counter-arguments. I didn't even call Patrick back, assuring myself I would do so as soon as my meeting was over.

We had pretty much reached my office by then, so I pulled into the underground garage, swiped my pass and, after another twelve minutes, managed to find an open space where I parked the car.

Angie got out and followed me to the elevators. I gave a quick thought to faking her out, getting back in the car and ditching her for the rest of the day and then I remembered 1. That it was my office and 2. That I was wearing four-inch heels and couldn't run faster than Angie on my best day. This was not my best day.

Resigning myself to the fact that she'd be following me around and packing heat (good lord), I walked to the elevators and pushed the button for my floor. Angie looked around the elevator as if expecting ninjas to drop from the roof and attack me. Her hand was in her unzipped purse, just in case I was in need of having someone shot. Alas for Angie, we made it up to my office unassailed.

We passed Jon's office on the way to mine and saw that he was already elbow-deep in the Reeves file. I could see his elbows because he'd literally rolled up his sleeves to get started. He waved as we went by but didn't engage me in conversation;

Jon would want to be completely up to speed on the case before he'd discuss it with me.

And most of the work wasn't even on paper; it was in computer files I'd sent him. Jon must have had everything printed out because he likes having it in a tangible form. Jon is old school.

I had barely made it to my own desk and sat in my own chair when there was a commotion of some kind in the outer office. Angie pulled the gun out of her purse – this is all based on some general rumblings in another room, mind you – and headed for the office door before I said, 'Hold it. Nobody's coming for us.' She flattened out her lips and stopped, but she clearly wasn't a fan of my assessment of the situation. 'In two seconds my phone's going to ring.'

It did, too. Possibly the first time I'd been right all day. I picked up the phone, listened to Janine on the line, said, 'OK,' and hung up. Angie stared at me.

'Show people,' I said. 'Never lost for a big entrance.'

I stood up and walked to my office door, which took six steps. I don't have a Bronson-sized office. Angie silently followed behind. I took a pause at the door and stood for a long moment.

'What?' Angie said.

'With egomaniacs it's best to make them wait for *you*.' I finished counting to fifty and opened my office door.

Angie, nodding, walked by my side to the small conference room, which would have required a Sherpa guide the first three months I had worked at Seaton, Taylor. I would have dropped breadcrumbs, but they have a cleaning service come in every night.

When we walked into the room, which I generally used for one-on-one client meetings that I didn't want to hold in my own office, Robert Reeves was standing next to the table looking impatient, which had been my goal. Penny was with him, of course, but she didn't look nearly as irritated as my client did. His arms were crossed over his chest and it's entirely possible that his foot was tapping on the floor, which did him no good because the floor was carpeted.

Next to him was a woman easily twenty years younger than

he was, and she was a confusion of people all in one very well-toned body. Trying hard to be chic but also youthfully casual and sexy but professional and knowledgeable while kooky all at the same time must have been exhausting, but she was doing her very best to pull it off.

'Ms Moss,' Reeves said. 'You've kept us waiting.'

'I know,' I said. I directed my attention to the even-younger-than-I-thought woman. 'You must be Patricia Reeves.'

She stuck out her hand and, despite my resolution to avoid shaking hands, I took it to establish some solidarity. 'You can call me Tracy,' she said.

I looked at Reeves. 'And you can go,' I said.

THIRTEEN

Reeves and I had the usual struggle about him leaving the room. He knew I'd already clearly stated the rules, but he wanted to show what a big important guy he was, particularly in front of his younger-every-moment wife. I, on the other hand, wanted Tracy Reeves to see without ambiguity that I was in charge here and could order her husband, major cinematic talent that he believed himself to be, to go away.

Then he agreed to leave but wanted Penny to stay, which would have been the same thing as him remaining in the room. So there was another round of hilarious banter, followed again by my usual threat to drop the case and let him deal with the public defender and Reeves telling me I'd never do that. I wasn't sure he was right.

After all the posturing, Reeves left the room, no doubt to go and terrorize Penny his assistant for mentioning Steven Spielberg's name in his presence. He seemed the kind of guy who would do that to make himself feel better.

The current Mrs Reeves was sitting with her legs (amply displayed in a short skirt) crossed at the ankle, no doubt as they had taught her in parochial school before she started wearing short skirts. Her hands were clasped in her lap. Her eyes were wide and open, not just literally but effectively, ready to take in all that might happen before her. She was the very model of a modern trophy wife, and no doubt owned her own yoga studio on top of it.

'Nice to meet you, Tracy,' I said. It wasn't the most original opening in the world but it did the job.

'Hi.' Did she even know why she was here? Angie, sitting as far to my right as she could to be out of the way, snuffled a snort and looked out the office window searching for threats. There were apparently none imminent.

'I'm glad you came in,' I continued, ignoring my best friend's editorial comment. 'I want to ask you about some of the issues surrounding Robert's upcoming trial.' I mean, his wife knew he was accused of murder, right?

'OK.' I'd had more interesting conversations with cats. And I've never owned a cat.

I had a pen in my hand, ostensibly for the purpose of making notes on a legal pad (I'm one of the chosen who can use them unironically) and noticed myself tapping it on my desk. I stopped.

'Robert is accused of sabotaging a stunt on the set of his movie in order to kill a stuntman named James Drake,' I told Tracy. Just in case. 'Did you know Mr Drake?'

She nodded dutifully. 'Oh yeah. We were screwing.' I guess it could have been worse.

'You were.'

Tracy nodded even more forcefully. 'Oh yeah. For, like, months.'

I was mentally crossing Tracy Reeves off my witness list. 'Why?' I asked.

She actually looked up, having not anticipated the question. 'Why?' she repeated.

'Yes. You were newly married and then you began . . . seeing another man. And *he* was married to someone else. Why did that happen?'

'Stuff just happens,' she said.

'No, in cases like this, stuff doesn't just *happen*,' I said. 'People make choices. You had a choice *not* to cheat on your husband and you decided you would anyway. Now, that was your choice and you had every right to make it, but I'd like to know about the decision-making process that led to it.'

'I don't know,' Tracy said. Like that settled it.

I'd circle back to this when I could wrap my head around what might have been going on in Tracy's. 'Did your husband know about your affair with Mr Drake?' I asked.

'Oh sure. He fixed us up.'

Huh? 'Your husband suggested that you have sex with a stuntman in his employ?'

'Well, he didn't say it like *that*.'

I was being spoon-fed information when I wanted to take large gulps. 'Suppose you just tell me how that happened and don't leave *anything* out,' I said. Maybe I could get more than six words out of her that way.

'We were at a party? And Jimmy came over? And Robbie said he thought we looked good together?'

Was she asking me if that was what happened?

'Is that what happened?' I figured it was best to clarify this as quickly as possible.

'Yeah?' Somehow that didn't help much.

Angie, no matter what role she might have in the current drama, was going to be Angie. It was one of the reasons – no, it was *the* reason – I had tried to avoid having her in my office while I was working. She took time away from security detail (but not taking her eyes away from the window into the main office) to say, 'You know your husband says you're crazy, right?'

That seemed to awaken Tracy from her stupor. '*What?*' she said.

'Yeah. He says you weren't cheating with this Drake guy and that you just think you were because you're nuts. So who should we believe?'

Tracy looked at me, the figure of authority she'd seen kick Robert out of the office only minutes before. 'Is this true?' she asked in a voice that was ten years older than the one she'd been using.

I gave Angie a poisonous glare that I hoped Tracy didn't notice and said, 'Robert has been making some statements that would indicate you might have some problems separating reality from unreality,' I said. 'That's why I'd like to have a doctor friend of mine meet with you next Tuesday so we can make a determination about whether you might testify at the trial.'

Tracy paled a little bit. 'Testify? Under oath?'

'That's how they like to do it,' Angie said.

'I'm not going to do that,' Tracy said.

This meeting was not going quite in the way I had hoped. 'Well, why don't you meet with Dr Chao and then we can talk again about how we'll proceed.'

'Not a chance, lady. I will *not* testify.'

It was an interesting response, but not one that I thought confirmed Robert Reeves's assertion that his wife was suffering from a mental illness. She was, however, dead set on not speaking on her husband's behalf in a court of law.

'Why not?' I asked.

'A wife doesn't testify against her husband,' Tracy said. She too was apparently a fan of courtroom dramas in movies and on television, because they tell you that all the time.

'A wife doesn't *have to* testify against her husband,' I said. 'But if you have evidence that your husband didn't kill James Drake, you'll be testifying *for* him, not against him.' Besides, she was under subpoena from the DA. It appeared Tracy didn't read her mail.

'It doesn't matter. I'm not doing it.'

I put up my hands like a very dedicated traffic cop, palms out and up. 'OK. You don't have to testify for the defense. But I would like you to see Dr Chao so we can deal with any testimony that might be about your state of mind. Is that OK with you?' It pretty much had to be.

'My state of mind?' Tracy said. It wasn't like Angie hadn't been particularly clear about what that meant.

'There's going to be a lot of talk about whether you were having an affair with the victim,' I began.

'And I was. So what?' There are witnesses and then there are living, breathing obstacles to getting an acquittal.

'So maybe your husband killed the guy you were sleeping with,' Angie said. Angie is my id.

Tracy shrugged. 'Maybe.'

I was starting to be happy she wouldn't testify. For me. Not so much the other way.

'They're gonna want to talk about that in court,' Angie went on, explaining like she would to a particularly bright pet ferret. 'So if your husband says you're nuts and you don't know if you were really *shtupping* the stuntman, we need to know if anybody has any evidence that you do or don't. Get it?' After that explanation even *I* didn't get it.

But Tracy nodded. Clearly we were dealing with kindred spirits here. Although I thought Angie could think rings around Tracy without a scintilla of effort. They were communicating on a level I didn't have, and I didn't know if that was good or bad.

It was time to get back to the point. 'So you'll see Dr Chao on Tuesday?' I said.

'Yeah. I guess. I'm not crazy. Might as well have that on the record. I guess.' Tracy guessed a lot. She was probably guessing when she married Robert Reeves that he would find out about her dalliances with other men, divorce her and then – under California's no-fault divorce laws and the pre-nuptial agreement I had not yet read – get a large sum of money in alimony and community property. But I was just, you know, guessing.

'Do you know anything about a Stacy Reeves?' I said. Sometimes if you startle a witness you get information they were not intending to give you. I figured the mention of Reeves's alleged other wife might move the needle a bit on Tracy.

Nothing. 'No,' she said with a look of indifference on her face that couldn't possibly have been faked; I don't care if Dame Judi Dench was playing the role. 'Is that, like, one of his cousins or something?'

'Something,' I said.

FOURTEEN

'If anyone is incompetent, it's Bobby Reeves.'

Burke Henderson, the stunt coordinator on the ill-fated set of *Desert Siege*, was surrounded by cars. Not all of them were in perfect working order, having been cut in half or with no visible engines under their hoods.

We were in Henderson's 'shop', the place where he devised some of the stunts that would appear on screens of various sizes. It was not attached to his house, as you might expect, but took up most of an old airplane hangar at a regional airport in Torrance, California, near enough to movie studios that it would not be much of a hardship to get back and forth during a shoot.

'Bobby?' I said.

Henderson, a broad man with a broad face, smiled a broad grin. 'I call him that because it pisses him off,' he admitted. 'Bobby's pretty easy to piss off.'

Nate Garrigan had suggested I talk to Henderson because no matter how much he liked to irritate my client, he might have information that could prove relevant to the case. The fact that 'Bobby' had suggested he, Henderson, was responsible for the death of a stunt performer under his authority seemed like a detriment to him being a good defense witness, but Nate had talked a bit to Henderson and was here with me and the ubiquitous Angie now to prove his point.

'How was the gag supposed to work?' Nate asked.

I took it that *gag* was insider jargon for *stunt* and filed that away in my head. It can help with witnesses to speak their language.

'I'll show you,' Henderson said. He walked over to a workstation inside this enormous space and reached into a drafting desk to pull out an actual rendering on poster board of the stunt – sorry, *gag* – that had been planned for the day James

Drake died. He brought it over and laid it on the table in front of our gathering.

'Why didn't the prosecution confiscate these images?' I asked.

'They did. These are copies. They have them digitally and the original drawings.'

'I'd have thought everything would be on a computer somewhere,' I said.

'It is, to be honest. But I like the look of something I can hold in my hand and look at in different kinds of light, so I always print it out or have it hand-drawn once the director gives me any storyboards he has or at least a description of what's in mind.'

The closest drawing in front of us, which I found beautiful and fascinating, was of a man wearing a jet pack flying through the air over a vast canyon. Next to it was a rendering of the mechanics involved, which included the infamous thirty-foot crane. Both appeared to be hand-drawn.

I'd seen the finished film on a screener at Patrick's house and was puzzled. 'This scene isn't in the movie,' I said to no one in particular.

Henderson looked a little stunned. 'Of course not,' he said. 'After Jimmy died it would have been disrespectful to him for us to include the gag, and I don't think anyone else would have wanted to do it anyway.'

'Doesn't that mess up the story?' I am so not part of the movie business.

'You can always work around it.' He looked at me with a little disgust in his eyes and I prepared to be offended or humiliated. But it turned out his distaste wasn't directed at me. 'You know Bobby Reeves wanted to film it with me in the harness, and when I told him we wouldn't do it, he was going to do the whole thing digitally, but it wasn't in the budget so he had to get the writer to plug the hole in the script. That's the kind of jackass we're talking about.' He seemed to catch himself. 'Sorry, Ms Moss.'

He thought I'd get upset at *jackass*? 'No need,' I told him.

'What happened with the cables?' Nate very intelligently took the reins of the conversation lest we enter into a discourse on what was and was not ladylike language. 'How long before you did the rehearsal were they last examined?'

'I looked at them personally less than an hour before Jimmy suited up,' Henderson answered. 'This wasn't the hardest stunt I've ever seen done but it was, obviously, a dangerous one. He was dangling over a big drop and we had an airbag on the ground but even that wasn't enough from the angle. He would have hit the bag if nobody had messed with the cables. It was just too high.'

'And when you examined them?' I didn't finish the question because I didn't want to supply Henderson with a possible answer.

'They were strong and safe.' No hesitation and no break in Henderson's gaze.

'What were you doing between the time you last checked on the cables and the time they began rehearsing the stunt?' I asked. *Gag* be damned. I was a layperson and a lawyer. I was questioning a witness, not trying to be discovered for a movie career.

'I was checking on other aspects of the gag.' Henderson *had* a movie career and, damn it, he was going to talk like that. 'I looked over the hydraulics and tested the controls of the crane. It took about twenty-five minutes, I'd say. Then we started setting up as soon as Bobby came in.'

'So Reeves wasn't there when you were preparing and examining the crane and the cables?' Nate asked.

Henderson pointed to the drawing on the right, the one that showed the man in the harness dangling off a huge crane positioned over an abyss.

'There were so many moving parts here that we knew prep was going to take a long time,' he said. 'Bobby doesn't like to wait. He was off auditioning an actress for a walk-on role. If you know what I mean.' He didn't even bother to leer.

'So Robert Reeves was cheating on his wife at the same time she was having an affair with the dead guy?' Nate said.

Henderson held up his hands in a defensive position. 'I can't say *for sure*,' he said. 'I know he asked not to be disturbed because he was *evaluating* an actress.'

I felt Nate had assumed too much. '*Was* Tracy Reeves

sleeping with James Drake?' I asked Henderson. 'So far all I have is rumors.'

'I mean, if you're asking me whether I ever *saw* them in bed together, then the answer would be no,' he replied. 'But it was pretty common knowledge on the set that the two of them were all over each other whenever she visited and Bobby wasn't in direct sight.'

'Are you married, Mr Henderson?' I asked. I knew that he was supposed to be gay, but that wasn't confirmed.

'Yes, to a lovely man named Stuart.' OK, so it was confirmed, or it would be once I had someone at the office track down the paperwork. It was still within the realm of possibility that Henderson might have been sexually involved with Tracy Reeves but less likely.

'But Mr Drake was married too, wasn't he?' I asked.

Henderson didn't wave a hand to declare the subject irrelevant, but he might as well have done so judging by his tone. 'There's married and there's *married*. Jimmy was a stunt guy and stunt guys as a rule make lousy husbands. They're either on movie sets doing all sorts of macho stuff that gets women interested, or they're at home nursing their injuries.'

I shut my eyes for the same reason Angie had turned away from Nate and Henderson. Strange how adultery never seemed to be the man's fault.

But hey. Law. 'Did you see Robert Reeves approach the cables while you were testing the other equipment?' I asked Henderson.

'No. But to be honest, I was looking at other things. He could have come over at any time.'

'What kind of tool would you need to cut through those cables enough that they would snap under Drake's weight?' Nate asked. 'The cops never found anything that they thought had done the job.'

Henderson put the drawing back into the drafter's table from which he'd extracted it. 'That's been driving me crazy,' he said. 'A regular pair of wire cutters, even the heavy-duty ones, wouldn't make a dent in these things. And the only tool I can think of that would do it would be a demo saw or a grinder, both electric.'

'Why couldn't one of those have been used?'

I got another oh-those-women looks from Henderson. 'They're electric tools and they would take some time to use and make a ton of noise,' he said. 'This was a set outdoors in a public park that had been closed for our use. There was crew everywhere. There's no way Bobby Reeves could have walked up with one of those things, cut just enough through the cables and walked away without *anybody* noticing.'

'And it's not possible it was done before you checked?'

Now Henderson looked insulted. 'I would have seen it,' he said through clenched teeth.

'Then I don't understand,' I said. 'If you don't see a way that Robert Reeves could have sabotaged the stunt, how do you think James Drake died?'

Henderson looked at me for a long time. 'I have no freaking idea.'

Except he didn't say 'freaking'.

That time he didn't apologize to me for language.

FIFTEEN

'You're stressed out,' Patrick said.

Patrick has a way of saying things you already know and making it sound like he's just invented them personally. Of course I was stressed out. I was defending a man accused of murder and couldn't figure out why the police had decided he was so guilty they'd stop looking at anyone else, or at the possibility that the whole thing had been a tragic accident. I had checked Renfro's witness list and found the expert on construction equipment who had determined that the cables on the crane had been cut purposefully. I wouldn't call him, but I had to find someone to counter the testimony in court and, oddly, I did not have the number of an expert on construction equipment in my contacts on the iPhone.

'Yes I am,' I admitted.

We were at Patrick's house – of course – and his suggestion

that I move in was hovering in the air above us. I hadn't definitely told Patrick I didn't want to go to his premiere because I felt like I had to be supportive, but I was sort of dreading it and trying to come up with emergency work things to do that would prevent me from going out that night. So far, 'finding an expert on construction equipment' seemed like the best bet, but why would I have to do that at night?

Patrick started rubbing my shoulders, which is what men think they should do when a woman is stressed. I'm willing to bet that Sergeant Roberts did not rub Lieutenant Trench's shoulders whenever things got a little dicey in the homicide and robbery division. But then, I liked having Patrick's hands on my shoulders. He told me he'd worked as a massage therapist for a soccer – sorry, football – team in England while he was still trying to get noticed as an actor. I don't know if the story was true, but his hands were convincing.

'It might help if you told me about your case,' he suggested.

'You know I can't do that. You're a . . .'

'Potential witness, I know. Just tell me if there's a way I can help.' There is absolutely nothing Patrick wants to do as much as help. Everybody, if possible. It's sincere and, after a while, truly annoying.

'Not unless you know an expert in construction equipment,' I said.

He stopped rubbing. And my neck had just begun to loosen up. 'You mean like the crane they used for the stunt?'

I'd said too much. 'Forget it,' I said. 'I didn't mean that at all.'

'Of course you did. And I know your man.'

I turned around to look at him. Patrick was behind me on the absurdly enormous sofa and kneeling on the cushion to get a better angle on my shoulders and neck. I knew I shouldn't say anything else about the Robert Reeves case to him, but the fact that he could drop that little glimmer of information so casually intrigued me. Because, let's face it, I really did need an expert on construction equipment *exactly* like the crane that was used in the aborted stunt.

'You're just saying this because you want to help,' I said.

'No. Sandy. I work in the entertainment industry. This was

not my first crane. I've been up on one or two myself, although always in a studio where it could be more carefully controlled. And believe me, I know the guys who maintain those things because even in the studio it can be really dangerous to fly up in the air. I can give you a name and phone number.'

I shook my head. 'I've already talked to Burke Henderson,' I said. Why did I keep giving him information about the case when I knew I shouldn't? Oh yeah, because I was in love with him. That kept slipping my mind.

'Burke is a stunt coordinator,' Patrick said. I pointed at my shoulders and he started kneading them again, making me a little dreamy. 'He knows how to make the gag work. But he relies on the technicians and construction crew to see to the equipment. Brady O'Toole is your guy.'

'Brady O'Toole? You're making up names.'

'I'm not.' The hands left my shoulders and went somewhere else. I could hear him fumbling around behind me. 'There. I've sent you his contact information.'

'Patrick, it's really unethical for me to be sharing anything about the case with you, and getting an expert from you borders on witness tampering.' The hands came back and my chin dropped down to my chest.

'I've sent it to you already. If you have problems with the concept, don't use the information.'

It was hard to argue with that. I'd talk to Jon about it on Monday. He had a strong sense of ethics and wasn't in love with Patrick.

I exhaled. 'My shoulders feel a lot better,' I said. I turned around to face Patrick. 'Thank you.'

'Now let's see about the rest of you,' he said.

The rest of the weekend was quite nice indeed but you don't need to know the details. But by the time I got to work Monday morning, I was back into my attorney mode and had decided that taking a name from Patrick was not unethical. I could evaluate this Brady O'Toole (if that was a real name) independently based on his qualifications and knowledge of the specific crane that had been used on the film the day James Drake had died.

But I did ask Jon before I made the call and he said it was OK.

Brady O'Toole answered my call on the third ring. He had a sort of high-pitched voice and sounded very little like the stereotypical idea of a big brawny construction worker. Patrick had told me nothing except his name and phone number, and the tiny bit about him meeting O'Toole on a set and discussing the general sort of stunt that had killed James Drake. So I approached him as a potential expert witness with very little information other than a simple Google search could provide. Which it had.

After I identified myself and explained why I was calling, O'Toole began by reiterating that he had not been part of the crew of *Desert Siege* and had never worked with Robert Reeves.

'That's great,' I told him. 'I don't want any information or testimony to be prejudiced by previous relationships you might have had before. I just want you to tell me from the standpoint of someone who has worked with this kind of equipment what might have happened and more specifically what *couldn't* have happened.'

'I can't promise I'll tell you stuff that will get your client acquitted,' he said.

Well, you could try. 'I don't want you to guarantee that,' I answered. 'I just want you to tell me the truth. If you tell me things that might be detrimental to my client, it's entirely possible, to be frank, that I won't ask you to testify on behalf of the defense.'

'I could call the DA then and volunteer to testify for them.' O'Toole seemed to be thinking out loud.

'I couldn't stop you,' I said. That was the cold, hard truth.

'OK. What do you want to know?'

'Well, I can send you the specifications on the crane and the cables that were used on that set as well as the harness James Drake was wearing and the setup of the set in Griffith Park. What I'm asking you to do is study them and give me your expert opinion on a number of points, including how cables might have severed or been severed and whether what happened could have been avoided.'

'I have a real general idea of the stuff they were using,' he said. 'I read the newspapers and saw the stories on the TV after Jim died.'

'You knew Mr Drake?' That could be an obstacle.

'Not personally. I worked on sets with him maybe twice.'

'Did you speak with him?'

He hesitated, maybe thinking. 'Just about whatever gag we were doing,' he said. 'I didn't ask him about his wife and kids.'

'Drake didn't have kids.'

'Well, there you are,' O'Toole said.

He agreed to look at the specs in my file and get back to me.

Jon walked into my office just as I was hanging up. 'You get your man?' he asked.

'That's yet to be seen.' I wasn't sure which man we were talking about but guessed there were no good answers to that question.

'The construction expert.'

'Oh. Yeah. He'll look at the specs and call me. What do you think is our line of defense?' I often ask Jon for tactical advice; he's a genius-level legal planner. I used to think he wasn't great in a courtroom, but I'd started to change my opinion on that point when I became a client of his after my arrest months before. It's a long story. I've told it elsewhere.

I gestured at the client chair and Jon took it. He still moved a little stiffly, a result of his having been badly wounded by a shooting in front of our office building. He was almost entirely back to being himself, but it had been about a year now and Jon had a little hitch in his walk and sat slowly.

He seemed to sift a lot of possibilities in his mind. 'First, I think it's really a good thing we still have a couple of months before this thing reaches a courtroom,' he said. 'The evidence against Reeves may all be circumstantial, but there's a lot of it. His wife is going to see Sidney Chao?'

I nodded. 'Tomorrow.'

'That's good. If he can testify that she's sane and competent, it might hurt because she insists she did have an affair with the victim and that means our client had the most classic motive in history, if you don't count Cain v. Abel.' That's Jon doing a lawyer joke.

'What if Sidney says she has difficulty distinguishing between reality and unreality?' I asked.

Jon spread his hands. 'Obviously, that would be better for us. Not for her. But if that happens, we can explore the idea that she did not have any physical relationship with James Drake and therefore our client had no reason to want him dead.'

I don't chew on pens anymore. I gave it up when we weren't allowed to touch anything for a while. 'If I'm the prosecutor, it's not bothering me too much if Sidney tells us she doesn't know the difference and only thinks she was sleeping with Drake.'

Jon's eyes narrowed. 'Why not?'

'Because if she *believes* she was having an affair and she told her husband she was, there's no reason he wouldn't believe her.'

'He says she's mentally ill.'

'Yeah, now. Then he wasn't on trial for murder.' I let out a long breath. 'Either way I'm not crazy about how this is going to look.'

'There's an alternative,' Jon said. I got the impression he was being careful.

'I'm not going to like this, am I?'

Jon shook his head. 'You can get him to plead guilty.'

'You think he did it?'

'The only way I'd be a hundred percent convinced is if we knew how the cables were severed,' he said. 'Otherwise I don't see anybody else who wanted to kill James Drake and had the ability to do it that day.'

'He won't plead,' I told Jon. 'It's not an option.'

'Then we have to go in full steam ahead and force the prosecution to show there's no reasonable doubt,' he said.

'How?'

'We have to determine exactly how those cables were cut,' Jon said. 'We have to figure out what's going on with Robert Reeves's wife, or wives. We have to find out if there's precedent for a film director being held criminally, not civilly, responsible for a death on the set. And more than anything, I'm afraid we need to know whether or not our client killed a stuntman on his movie because he was jealous.'

I was suddenly very weary. 'I hear what you're saying and I don't disagree,' I said.

Jon half-smiled. 'I know it's not what you want.'

I flattened my mouth out and nodded. 'But we have to do it.'

'What's this "we" stuff, Kemosabe?'

I probably grunted. 'Fine. *I* have to talk to our client.'

SIXTEEN

Robert Reeves had learned by now that there was no point to refusing when I called and said we had to talk. But he did understand his place well enough to insist that I come to his office (he said 'offices') rather than the other way around. After all, he was a busy man, and all I was doing was trying to keep his ass out of jail. You have to have a sense of the pecking order in Hollywood. I was still having trouble adjusting. I wasn't going to peck.

So I showed up at Reeves's office (and it was one office, for those keeping score at home) on the lot of Majestic Pictures, where apparently he had a first-look deal, whatever that was. Maybe it meant that whenever he made a movie, the staff at Majestic got to look at it first. That would be nice.

Angie would not be denied but Nate was not with me. Jon was absent as well, having maneuvered for himself to be back at the office going through case law to see what we could do about showing that a film director might be sued for a death that took place under his watch, but not prosecuted for it. I did not have high hopes for that strategy, but it had kept Jon out of this meeting and that showed some shrewd ingenuity on his part.

The office was large and opulent in a very modern, pretentious and ultimately hilarious sort of way. Everything was square. The walls were square. The logo appearing above the front desk (which was square) was square. Square lamps, waste baskets, rugs, sofas and desks abounded. And it was all done in black and white, I assumed to associate Reeves with the classic films of some decade he thought he should have lived through.

Angie, who was decidedly *not* square, was barely containing her amusement, but she knew her supposed job was to protect me wherever I went, so she was sitting on the 'guest' sofa and watching the door (the only potential entrance for an assailant in sight) like a hawk. Assuming a hawk was watching the door.

Reeves made us wait because of course he did. I had made him wait for the same reason, so I had no right to act insulted. So when he walked in I acted insulted.

'I'm trying to save you from a lifetime in prison, Robert,' I told him as he made his way to his impressive (square) desk. 'If I say we need to meet, you have to clear off the time and be ready when we have agreed to talk. Are we clear going forward?'

He waved his hands in a dismissive motion. 'I was five minutes late,' he said.

'You were eight minutes late and that's not the point.' It was totally the point. I was showing him that I paid attention to the time and that mine was as valuable as his, if not more so.

'Fine.' He sat down heavily. 'I'm here now. What's so important?'

What's so important? Did this guy want *to keep his freedom?* 'There's a lot I don't know and much of it is because you're not telling me everything,' I said. 'I can't mount an effective defense if I don't know what I'm dealing with.'

'You know everything I know,' Reeves said as Penny entered the office and sat opposite Angie in an upholstered chair nearer to her boss. I guessed Reeves didn't want to be outnumbered in the meeting. I considered telling her to leave just to show Reeves I could, but I didn't want to interrupt the meeting itself and, frankly, I didn't care if Penny was there or not.

'You seem to see me as the enemy,' I said. 'I'm the only person you can be certain is on your side. And until you get that through your head, you're going to be tying my hands behind my back and making the possibility of an acquittal more remote. So you need to accept that I'm trying to help you, and you need to do it right now.'

Reeves pushed his hands up into the space above his head. 'I hired you, didn't I?' he said. 'Doesn't that indicate that I want you to help me?'

'Cooperation is necessary,' I told him. 'You're just not trying to stop me from helping you. It's not the same thing. To begin with, you claim that you weren't jealous of your wife regarding the victim, James Drake.'

'I wasn't, because she wasn't having an affair with the guy.' Reeves sounded exasperated. Did we have to go over the details of his impending trial *again*?

'For the time being, let's pretend that's true,' I said, and didn't wait for him to protest because I'd thrown that in just to get him annoyed. I can be petty as well as anybody. 'Even if she weren't sleeping with Mr Drake, you must have heard the rumors around the set, didn't you?'

Reeves pursed his lips like he was eating fish. I'm not sure if the recipe was tasty or not. 'Sure, you hear rumors,' he said. 'It's a movie set. There's no place on earth that's anywhere near as gossipy and incestuous. There are always rumors about who's having sex with whom. So what?'

'It didn't bother you that your wife was the subject of some of the rumors?'

He waved his hand again, swatting at the very suggestion. 'If I worried about every rumor, I wouldn't have time for anything else. Look. My wife is a very attractive woman and yes, she's considerably younger than I am. So, guess what, people talk. She and I know what's real between us and it doesn't matter what anyone else thinks. So no, I did not kill Jim Drake because I thought he was screwing my wife and I didn't kill him because *other* people thought he was screwing my wife. I didn't kill him. Period.'

He had to give me something other than his word. 'OK,' I said. 'You're the director of a very expensive, very difficult action movie. And you're in charge of essentially everything that goes on when you're filming.'

Reeves tried really hard not to look too drunk on power

and failed. His smile was slight but definite and we were talking about a man dying. 'That's right.'

'So tell me. How does someone, less than an hour after the stunt coordinator personally checked the cables—'

'That's your problem,' Reeves said, interrupting me as I would have bet my month's rent he would. 'You believe what Burke Henderson told you. The man is a pathological liar and my first choice for a suspect in Jim Drake's death.' Penny nodded her agreement, as if that were ever in question.

I nodded in Reeves's direction to concede the point. 'I have no evidence either way to support that idea, but let's say you're right and Henderson is the killer,' I said. 'You're on the set. He's on the set. There are how many other people on the set when the rehearsal is being arranged?'

'Somewhere in the area of a hundred,' Reeves acknowledged.

'And those were thick steel cables being used on the crane. You don't cut those with something you get at Home Depot. So, being in charge of the whole production, I'll put the question to you: how did Burke Henderson cut those things down just to the point that they'd snap once James Drake was suspended over a thirty-foot cliff without any of the other ninety-nine people on the set – including you – seeing or hearing anything?'

'I couldn't begin to speculate,' Reeves replied, looking at Penny.

I suppressed the urge to glance over at Angie as a retaliatory gesture. Angie was not a prop. 'I thought you were the expert on that set,' I said. 'That you didn't miss so much as a tiny detail. I'd think you'd know how something as big as a dangerous stunt would work and that you'd have checked on it yourself.'

That was designed to get under Reeves's skin and more specifically his ego, and it seemed to work perfectly. His face reddened just one shade from normal and, while his eyes did not bulge, the lids widened enough to signify an insult of the most heinous variety. Good. Even if I didn't get a plausible response, at least I was having a fun moment. You have to fill your days with something.

It's not that I didn't want to win Robert Reeves's case, or that I wanted him to be guilty of the charges before him. It was that I don't respond well to pomposity and Reeves appeared to be the west coast distributor of pomposity. Some things are reflexive and immune to my professionalism.

I let his head vibrate for a few seconds and did not (I checked later with Angie) show my pleasure in his discomfort. Then he said, 'I trust the people on my set,' he said. 'They're professionals and they know how to do their jobs. If I didn't trust them I wouldn't hire them. If they tell me it's safe, then I believe to my core that it's safe.'

'But you said this Henderson guy was a snake and that he probably killed the stuntman himself,' Angie very helpfully pointed out.

'That's how I know he did it,' Reeves said. 'He knows his job is to make the gag safe beyond question, and it happened anyway.'

Feeling less satisfied with the answers I'd gotten than I had hoped I would be, I ended our client meeting, but not before informing my client that we would have another one in three days after I got the results of Tracy Reeves's psych evaluation from Sidney Chao. He did not protest, which I found refreshing.

Penny looked downright defiant as we left, which was odd since she hadn't won anything and in fact hadn't spoken the whole time, simply providing visible support for her boss. He could have had a loyal beagle in the room and it would have done what Penny had done.

We got back out into the hot California sun in a few minutes (I believe that movie studio lots are harder to navigate than anything Lewis and Clark ever had to deal with, and there was no Sacajawea in sight), and were trying to remember exactly where my Hyundai was parked, when two men got out of a silver van marked 'Craft Services' nearby and walked over to us. Angie immediately reached for her purse and I told her to stop that because the reminder that Angie of all people was carrying a gun would be enough to keep me awake at night.

They were about our age, I'd say, and smiling pleasantly

as they approached. I wondered if they were employed here at Majestic. Couldn't be security; we had valid visitor passes to be on the lot. 'Excuse me,' said the one with darker hair. 'Is one of you two ladies Sandra Moss?'

Angie's back suddenly got straighter and she did reach for her purse.

She actually even got it open before the blonder man produced a handgun from his Dodgers jacket and pointed it at her. 'You'll never get it out of the bag,' he said. Angie withdrew her hand from her purse. Slowly, and empty.

'What's this about?' I asked. Because, honestly, at that moment I didn't have the faintest idea what it could be about.

'You were told to drop a certain court case,' the dark-haired man said. 'You didn't.'

Seriously? The guy in the restaurant sent these two? 'Lawyers don't do that,' I told him.

'You should have.'

The world went dark and I realized something had been placed over my head. I heard Angie yell, 'Hey!' at the same time I did. I tried to hold up my hands but suddenly my arms were being held behind me. Angie hollered, 'That's my *purse!*' while I felt my hands being bound with . . . something . . . and then I was either being lifted or pushed, but I was sitting on a cold metal floor and a loud metal sound, like a car door closing, reverberated around me.

An engine started and I could tell that whatever I was in, probably the craft services van, was moving. It was a moving van. And I was the cargo.

'Ang?' I said hopefully. And I breathed a massive sigh of relief when I heard my closest friend's voice come back to me.

'Hey, Sand,' she said.

'What?'

Angie sounded almost giddy. 'We've never been kidnapped before!'

SEVENTEEN

The van rolled on while Angie and I, we managed to establish, tried to get our bearings. I could tell from her voice that she was less than six feet away and we managed to figure out that the two guys we'd met had put bags over our heads and tied our hands behind us, then thrown us in the cargo area of the van. The bag over my head was not tied, so it felt loose, and I was trying to stand so I could bend over and make it fall off.

'Can you see anything?' I asked Angie.

'No, but my other senses are heightened.' Of course they were. 'The thing over my head is burlap. I like the smell of burlap.'

'You do?'

'Yeah. It smells like grammar school, or something.'

The bag wouldn't come off my head. 'They took your purse?' I asked. That would mean they had her gun.

'For all the good it'll do them.'

I knew she wasn't really going to shoot anybody. 'You're right about that,' I said.

'Yeah. Do you think we should sit back-to-back and try to untie each other?' Angie watches a lot of movies.

'Do you really think that'll work?' I asked.

'What else do you have to do?' she countered. She had a point.

'OK.' I sat down, which made my life easier, if not less dark. 'Where are you?'

'In the back of a van.'

'You're a million laughs. If we're going to sit back-to-back, I need to know where your back is.'

We managed to find each other's backs, but any efforts to untie hands with hands that were also tied were, we discovered, doomed to failure. We gave up after only a few minutes.

'They didn't cover this possibility in law school,' I said.

'Where do you think they're taking us?' Angie, who had seemed more excited than scared the whole time we were driving on the magical mystery tour, had moved on to the next thing.

'I don't know. I'm hoping it's not someplace where it's easier to dispose of the bodies.' I was – and I'd like to make this clear for the record – *not* excited. Terrified, sure. Angry, you bet. Plotting hideous revenge? I wouldn't put it past me. But definitely not excited.

'Hey Sand.' Angie wasn't concerned with where our bodies might end up, which was remarkable given that she had the better body according to pretty much any metric you could use to make your computations. 'How come they put bags over our heads?'

She had distracted me from my self-body-shaming. 'What?'

'Why'd they put bags over our heads?'

That seemed an odd question. 'I don't know. Isn't that what you do when you kidnap somebody?'

'We'd already seen their faces. They're putting us into a van that, if I remember correctly and I do, has no windows. Why'd they put bags over our heads?'

It seemed to me she was concentrating on the wrong aspect of our predicament. 'Shouldn't we be working on how to get out of the van?' I asked.

'While it's going along at forty miles an hour? Probably not. Do you have your phone? Mine was in my purse.'

My phone! Of course! If I could call the cops, or at least Trench, or Patrick, who always seemed to be able to make anything you need appear in seconds . . . 'I think it's in my jacket pocket,' I said.

'Great!' My friend, overlooking the obvious.

'My hands are tied behind my back, Angie. Really hard to get to the inside pocket on my jacket right now, and I can't see anything so I wouldn't know who I was dialing.'

'Hang on.' Angie started to make noises that I would have associated with her only if another person, probably male, was present, and I wasn't. 'Dammit! I can't walk my way out of these ropes.'

The van slowed down and I did not consider that a great

sign. 'Nothing you've seen in the movies is gonna work, Ang,' I told her. 'We've got to figure our own way out of here and promise never to tell it to a screenwriter.'

But the grunting went on even as the van came to a halt. 'It's all about my butt,' Angie said.

'You've met guys who thought so.'

'Not the good ones.'

It felt like the van parked, possibly on gravel from the sound of it. 'We should have been thinking of a plan,' I said.

'Oh, I have a plan,' Angie assured me.

Then the van doors opened and I felt someone pulling on my ankles. I must have been facing toward the door with my back toward the cabin of the van. I thought about kicking but that wasn't getting me out of this burlap bag (which, just so you know, smelled like burlap and that was not great) or these ropes.

The hands pulling me were not rough and calloused. I couldn't tell whether they were different hands than had dragged me into the van. Either way, this guy was going to have some major problems with the American Bar Association when I was done with him. 'Hey,' I said involuntarily.

'What?' Angie, not my abductor.

I didn't answer her other than to say I was all right. My hands were tied behind me and I had a bag over my head, so it's possible I wasn't in the best mood.

They stood me up (and I assumed Angie as well but how would I know?) on what felt like a paved surface. Then the bag was lifted off my head and I blinked in the increased light. I mean, burlap isn't *that* thick.

The two men from before were standing between Angie – whose burlap sack had also been taken off her head, which probably made her think of high school or something – and me. It was like a weird sandwich, casting the two guys as filling and Angie and me as the bread.

We were no longer on the studio lot, which was not even a tiny surprise. But it was a little odd that we appeared to be in the actual middle of nowhere. It was paved, with asphalt, on the small stretch where we and the van stood, and appeared to have once been a driveway for some structure that had long been demolished and overgrown. Everywhere around us there was nothing but dirt and weeds. It was like being in the least exotic desert on the planet.

'So let me get this straight,' Angie said as soon as we were upright and unmasked. 'You put the bags over our heads and drove us here, then took the bags off. Were you afraid we'd know what the inside of the van looked like in the dark?'

'Turn around,' the dark-haired man said. 'We'll cut the ropes.'

Not wishing to question our good luck but wondering whether they thought this would make the bodies look less like they'd been abducted, I turned my bound hands toward the dark-haired man. The blond held a gun on me while the one I'd decided was *my* kidnapper pulled a knife out of a sheath on his belt and cut the ropes.

All the clichés are true. I shook my hands and rubbed my wrists. It's what you do when your hands have been tied. I told you that so you won't feel that you have to experience it yourself.

As soon as my bonds were cut, the blond put the gun in the pocket of his jacket and my kidnapper turned toward Angie.

Except she was already holding her gun on him, hands still tied but in front of her. The blond, completely flatfooted, reached back into his pocket. 'Don't,' Angie said. 'I've never missed anyone I've aimed at.' That was, I assumed, technically true, since she'd never pointed a gun at anyone before in her life. 'Now reach into that pocket and pull out the gun using your thumb and your pinkie and nothing else.'

'How'd you get your hands free?' I asked her. 'And I thought they'd taken your gun.'

'They took my *purse*.' Angie was still intent on her target. My guy, still holding the knife, was clearly trying to figure out if he should rush her. The look in her eyes convinced both of them to make no sudden moves. 'I had the gun out of it as soon as I saw the van when we left Reeves's office.'

'Drop the knife,' I said from behind the dark-haired man, who had his back to me. 'And don't turn around or you're a dead man.' I didn't know what I meant but it sounded good.

The guy dropped the knife and I picked it up. I wanted to ask him for the sheath too. 'Take off your belt.'

'Sandy!' Angie found that amusing. Meanwhile the blond-haired man had removed the gun from his pocket just like she'd instructed and laid it carefully on the asphalt in front of him.

'Don't be gross,' I told her. 'And how'd you get your hands free?' It was worth asking again.

'Yeah, how?' asked the dark-haired man. 'I tied those ropes tight.'

'The belt,' I reminded my kidnapper. 'Now.'

The guy started undoing his belt. I glanced back at Angie.

'I told you it was all about my butt,' she told me. 'I managed to squeeze my way out right at the end there. I'll be sore for a couple of days but it was worth it.'

'I'll say.'

'See?' Angie exulted. 'Sometimes the movie stuff *does* work.'

The dark-haired criminal had his belt off. 'The pants now?' he asked.

'Ugh, no. Just give me the belt.'

He did and I removed the sheath to put the knife in. Then I made the guy take off his jacket and found a small handgun in the right-hand pocket. I put that in my own belt but did not remove it to put the knife and sheath on my waist. It would have ruined the line of my outfit.

'OK, let's hear it,' Angie said. 'Who sent you and what did they tell you to do with us?'

'I got a call from a guy I don't know,' the dark-haired guy said. 'They offered us money to take you two out here and leave you here.'

Angie and I looked at each other. That gave blond guy the idea that he had a moment to act, and Angie immediately fired directly into the ground in front of his feet. A piece of asphalt flew up and missed his head by inches. The guy put his hands up, visibly shaken.

The shot reverberated in the nothing around us for a good few seconds.

'Get the message?' Angie growled. The guy nodded his head convincingly.

I directed my attention at my personal prisoner, who had at one time been my captor. It's funny how things work out when you're with Angie. 'This anonymous person just calls you out of the blue, doesn't identify himself, and asks you to kidnap two women and leave them in the middle of nowhere for no particular reason?' I shook my head. 'Couldn't you have gotten into at least a community college?'

'The money was good.' He was looking at his shoes, probably in shame.

I tied my abductor's hands behind him using his belt. Then I used his knife to cut the ropes on Angie's hands but made sure to leave enough length to tie *her* kidnapper up. We got them into the back of the van without putting our hands on them – a technique that hopefully they would learn from the next time they decide to take hostages – and locked the door behind them. The keys were actually left in the van's ignition.

'Those are some really bad kidnappers,' Angie said as she slipped behind the steering wheel.

'Be thankful they are,' I said.

'By the way, when I shot the ground in front of that guy?' Angie looked sideways at me.

'Yeah?'

'I was aiming for his leg.'

EIGHTEEN

Patrick was waiting outside Lieutenant Trench's office while the good policeman, as usual doing nothing that would betray a human emotion, flayed me verbally for having brought him a van full of kidnappers. You'd think a cop would be grateful for such a thing.

I had called Patrick first, of course, and then Trench, while we were driving our haul to his office in the Los Angeles Police Department headquarters, a strange-looking building that seemed to be leaning on one side. Trench, meanwhile, was upright and straight as a rail like always. At the moment he seemed to be having a rhetorical conversation with himself while aiming it at me.

'You hold two men at gunpoint, tie them up and trap them in a van, all of which you admit to, and then you expect me to charge them with conspiracy to inconvenience?' Trench was in rare form. 'You say they told you the idea was to strand you in an area less than twenty miles from the center of the city. And you brought them specifically to me, so I wonder why you think this has anything to do with your case in the James Drake murder.'

'I'm not thinking about the James Drake murder!' I shouted. 'I just got kidnapped and you want me to care about Robert Reeves?'

Trench grimaced the slightest bit, which for him was the equivalent of a public mental breakdown. 'I am an officer of the law,' he said. 'My only connection to you right now is the Robert Reeves case. So I am asking where you thought they were taking you so I can draw some connection.'

'Forgive me for not knowing how to calibrate my position while being blindfolded and tied up in the back of a moving van with no windows,' I countered. 'How exactly is what these two guys did *not* kidnapping with a side of terroristic threats and assault? Why are you aiming all this at me when they are the ones who abducted Angie and me because they were following up on the threats that guy made in the restaurant the other night?'

'Did they tell you who they were working for?' Trench asked.

'No. You're always telling me I should let the police do that sort of work, so I delivered them directly to your door. You're welcome, by the way.'

Patrick, I should point out, had been considerably more understanding, meeting Angie and me at the cop shop and following us in his Tesla to the drop-off point, where he watched as our sheepish abductors were loaded off the back of the van and marched into police headquarters without saying a word. Not even Angie's taunt of, 'You got tied up and taken by a couple of chicks!' appeared to register. Some days it's hardly worth having a Jersey attitude in California.

'Don't worry, Ms Moss.' Trench's voice took on a tone of

weariness that I'm sure he was putting on. 'We'll be happy to charge your two new friends with everything we can possibly conjure. And we will try, unsuccessfully I'm sure, to get them to tell us who employed them to take you on that little adventure. But with all you and your accomplice have done, I'm not sure we can convincingly tie them to the murder charges against Robert Reeves.'

Was this some odd Trench pod person who didn't really want to be a cop? 'They *told* us the message was to get me off the Reeves case,' I said. 'What more do you need?'

'The only thing they said before their attorney arrived – without the benefit of their obligatory phone call, mind you – was that they didn't know why you were so angry with them. They claim they were driving by in their van when you and your partner in crime flagged them down, pulled a pistol on them and abducted them.'

I lowered my eyelids to half-staff. 'With the purpose of driving them to the police?' I said. 'How's that going to stand up in court?'

'Not my department, Counselor.'

A stress headache was starting up in my temples and I didn't blame it a bit. 'Lieutenant,' I said. 'Their attorney showed up despite them not calling. Who's their attorney?'

'Samuel J. Cogley.' Trench certainly knew the name well.

I'm not familiar with the Los Angeles criminal law community the way I was in New Jersey, but I had heard of Samuel J. Cogley. 'Isn't he a mob lawyer?' I asked.

Trench didn't miss a beat. 'Alleged,' he said. 'None of his clients has ever been convicted.'

'Alleged,' I said.

He'd taken my statement personally while Sergeant Roberts dealt with Angie. The two guys who had just been arrested were somewhere in the bowels of the building, conferring with the Perry Mason of mob lawyers, and Patrick, wearing an expression as much like the one my mother would have (if I were ever foolish enough to tell her about this) as I was willing to admit, was almost pressed up against the glass separating Trench's office from the police station bullpen.

Almost.

The one tactic I've ever used with Trench that had gotten even a modicum of information out of him has been the just-short-of-combative direct approach. So I looked sideways at him. He was looking at the lone piece of loose paper on his desk. I assumed that everything else he received had been memorized verbatim and then burned in a Trench ritual that took place at the end of every shift he worked.

'How come you're not treating this whole thing more seriously?' I said.

'*I'm* not treating it seriously?'

'You are the most organized man I've ever met,' I told the lieutenant, and it was true. 'You never miss anything and you never dismiss anything. But I come in here with a couple of kidnappers all trussed up and ready to go, and you're falling just short of asking me why I'm bothering you with such a trivial matter. That's not the Lieutenant Trench I know. So tell me what's different.'

Trench actually looked up from whatever document he'd been studying and locked eyes with me. 'Ms Moss, it never fails to astound me that you seem to believe the Los Angeles Police Department exists for the sole purpose of seeing to your needs. You brought me two men whose alleged crimes do not in the least overlap with my area of the department and I have seen to their arrests. They have been processed and are seeing their attorney as we speak. I'm wondering exactly what other services you expected from your friendly neighborhood policeman.'

I sat there stunned for a moment. Coming from Trench, that was the equivalent of an expletive-heavy dismissal with an invitation to never darken his doorstep again. Finally I stood up, nodded and walked out of the room.

Patrick engulfed me in his arms the second I was in the corridor outside Trench's office. 'What's wrong, love?' he asked. 'Did the lieutenant tell you that you're in danger?'

I held onto him a little longer than I probably should have but I'm sure Patrick would not have complained. 'Let's go someplace warm,' I said.

NINETEEN

The next morning Angie and I went to see Nate Garrigan. It was Angie's 'official' day to tag along with my investigator, and I wanted to see the video footage of the stunt that killed James Drake, which Nate had told me he'd have by today. Win-win.

But Nate, after the usual grumbling about being 'saddled' with Angie because Patrick was a lunatic and so on, had other developments he wanted to discuss first. 'I've been looking into our client and his wife Stacy,' he said.

'Tracy,' Angie corrected.

Nate waggled a finger. 'No. I've been able to trace back to a marriage certificate issued in San Bernardino nine years ago to Robert T. Marciano, which by the way is his real name, and Stacy Rabinowitz. There is no record of a divorce, legal separation or Mrs Reeves's death, so as far as I can tell they're still married.'

I had known that Reeves had changed his name through the police report of his arrest, when he'd been compelled to answer after giving his professional name four times and then admitting to his birth name. He'd had every right and opportunity to change it legally and had not bothered to do so. People make choices. Personally, I thought Robert Marciano was a perfectly good name.

'So how did he get a marriage license for Tracy?' I asked.

'As far as I can tell,' Nate answered, 'he didn't. There's no record of the marriage to Stacy ending and there's no paperwork I can find that indicates he's married to the woman he's introducing to everyone as his current wife.'

Angie, who could have seen the devious side of Mahatma Gandhi, took on a concerned expression. No doubt a conspiracy theory was on its way.

'So did Reeves – that is, Marciano – ever divorce his first

two wives, or are there four women running around thinking they're married to this guy?'

Nate shook his head. 'The first Mrs Marciano divorced him while he was still Marciano,' he said. 'The second one divorced him ten years ago. It's just the third one who's still hanging in there.'

'But Tracy,' I said.

'Hey, you're the lawyer,' Nate reminded me. That was helpful, because for a minute there I thought I worked at the M&M Store. 'If there's no marriage certificate anywhere and no divorce decree from Stacy, is the current Mrs Reeves the current Mrs Reeves?'

'It doesn't make sense.' I felt like I was trying to rouse myself from a deep sleep. First Trench was acting like I was even more of an annoyance than he usually considered me, and now my client had been lying to me about his marriage(s). I'd have to call my mother later and see if she still remembered me. 'Why would Reeves introduce Tracy as his new wife and listen to all the rumors about her sleeping with the stuntman on his movie if they're not really married and he has another wife somewhere else?'

'Variety?' Angie attempted.

Suddenly it occurred to me that I was at least theoretically in charge of this ragtag band of investigators. 'So it seems to me that you need to follow Reeves when he goes home at night and see which wife greets him at the door,' I said. 'But if that's Tracy, we need to find out where Stacy lives so we can go talk to her as well.'

'I can't be in two places at once,' Nate said. Then he looked at Angie with an expression men don't usually have when they look at Angie. He had a shifty smile on his face. Wait. That *was* the expression men usually have when they look at Angie. 'But I can send an operative to do some of that, can't I?'

Angie looked positively flattered. 'An operative?'

There followed a good deal of commotion, much of it devoted to the proper title Angie should hold in the investigation agency that Nate was now apparently opening just for her while she was still working full-time as Patrick's executive assistant. On the prospect of pay, Nate was quite clear: there wouldn't be any. Angie, no doubt wondering if she'd have to pay all the rent on our two-bedroom should I move out and live with Patrick, spent some time trying to convince him otherwise and came up short.

When all that had been settled (Angie was essentially in exactly the same position as she'd been when she woke up this morning, except now she had a task to perform), I asked Nate about the footage he'd supposedly been offered that showed James Drake falling to his death. I wasn't exactly looking forward to seeing it, but I had to know if it hurt or helped my client, and especially what effect I might expect it to have if shown to a jury.

'You told me not to look at it yet so I didn't look at it,' he said. That's Nate being evasive.

'You listened to it, didn't you?' I asked.

He looked sheepish. 'A little.'

I put my hands on my hips. 'Nathan, what did your father and I tell you about stretching the truth?'

No response other than a sour expression. Some people just can't take it. 'What'd you find out?' I said.

'Not that much. Let's take a look.' Nate gestured toward the sofa, so Angie and I sat down, facing the ginormous flat-screen TV he had in his office for, you know, investigating stuff.

'Did you get this on Blu-ray or DVD?' Angie asked. It's possible she was making an age joke. It's equally possible she wasn't.

'No. I'm mirroring it from my desktop to the TV so it'll be bigger and we can see it better. Welcome to technology.' No doubt that was a dig to counter the comment I'd made when I was his mother a minute before.

He clicked the right icons and keyed in the proper commands, and in another minute we were all paying close attention to the big – and I mean *big* – screen.

As might be expected from video taken on a phone, particularly when the person taking it didn't know something momentous was about to happen, it began with some chaotic panning around and looking at people's backs. Because it had been recorded on a phone held vertically, there were bars on either side of the image. It was clearly taken on the movie set in Griffith Park, but was not really clear or focused on anything in particular. I might have to look away in a moment to avoid motion sickness.

'Who's taking the images?' I asked Nate.

'How bad do you need to know?'

'If I'm putting someone on the witness stand, I generally like to know who they are ahead of time,' I said. 'Call me quirky.'

'You're quirky,' Angie said. She's so accommodating.

'Let's take a look at it first and if you think it's going to make a difference you can ask me where I got it afterward,' Nate said. 'I kind of promised I wouldn't give that up if I didn't have to.'

That wasn't my preference, but it was fair enough and I told Nate so, then turned my attention back to the video.

The cameraperson seemed to be walking through the set. No one greeted him or her or I would have at least gotten a first name for my potential witness. They all seemed too intent on their individual jobs to take notice of whoever this person might be.

There was plenty of sound, however. Hammers were hitting nails. Electric tools were whirring (which made me want the videographer to get closer to the crane where James Drake was no doubt getting ready for what he thought would be an easy rehearsal). There was plenty of foot traffic. The park was obviously closed to the public – at least this area of the park was – and it was *very* early in the morning, judging by the light to the west. It almost looked like night but light was starting to bleed through the black sky.

The motion slowed down, which made my stomach give thanks. Loudly. Nate glanced at me but Angie just smiled and kept her eyes on the screen.

Eventually the videographer arrived at the base of the crane, where they focused on the top first and then panned down slowly, making me wonder if the person taking the images was a cinematographer or one of the area's vast army of aspiring directors. Most likely the latter. The image ended looking down off the edge of the cliff, which looked less threatening than the circumstances might have suggested. It was a hillside, but the crane was extended out over it and that made the drop considerably more precarious.

Then the person taking the video tilted back up and there on the screen was my client Robert Reeves, acting very much the director, in jeans and a blue shirt but with a red scarf around his neck, no doubt to obscure any possible signs of aging. Now that I came to think of it, Reeves had been wearing a scarf every time I'd met with him, too.

Next to him, deep in conversation with Reeves, was a man in khaki, clearly wearing a harness that would be latched to the crane in a few minutes. He was a large, easygoing-looking man, listening intently to what his director might have to say.

James Drake.

'You're being thrown from a catapult, sort of,' Reeves was saying. It was hard to make out his voice through all the ambient noise, but my client helped himself be more audible by yelling at his stunt performer, something that would undoubtedly make him more endearing to a jury. It's sarcasm. I'm from New Jersey. 'You're a Nazi! So you're terrified, but you're trying your best not to show it because you want to appear invincible. Get it?'

'So I'm not afraid of falling over the cliff?' Drake asked, to all appearances sincerely.

'Of *course* you're afraid!' Reeves put his hand to his forehead in a gesture of amazement at the stupidity of his companion. 'I just *told* you that! But you're *pretending* not to be afraid so you can impress the girl!'

Drake looked over at an actress who was standing nearby, holding a blanket over her shoulders because it must have been the California version of cold that morning. 'How am I going to impress a girl by falling off a cliff and dying?' he asked Reeves.

The director made a show of not losing his temper, but you could see the veins in his neck bulge even in a cell-phone video. He spoke very slowly, trying to control his volume and pitch. 'You don't know you're going to die. You only have a split second to realize what's happening.'

Drake looked up at the crane, maybe having an eerie premon-
ition, maybe just gauging the distance. Maybe he was thinking
about whether having breakfast from the craft services table
just now had been a good idea. He wrinkled his nose. 'What
stinks around here?'

'Everything. Now let's get this going, for crissakes! We're
already overbudget!'

'OK,' Drake said. Then he got an impish grin on his face
and looked at Reeves. 'You don't want to try it first, do you?'

'*No*, I don't want to try it out first! Come on! Let's get
the rehearsal done so we can shoot the real thing before they
kick us out of the park, OK?' Reeves walked away in a
mumbling huff and Drake stood there with a look on his face
that indicated he didn't know why his joke hadn't landed.

He shrugged and walked away.

I thought the video would cut there and turned to look
at Nate. 'That's it? All it shows is that Reeves is a jerk to the
people who work for him. That's a bad thing to be but it
doesn't prove he did – or we're hoping didn't – set up that
stunt to fail purposely so James Drake would die.'

'Keep watching,' Nate said ominously.

With the obvious drama concluded, our intrepid videographer might have just quit shooting altogether – something
I would later wish they had done – but no, whoever it was
felt the need to document the entire process for posterity. And
what they recorded was at best confusing and at worst . . .

It started with a pan around the set – again – and glimpses
of the crew, electricians laying cable on the ground and
making sure it was insulated from moisture, technicians
setting up lights, the standard videographer in this case *not*
taking any footage because it was a technical rehearsal and
not a camera rehearsal.

Then two things happened quickly that left me sitting
frozen on Nate's sofa. First, about two minutes after he'd
stormed away from James Drake, the figure in jeans and blue
shirt, Robert Reeves, casually sauntered over to the area of
the crane. And just for a second, just enough to see it on the
video, he pulled a small . . . something from his pocket and
leaned over the crane toward the base of the cables.

'Uh-oh,' I said aloud.

But the person taking the video must have been distracted because the image left Reeves to his 'work' and panned to the left, where some of the cast had assembled to watch the spectacle. There was the female lead, who must have been there to lend emotional support and context to the stunt performer. There were a couple of supporting players, clearly actors because they were in desert costumes and way too attractive to be crew members (my apologies, but it's the truth). And standing just to the side, looking – a little awed – in the direction of the top of the crane, was the star of *Desert Siege*.

Patrick McNabb.

TWENTY

'I honestly don't remember being on the set that day,' Patrick said.

I hadn't called him from Nate's and I hadn't called him from the car. I wanted to see my boyfriend's face when he explained his presence in an almost definitely incriminating video on a day he had told me directly that he hadn't been present. So we were in his office at Dunwoody Inc., sitting on the sofa facing each other, with Angie in the chair behind Patrick's desk. She resisted the impulse to put her feet up on his desk, which I knew must have taken a great deal of willpower on her part.

'I saw you with my own eyes,' I told him. Like I could have seen him with someone else's eyes. 'You were there and you were looking up right at the crane where James Drake fell and died. How could you forget that?'

Patrick shook his head in wonder. 'I have no explanation.'

He turned toward Angie. 'Please call the studio and find the call-in sheet and the log for that day,' he told his executive assistant. 'I want to see if my name is on the sheets, because I'm sure that I finished shooting the week before this happened.'

Angie, now in full assistant mode, nodded and pulled her phone from her purse. Quietly I heard her start to make inquiries. She had not had to consult any database for the phone number. That's Angie.

'You didn't just drop by to watch?' I asked, suggesting a way that the lie could be innocent. 'It was a pretty big stunt. People like to watch that stuff.'

'That's just my point,' Patrick answered. 'If I were there for something like that, I'd certainly remember it. And you know me, Sandy. My memory is not faulty.'

That was true, but his perception was sometimes skewed. Patrick didn't like anyone, especially me, to see him in a bad light. 'Maybe you came by first thing in the morning and then left before the accident happened,' I suggested.

That was a convenient out and Patrick refused to take it. He shook his head. 'I wouldn't have done that, and if I had, I'd remember it. I wasn't there, Sandy. Could it have been my stunt double? I mean, he is paid to look like me.'

'They're looking for the log-in sheet,' Angie reported. 'Back to us within ten minutes.' She put her phone back on the desk.

'Thank you, Angie.' Patrick is, it should be noted, nothing like Robert Reeves as a boss.

I had made a copy of the file Nate had on his hard drive and showed it to Patrick. 'Does that look like your stunt double?' I asked. 'Because if it does, maybe I'll move in with him.'

Patrick looked up. 'So you're moving in?'

'One thing at a time. First let's find out if you were actually on the set or not.'

Angie's phone buzzed and she picked it up.

'That's not Henry,' he said, looking at the screen. 'It's me all right.'

'So you were there.'

'Not necessarily.' Angie had one hand on her ear and the other ear to the phone. 'The studio's records are not definitive. Patrick's card was scanned at the entrance to the set but then never scanned out, and he clearly isn't still there.' That was evident, I thought. If he were still on the set of *Desert Siege*, I wouldn't have seen him again after his trial. And my life, while certainly less complicated, would not have been as interesting.

'Check on the set of *Torn*,' Patrick told her. 'See if they have a record of me being on set that day because I think I was. And if so, what time.' Angie nodded.

A completely random thought that had nothing to do with the case occurred to me. 'Why is it called *Torn*?' I asked Patrick. 'You'd think *Split* would be a better title for a character with multiple personality disorder.'

'*Torn* tested better,' he said. Of course it did. 'I don't understand it. I have no memory of being in Griffith Park that day. I've only been there a couple of times, mostly when you and I went to the observatory, Sandy.' (That had been a lovely evening, for the record.) 'You tend to get noticed in big spaces like that and there's nowhere to hide.' That's Patrick being modest; he loves the attention and sometimes goes out in public just to be noticed. Don't let him fool you.

My cell phone rang and I was surprised to see the caller identified as LAPD. Not Trench, because his line is in my contacts. Just the cops. You get a twinge in your intestines when you see that, but pretty much everyone I care about in Los Angeles was here in the room with me. Not that it helped my intestines. Those things just can't be reasoned with.

I picked up the call. 'This is Sergeant Roberts.' Trench's assistant. His aide-de-camp. The Watson to his Holmes. You get it. And that's how bad things had gotten: Trench had something he wanted to tell me and he didn't even call himself.

'Hello, Sergeant.' I'm pretty sure Roberts's first name is 'Sergeant'.

'Ms Moss, I'm calling because Lieutenant Trench' – the coward – 'has some information he wanted me to pass along.'

'What's that?' No doubt Trench had found some new way to prove to me that I was an annoyance and a hindrance but felt it was beneath him to pass that along in person. I wondered if Roberts ever got tired of being in his shadow. But it would probably have been a bad idea to ask.

'He said to tell you that the two men who abducted you yesterday have been arraigned and released on their own recognizance. He said that if you have not taken security measures you might want to do so, and if you have you should probably increase them.'

I looked over at Angie, who in her third job after being Patrick's executive assistant and Nate's intern was also my security detail. She was on the phone with the production office at *Torn*.

'Thank you, Sergeant,' I said. 'I'll make sure to do that.'

I disconnected the call because I didn't want Roberts (and by extension Trench) to hear me cry. But my face must have registered the way I felt.

'What's wrong?' Patrick asked immediately.

'Nothing,' Angie said. 'We have records of you being on the set of *Torn* the day the crane dropped Jim Drake into a ditch.'

But Patrick was intent on me. 'Sandy?' he asked.

'I think we need to call in the Marines,' I said.

TWENTY-ONE

I have never known her as anything but Judy. At least six feet tall and resembling the Washington Monument, she had the personality of sandstone and the affect of someone who is currently in a coma.

She was the perfect bodyguard, and had saved my life more than once. Angie had called the agency from which we'd hired her before and requested Judy specifically. Luckily she wasn't keeping anyone else from getting killed just at the moment, so I had hired her again and this time had the firm paying for her services, over Patrick's objections because he loves to pay for everything I need, which isn't as terrific as it sounds.

I had hoped never to see Judy again, but then I hadn't put *get kidnapped* on my bucket list either. Now, my priorities rearranged, having her in the room with me while I sat down with Penny Kanter, Robert Reeves's assistant (possibly executive assistant, because I don't care about those titles but Angie would know), on her own, which was clearly making Penny nervous. Not having Reeves there for her to constantly monitor appeared to be a very nerve-racking situation for her.

Judy stood by the door, back straight, shoulders proud, face as impassive as a figure at Madame Tussaud's. That is the wonder that is Judy.

After we'd settled in for our conference, I felt it was important to state the objectives and get right to the important issues so I could release Penny and let her go lick Reeves's boots or something. (It should be noted that even working for Patrick, Angie is never in any way subservient. She is Angie and that is a force of nature. Luckily Patrick loves that about her.)

'What I'm trying to establish is where everyone who might be a witness was when the accident happened,' I began. I had decided that calling the murder an accident might have made some of my witnesses more comfortable, and you want them relaxed so you get unguarded answers. Unfortunately, I was getting the impression that being relaxed wasn't in Penny's skill set. 'So tell me where you were that day.'

The opposite of good happened: Penny tensed up more. 'Am I considered a suspect?' she asked.

'I can't see why you would be.' And I couldn't. For one thing, I'm not in charge of who's a suspect. I just needed to create reasonable doubt that my client did it. 'I'm gathering information and you were there, so you might know some things that could be of help. For example, were you with Mr Reeves the whole day?'

'Yes.' Immediate, like a doctor had hit her Reeves-response-knee with a rubber hammer. 'Wait. No. I left the set for an hour after the police said I could leave.'

'After the incident that killed James Drake,' I said.

She nodded. 'I was there the whole morning until that.' She gave no sign of distress or a painful memory. She was Robert Reeves's assistant and the guy who had died wasn't her concern. The focus was a little terrifying.

'What were your duties that morning? When your boss is directing a movie and he's on the set, what are you required to do?' I actually had a decent idea of what the answer was, but this was a test of what kind of witness I could expect Penny to be.

'For that particular day I had to coordinate his meeting with the stunt coordinator, the stunt performer and the camera operator as well as the cinematographer,' she said without consulting notes of any kind. 'But the usual things were also part of my work, making sure his bills were paid, managing appointments with the ex-wives and visits with his children. Also there was a meeting with his manager that didn't occur because the police questioning took longer than we might have expected.'

'Longer than you might have expected?' I said.

'Yes.'

'You were expecting police questioning that day?' It seemed an odd breakthrough in the trial, and not one that was going to make my job easier. 'You knew James Drake was going to die?'

Penny looked confused, then shocked, then worried. 'Oh no,' she said. 'I meant it took longer after the . . . incident occurred than I might have anticipated. Either way, Mr Reeves did not make the meeting with his manager that day.'

I think better on my feet, and without thinking about it I got up and started to pace around my office. I don't have a very large office so I ended up pacing in a fairly tight circle around my desk. Penny's expression indicated that she was afraid to be in the same room with someone this deranged. I didn't care. I looked at Judy, who was not pacing. Or moving. Or anything. Occasionally she blinked but I think it was a source of great embarrassment to her.

'Do you have a list of the personnel who were present in Griffith Park that morning?' I asked. I already had the studio records but it would be interesting to see if Penny's – and I was sure she'd have some – matched up. Mostly I wanted to see if they agreed on the whereabouts of the guy who wanted me to live in his house with him.

'No, I don't keep those,' Penny answered. 'You'd have to check with the studio's records.'

That seemed uncharacteristic but there was no point in pushing it. I decided that another way to loosen Penny up as a witness was to ask about herself. 'How did you come to work for Mr Reeves?' That seemed easy enough.

Penny did appear to relax a bit. She still had a look in her eyes that evoked Bambi standing out in the middle lane of the 405 at night, but her shoulders got less taut and her face overall indicated she was on more comfortable ground. She didn't smile, but I wouldn't have asked her to violate her religious beliefs.

'I came out here like everyone else, from Nashua, New Hampshire,' she began. I didn't want to point out that not everyone came from Nashua, New Hampshire, because that seemed just a touch mean. But in my own head I stored that one away. 'I had a degree in film and video and figured I could take the movie business by storm.'

'You wanted to be a director?' Everyone in Southern California wanted to be a director except the directors, who wanted to be something closer to a deity as far as I could tell.

'No, I wanted to be a special effects artist.' Penny's answers were always not what I expected them to be, which was why I was glad to be having this conference. She was the last person you'd want to get on the stand and wing it. 'I had a background in computer technology and imagery and I figured I would be working on the next superhero extravaganza within days of getting my apartment in Burbank.'

I leaned on the edge of my desk because pacing hadn't gotten me anywhere, literally. 'But the jobs weren't so easy to find.'

Clearly Penny was reliving her struggles because she looked off into the middle distance and sighed. 'No.' I'm not sure but I think Penny liked to say 'no' to me. 'But I had gotten to know someone who worked on effects on a freelance basis, and he knew that Mr Reeves needed an assistant. Luckily I had a minor in business administration and I'm very detail oriented. I met Mr Reeves and he offered me the job that day.'

'Is he a good boss?' I said. Character matters in criminal cases, and for that matter in civil cases. Anytime a jury or judge is going to pass judgment on a client you want them to like the client. Or at least not hate him. Hate is bad.

'He pays very well,' Penny said. I waited but that was it.

'I mean, you hear stories about people in the industry mistreating their employees, berating them, throwing things,' I explained. 'Does Mr Reeves ever do stuff like that?'

'Oh, never.' Eyes so wide they could be a studio apartment in Manhattan. That was when I started to realize Penny had been lying. Perhaps for the whole interview.

There was no point. 'Thanks for coming in,' I said.

Penny, used to taking orders without question, got up, nodded in my direction and walked out of the office past Judy, who stood by vigilantly. I suppressed the urge to tickle her just to see if I could get a response.

Instead I nodded in Penny's direction as she raced for the elevator in relief. 'She's hilarious,' I said.

'Yes ma'am,' Judy said.

TWENTY-TWO

'Why would someone want to intimidate me off this case?' I asked Holly Wentworth.

We were sitting in the cafeteria at Seaton, Taylor and supposedly having a quiet lunch. I was hunched over the salad I'd ordered for myself out of food guilt, elbows on the table and head hunched over the plastic container full of various vegetable matter. I poked at the salad with a fork as if trying to determine if it was still breathing. Holly had a lovely selection of sushi which she had ordered in (Holly doesn't do the cafeteria and neither should I) and was eating elegantly with chopsticks.

Judy sat at a table to my left, not eating anything. I've never seen Judy eat. I've seen her sit at tables in restaurants, coffee shops and, in this case, a company cafeteria. But she has never eaten in my presence. She has occasionally had a drink of water, which probably made her feel inefficient. Real robots don't require hydration.

'Because someone doesn't want Robert Reeves to be acquitted,' Holly answered sensibly. Holly is extremely sensible, but then I've only seen her in the office. For all I know at night she's a wild woman throwing caution to the wind and indulging in debauchery of the most vulgar and decadent variety. But sensibly.

'That's it,' I said. 'If I'm off the case he'll get somebody else to defend him. There's no reason to think that I'm more likely to keep him out of jail than anybody else.'

Holly put down her chopsticks. 'Sandy,' she said. 'You really don't get what you've done here in two years. You got both Patrick McNabb and Cynthia Sutton off on murder charges when nobody thought that was going to be possible. You have a real reputation in the LA legal community. People are in awe of you. Of course they want you off the case.'

I was probably blushing; I blush at the drop of a compliment. I don't handle them well, I'm saying. 'Oh, come on. I got lucky both times.'

Holly could just barely suppress her eye-roll. 'No you didn't. You were exceptionally clever and inventive in court and you found evidence in both cases that resulted in acquittals for your clients. In fact, you've never even had to go to a closing argument because the charges were dropped before you had to go to a jury.'

That was all beside the point; it was mostly Nate who had helped in those cases. And to prove it he texted me at that moment: *Trailed Reeves home. Went to Stacy, not Tracy. Sending address to Angie.* OK. I wasn't sure what that told me so I looked back at Holly.

'Nevertheless,' I said. 'Someone sent two men to kidnap Angie and me and . . . I guess strand us somewhere. That's not normal intimidation behavior. Who does that?'

Holly seemed to think about that while chewing a piece of tuna roll. 'I assume Lieutenant Trench is working hard to find out.'

'Don't get me started on Lieutenant Trench. Somehow I got on his bad side and he's not talking to me.' Kale, in case you're wondering, is overrated. It's spinach with a press agent.

'He's just being Lieutenant Trench,' Holly said, and her eyes got a little dreamy. Did she and Trench have a thing?

Did she know what K.C. stood for? (I couldn't imagine a level of intimacy deeper than that for the homicide cop.)

'I'm dancing around it, but I am a little afraid,' I told Holly, and maybe myself for the first time. 'I've gotten shot at and threatened since I took this job, and I moved out here because I thought the change to family law would be less stressful.'

Holly chuckled to herself, sensibly. 'You need to own up, Sandy. You actually love this kind of case and you should be actively seeking more of them. You like the adrenaline rush and you like dealing with things that you're really good at. You're fine on the divorces and the custody cases we do in family law but guess what? You really shine when you're defending a client against criminal charges. And that's because you like it better.'

I was about to dispute everything Holly had said with cogent, well-considered arguments that would leave her a quivering heap over a small platter of raw fish, but my telephone rang and the caller was Sidney Chao. I had to answer that one, no matter how devastatingly convincing I had been prepared to be.

I pointed to my phone and Holly showed me her palms to say it was OK for me to take the call. I was going to do that anyway, but it's nice when your boss gives you permission. 'Sidney,' I said, 'give me good news.'

'What would qualify as good news for you?' the psychiatrist asked. 'I've completed the evaluation on Tracy Reeves and I will be writing a detailed report for you, but I'm wondering whether you prefer she be competent to answer questions about the case or not.'

'Stop psychoanalyzing me, Sidney. If I need help I promise I'll call you.'

'You need a great deal of help, but that's a subject for another conversation or twenty,' he said. Now I was starting to wonder what he meant by that. 'But it seems to me, and remember I'm not a lawyer, that if your client is to be found innocent, his wife needs to be considered incompetent and his claims that she can't distinguish between reality and fantasy must be true.'

He was right, of course, but I had to sound more confident

than I really was. 'That's not entirely true. I can defend him into an acquittal even if she's as clear as water about what's real. But it would probably help if she's not. So what kind of news am I getting from you today?'

Holly, pretending to look at something on her phone, was really watching me out of the corner of her eye. She'd make a terrible actress.

'Keep in mind that the short time you gave me . . .'

'That the court gave me,' I corrected.

'Yes, but the time didn't allow me to see the subject more than once, but I think the indications are extremely clear. That woman is among the saner people I've met in Southern California.'

That wasn't the best news I'd ever heard. 'OK,' I said to Sidney. I said that because, 'I'd like to resign from the legal profession and take up upholstery as a career' seemed a little over-the-top.

'There's more,' Sidney said. Sidney is a fan of the dramatic reveal. In New Jersey shrinks give you antidepressants. In Los Angeles they give you storylines.

It was now my duty to provide the straight line. 'What?' It doesn't take much.

'You understand that this woman is not my patient and that I examined her specifically on your request to prepare for trial,' Sidney said. Apparently telling me things I already knew was part of his carefully calibrated presentation. 'So I'm not violating doctor/patient confidentiality but I am going to speak based on my considered professional opinion and not on anything that the subject told me directly. Do you understand, Sandy?'

A relatively stupid manatee would have understood but, once again, I had to come up with the setup. 'I get it. You're telling me what you believe to be true and not anything that Tracy told you to your face, either as an answer to a question or otherwise. Right?'

'Excellent.' I was one of the brighter students in Sidney's class, apparently. 'So I think this information will be useful to you. In my professional opinion, the woman you sent me is not suffering from a mental illness.'

'You said that already.' Don't build me up just to reiterate your point. I don't have that kind of time.

'Yes, but I left this out: I also believe that there is almost no chance her name is Tracy Reeves or that she is or ever has been married to your client.'

I sat for a moment. Holly looked over at me. 'What?' My face must have been pretty blank.

'You sure?' I asked Sidney.

'In my business there's no such thing as sure, but yes.' I wasn't sure whether Sidney was a real psychiatrist or someone who played a psychiatrist on TV. But he had thrown a complete monkey wrench into my case just now and I hadn't even started considering the implications yet.

I thanked him and hung up, not noticing whether Sidney sounded offended by my abrupt departure. Then I looked over at Holly.

'I need to see Robert Reeves again,' I said.

'I'm sorry,' she said, and she was being sincere.

I put in a call to Penny and went through the usual excuses about what a busy guy Reeves was and the ritual of me threatening to drop his defense if he didn't show up in my office within the hour. Then I hung up the phone and worked on the Siperstein divorce for forty-three minutes and sure enough Penny's cry of, 'Robert Reeves is here!' filled the reception area. I was impressed they'd managed to ford the traffic that quickly, but for all I knew Reeves had been around the corner when Penny called him and it had taken him forty-three minutes to walk here just so I'd be annoyed.

Just so *he'd* be annoyed, I let him sit in the waiting area while I took a call from Angie. 'I'm at Stacy Reeves's house,' she said, almost whispering.

'Are you in her living room?' She hadn't broken in, had she?

'No, I'm in my car.'

'Then why are you whispering?'

'I dunno,' Angie answered. 'It seemed appropriate. Anyway, I saw Mrs Reeves.'

'Did you talk to her?'

'No. Should I?'

'Ang, we're trying to find out what's going on with our own client and his seemingly multiple wives. You might want to ask her about that.' I looked out into the waiting area. Reeves was standing and, in true melodrama fashion, tapping his foot. I half expected him to don a tuxedo, grab a cane and start a musical number with hundreds of extras.

'That seems awful personal,' Angie said.

'I'm a lawyer, not a detective,' I told her. 'I just want to know if she's legally married to Robert Reeves the movie director. And if you want to drop it into the conversation, find out whether she knows about the other current Mrs Reeves.'

'I saw her out in her garden,' Angie said. 'She doesn't *look* like the other current Mrs Reeves, I can tell you that. She's got to be in her late forties.'

'Reeves's age,' I noted.

'And she's in dingy clothes.'

'Angie, she's gardening. You want her to wear an evening gown?'

'I mean, she's *dowdy*, you know? She looks like a housewife.'

'Do they still have housewives?' I asked. No idea why I said that.

'I don't want to take her picture. I mean, she's not wearing makeup or anything. That'd be cruel.'

'Nobody's asking you to take her picture. Ang, I'm gonna hang up now. I've got her husband and maybe someone else's waiting to see me.'

When Janine led him into my office Robert Reeves did not look pleased, which I had expected. No conference room for my client this time; I wanted things as much on my turf as possible. He had barely sat down and started to complain about the interruption to his easily-more-important-than-mine life when I slapped my hand down on the surface of my desk to make a loud noise that demanded his attention. Reeves looked shocked and offended, even if he didn't know by what.

'I'm done screwing around, Bob,' I said.

'Robert.'

'I will call you what I want until you start acting like someone who's facing a life sentence in prison and realizes his attorney is his only way out.' Give the crowd the greatest hits before you start blending in the new material. 'Until then, you're going to be *Bob* to me.'

He tried to rise from his seat. 'I don't need to listen—'

'Yes you do, Bob. And you're going to. I want to know exactly what's going on with you and your multiple wives.'

That stopped him. He sat back down. 'What are you talking about?'

I waggled a finger at him. 'No, no. We're not playing games anymore. I know about Stacy and I know that Tracy isn't actually your wife and that her name is likely not even Tracy. So how about you finally open up to me, because I'm convinced now that your attempt at bigamy is related to the murder of James Drake and that's my business. Start talking.'

But this time my tough talk was just pissing him off. I was getting into his personal life and Reeves didn't like it. I didn't care much for it either, but I was the one who knew it was necessary. 'I don't know what you're talking about,' he said.

I moaned and not in a good way. 'I'm not doing this,' I said, both to Reeves and to myself. 'I have other cases I can concentrate on. If you want me to be your lawyer, you're going to open up to me. If you don't, I'm on my way.'

Reeves folded his arms across his chest. 'Really,' he said.

'Really.'

'Ms Moss, you've made that threat at least three times before and I always backed off because I'm told you're the best in LA at this. But you're still my lawyer, no matter how much I decide to share or not share with you and, frankly, the threat isn't playing the way it used to. You need a better director, Sandy.'

I picked up the landline on my desk and punched in the number for Judge Franklin's office. His secretary Frances picked up the line, and when I told her it was an emergency she put me through to the judge himself.

'Ms Moss, this had better be good.'

'I'm not sure you'll think so, Your Honor, and I apologize in advance. But I'd like to ask your permission to withdraw from the Robert Reeves defense.'

Reeves sat back in his chair (really my chair but let's not be petty) and clasped his hands behind his head in a gesture of supreme smugness. He thought I was pretending.

So I put Franklin on speakerphone.

'You're right, Ms Moss. I'm not happy about that request. I'm going to need some context. If you want to withdraw you have to give me a very good reason.'

I put the judge on mute and looked at Reeves. 'What'll it be?'

'You're bluffing.'

'Don't underestimate me, Bob. You're going to come clean to me – and I mean spotless – or I'm not your lawyer anymore. Make up your mind.'

Franklin said, 'Ms Moss?'

'Sorry, Your Honor.' Yes, I had taken him off mute first. 'Just one quick moment.' I looked at Reeves again. 'So?'

The color had drained from his face. His eyes looked like he'd sat on a very sharp block of ice. He shook his head. 'OK. OK. I'll tell you whatever you need to know. Don't drop the case.'

I took Franklin off mute again. 'Sorry to bother you, Your Honor. I've decided not to request withdrawal.' Then I looked Reeves right in the face. 'At this time.'

'I'm both pleased and puzzled, Ms Moss,' the judge said. 'Someday you must explain yourself to me.'

'It's a promise, Judge.' We disconnected the call. I put down the phone and put my elbows on my desk, resting my chin in my hands. 'I can call him back, Bob. Let's hear it.'

'OK,' Robert Reeves said.

PART TWO
There?

PART TWO

Theory

TWENTY-THREE

'**Y**ou have to understand what this business is like,' Robert Reeves said.

I had been, at the very least, an interested observer of 'this business' for more than a year now and, frankly, there wasn't a lot of it I was eager to understand better. But I let my client begin that way because it would have taken too long to get him to start over again. He was finally in a compliant mood and I wanted him to stay that way until I could get a handle on how to defend him.

Because so far it wasn't seeming all that possible.

'What about it?' I threw him a lifeline.

'You work for years, from the time you're in high school, to get to a point where you can make movies that people actually want to *see*,' he said. 'And it takes a long time but that's OK because you can see the prize at the end.'

'*Desert Siege*,' I said. It slipped out.

But Reeves didn't catch the irony and luckily Patrick wasn't there. But I'd seen their film and it was, in a word, silly. Not in a good way. 'Exactly,' my client said. 'An action movie with a big budget and you get to direct those because the people with all the power have come to trust you based on all your years of experience.'

I didn't see how this woe-is-me diatribe (if that's what it was) pertained to his having two wives, at least one of them legally wed to him, but I figured he was getting there sooner or later. 'I understand,' I lied.

Reeves shook his head; no, I *didn't* understand, but he was going to explain it to me in great detail. 'The problem is this town is obsessed with youth. Oh sure they love Spielberg because he can buy and sell everyone he knows, and they love Scorsese because the critics told them they have to, but they really want the next kid making two-minute videos on TikTok because they think he'll bring in the eighteen-year-olds and he'll work cheap.'

Still nothing about any of his numerous wives or whether or not he'd sabotaged the cables that snapped and sent poor Jim Drake to his grisly death. But did I show any impatience? Did I tell the film director to cut to the chase? Did I point out that the next kid making TikTok videos to work their way up might be a she or a they? I did not. I was the very model of restraint.

'You're worried you're aging out of action movies?' I asked.

Reeves looked at me as if wondering whether he should have let this idiot woman resign from his case after all. 'No. I am at the peak of my craft right now and my experience leading up to this point in my career is exactly why I should be doing what I'm doing.'

I was trying to follow him but he was blending into the surroundings like a chameleon. 'So what's the problem?' I said, still graciously not adding, *and what the hell does it have to do with you being married too much?*

'The problem is that *they* could think I'm aging out of action movies,' Reeves said, his face so forlorn that two basset hounds came to my office door to observe out of professional courtesy but Judy shooed them away. 'And in this town . . .' (People in Los Angeles always refer to the movie business as 'this town'. In New Jersey we refer to New York as 'The City', but it doesn't mean the same thing.) '. . . people see you as being as old as the person on your arm when you're on the red carpet.'

Immediately images of me and Patrick on red carpets leapt to my mind. I mean, we weren't really all that far apart in age, and Patrick is actually two years older than me but . . .

Hey. Wait a minute!

I tried to hold my temper in check but my fury on behalf of all women was boiling just under the surface. I hoped. 'So you're saying that you married Tracy so you could be seen with a younger woman and be thought of as younger yourself?' My teeth weren't clenched but they wanted to be.

'Oh, no,' Reeves said. 'That's not what happened at all.'

OK. So the system wasn't as awful as I'd thought it was

and my client wasn't a shallow, career-driven misogynist and nobody was looking at me and Patrick at a premiere and wondering why I wasn't younger and let's face it, prettier. My body temperature went down a degree or two.

'Then what did happen?' I asked.

'I never married Tracy,' he said. 'I hired her to be my wife.'

Naturally. This was definitely not helping my case. 'There's a name for that and it's not legal in this state,' I pointed out.

Whatever Reeves was about to tell me was clearly extremely painful to him. I could tell by his face and the way he suddenly refused to meet my eyes. There was a spot on the ceiling of my office, just to the left of the hanging plant, that appeared to fascinate him beyond any reasonable level of polite interest. Besides, it was a fake plant. I tried very hard to remember that he was a human being and by virtue of that worthy of my empathy. I tried.

'Don't be ridiculous,' he said, but his voice had lost the arrogance it had featured . . . every other time I'd spoken with him. He was putting on a front. 'Tracey and I are in a business relationship. We have never' – he coughed – 'been *intimate.*'

My mind was racing ahead but at the same time I was trying to take stock and some of it spilled out of my mouth as I did. 'So you hired a young woman to pretend to be your wife in public and then went home every night to Stacy, who I'm assuming is your real wife?'

He nodded. He might have brushed a tear from his eye.

'Tracy is not pretending,' he said, with just a hint of condescension. 'She is playing a role.'

Naturally. 'She's an aspiring actress,' I said, thinking out loud. 'She took the gig because as your wife she might get some movie roles.'

Reeves actually sat up and took his eyes off my ceiling. No, that's not a double entendre.

'She took the *gig* because it is prestigious to be seen as my wife and because I pay her very well, in cash.'

'Sure. You can't deduct *fake wife* from your income tax form.' Oh my, I'd said that out loud. Should really watch that habit.

But Reeves did not seem to be offended by that, which was unexpected. 'No. But my accountant says if I give her a role in my next movie it will save me a bundle and the studio will pay much of her salary.' No irony at all. None.

'Why didn't you just divorce Stacy and marry Tracy? And what's with the names? Is that just a coincidence?'

His lips flattened out at the very mention of the word *coincidence*. 'I don't believe in such things. They're bad story-telling. No, I asked her to take the name Tracy *because* it was so close to my wife's name. So if a name sounding like that was mentioned, I wouldn't react badly. If we'd used Virginia, her real name, and someone referred to my wife Virginia, I might not always immediately respond the way I should. It was a safety mechanism.'

This is the kind of logic the movie business encourages. Considering his first three marriages, I pressed on. 'Again, why didn't you divorce Stacy and legally marry the young thing you wanted on your arm at the Oscars?' (Like Reeves was ever going to be invited to the Oscars.)

He looked offended by the question. 'I love my wife.'

Of course he did. 'Listen to me. We need to plot a strategy for your trial, which will be here before you know it,' I told my client. 'And if you think that this dizzy scheme won't be uncovered, I'd advise you to start thinking of ways to "divorce" Tracy because if I can find this out the district attorney definitely can and they'll use it against you.'

'How?' Reeves said. 'The only reason I told you is because it would prove that I wasn't the least bit jealous about any supposed affair that Tracy was having with Drake. Why would I care if we weren't even dating?'

'For that to work I'll have to reveal your secret in court,' I reminded him.

'Then reveal it. Just don't ask me why I did it on the stand.'

'Then I won't put you on the stand,' I said. 'You can't testify. But Tracy will because she'll be subpoenaed, and she can't refuse because you two aren't really married. She had better not consider committing perjury.'

Reeves looked like there were fishing swimming around

his head and he was watching them go by. 'This just keeps getting worse,' he said.

'You ain't seen nothin' yet,' I told him. 'The trial hasn't even started. We have a few weeks to figure out how your marriages impact your defense and you need to come extremely clean with me about what happened right before Mr Drake fell off that crane. And I mean now.'

My client – I had to keep reminding myself that this was my client and not the opposition, because frankly I would have been much more comfortable prosecuting this case – had the nerve to look confused by what I'd said. 'I have been completely open with you about all that,' he said.

'You told me you barely knew the man and had probably never spoken to him,' I reminded him.

He gestured with his hands: *OK, so mostly.* 'I was almost completely open. So I knew him a little and I'd heard rumors that he was sleeping with my wife, who wasn't my wife, so I truly didn't care. Why is that a big deal?'

'It's a big deal because you left out the part where you tampered with the cables that held James Drake up, right before they no longer held him up and he died,' I said. I really felt like I was cross-examining a hostile witness and dropping the damning evidence right in his lap. I waited for Reeves's humble plea for forgiveness.

Instead he stared blankly at me. 'What are you talking about?'

I had expected something more humble but I was prepared. I turned my laptop around to face him. He looked at the screen and the lost expression in his eyes only deepened. 'What's that?' he asked.

'Watch.' I started the file of the home-video footage Nate had supplied, edited down to begin at the time Reeves started talking to James Drake at the base of the crane that would reach down to lift him up once he was properly outfitted . . . he thought. Reeves watched the beginning of the video and his face took on a look of impatience.

'This is terribly shot,' he said. 'So I was a little short with the stuntman. So what?'

'Keep looking.'

He rolled his eyes a bit but did as directed (see what I did there?). And then, I could tell from the sound, he got to the moment where the video showed him very clearly tampering with the cables on the crane.

'What's that?' Reeves's voice was almost breathless, strained. 'Who filmed this?' Was he finally going to confess now that I'd caught him dead to rights, with the evidence clearly exposed in front of his eyes?

Of course not. 'That's you messing with the cables on the crane,' I said. 'I can't see what kind of tool you have in your hand, but it's clear you weren't testing them for strength. Fifteen minutes later James Drake would fall seventy-five feet to his death. So what do you want to tell me now?'

'That's not what happened,' he said.

This case wasn't getting any easier.

That was equally true when Brady O'Toole called me later in the day. Already having the kind of week that would cause a lesser woman to regularly dissolve into tears – which I'd only done once – I picked up my phone with my thumb and forefinger only, as if afraid it was going to explode. It didn't.

'Tell me something I want to hear, Brady,' I said. 'Hello' is so mundane.

'I'm not sure whether you'll want to hear this or not,' he answered. 'But I've been doing some research on the type of crane that the production you told me about was using and the cables that would have been primarily responsible for holding up the stuntman.'

'Primarily responsible?' Already I was in over my head.

'Yes. There are backup systems and fail-safes all over these things. Remember they're usually used on construction sites in populated areas and insurance companies insist on cranes not dropping heavy things on innocent bystanders.' Brady clearly had been doing his homework, and had started off with considerably more knowledge of the subject than I'd had. 'This one wasn't the best I've ever seen but it wasn't the worst, either.'

I braced myself because I felt like the news wasn't going to be great for my case. 'What'd you find out?' I asked Brady.

'The good news is your client definitely didn't cut those cables,' he started.

I knew enough to brace for the rest of the information. 'What's the bad news?'

'Nobody cut through those cables. There's really no implement that would do the job right there in front of anybody and not be incredibly noticeable.'

'So how is it that James Drake fell from five stories up and died?' I asked. I'll admit I closed my eyes after the question.

'The cables were burned through,' Brady said. 'From what I can tell from eyewitness reports and the police documents, somebody had given them regular treatments of hydrochloric acid for at least twelve hours before the rehearsal took place.'

'What do you mean, regular?' I asked.

'It couldn't be done all at once. You can't just pour the whole bottle of acid on the cables and have them burn through just enough so no one would notice but ready to snap when the stunt performer was dangled over the edge. Whoever did this did it a little at a time, progressively over maybe twelve to – at most – fourteen hours, and could tell when to stop, which probably would have been shortly before the rehearsal began.'

I'd sent Brady the video footage Nate had provided. 'You saw the video,' I said. 'Is that what Robert Reeves is doing at the end of that clip?'

'I can't say for sure, but it's entirely possible.'

'I'm not going to ask you to testify, Brady,' I said.

'That's OK. The DA was happy to take my call.'

TWENTY-FOUR

'Even by Hollywood standards, Reeves's love life is a corker,' Patrick said.

I had been very careful not to tell him any of the legal maneuvers I intended to try in my defense or anything that, as a potential witness (especially given the footage of him standing and watching as the stunt was being prepared and while Reeves, who denied it unequivocally, appeared to be sabotaging the instrument by which Drake had died), he should not know ahead of the trial. But the stuff about Reeves's scheme to be seen with a younger, less 'dowdy' (per Angie) woman had resonated with me.

Since moving to Los Angeles I'd been comparing myself, just barely subconsciously, to the many actresses and other women I'd seen in the streets and offices where I worked. And I'd been coming up short in my own mind. It was strictly a physical thing, and I didn't think I was a hideous beast or anything, but the competition in Southern California is just a hair more intense than it is in Central New Jersey. Don't get me wrong; the Garden State has its share of lookers, but they're not *everywhere*. Even if you're not concentrating on it as you go through your day, the intimidation becomes ingrained.

So yeah, I'd told Patrick about Stacy and Tracy and why they were Stacy and Tracy. I'd told him because I wanted to see how he would react to such a thing. Because he wanted me to move in with him *now*, but in a couple of years?

'I mean, I understand why he did it, but it is still quite the scheme,' Patrick went on.

That wasn't boding well for me.

We were at a restaurant called OK, which was less intense and upscale than Voilà! Because I had better defined my idea of 'easy' with Patrick and he had, being Patrick, taken it all in and overcompensated. If Applebee's was a touch less fancy, it would look like this place.

'You understand why?' I said.

'Certainly. I don't agree with it, but the business does have a focus on youth because that's where most of their ticket buyers are,' he said, scanning the menu, which featured items like the OKBurger and the Chicken Fried Chicken. I'm not a food snob but this place was testing my limits. 'Being seen as an older man might limit the kind of projects Robert might be offered in the future.'

Did I really want to be eating in a place where the only alternate side dish to French fries was curly fries? 'That's not the point,' I said. 'I mean, it *is* the point but it's not the one I'm trying to make right now. It's ridiculous that people in your business think a guy over forty can't direct a movie people under twenty-five – and oh my lord maybe even people *older* than twenty-five – might want to see.'

'Then what's the point?' Patrick had given up looking at the menu and was scanning the chalkboard over my right shoulder for hope of a special for the night that would fall into the general category of Food.

'I'm amazed you don't see it, Patrick. Even if it were reasonable for an industry to force its key staff to at least appear to be young, which it's not, for the record, the idea that Reeves can look however he likes but his wife must be young and sexy is not just stupid, it's offensive to women everywhere.'

At the table to my left, Judy had ordered a small diet soda and was nursing it while scanning the premises for possible threats. She probably didn't even want the diet soda.

Patrick raised an eyebrow. 'That's not entirely true,' he said.

I had been hoping he'd rail against the idea that the significant others of showbiz big shots had to be in their twenties and wear a size zero, but it was not going the way I wanted, which frankly had sort of become my life. 'What isn't?'

'You're right that it's silly the business requires that level of physical attractiveness, especially for people who don't appear in front of the camera,' Patrick said. 'But it's not true that Robert himself can look any way he pleases. He's not important enough a director for that to be true. He watches everything he eats lest he gain a pound. He pores over photos of other directors to see what they're wearing. And I'd be frankly amazed if the face he's wearing right now is his original. That's a loaner if ever I saw one.'

'You think Reeves has had cosmetic surgery?' I asked. It hadn't occurred to me.

Patrick smiled. 'Look around this room. I'll bet fewer than ten percent of the people eating or working here are in the movie business. But maybe eight out of ten have visited the friendly doc at one time or another. It's more pervasive than you think, Sandy.'

There was no way I was ordering an OKBurger now. 'Do you want to eat somewhere else?' I asked Patrick.

'If you do, love.' You think only mothers are passive-aggressive?

'I do,' I said. 'It doesn't have to be Voilà! fancy but the cholesterol level should be considerably lower.'

We stood and Judy was immediately on her feet. Patrick put too much money for the nothing we'd ordered on the table and we headed for the door. A couple of diners recognized him on the way out and he did his friendly-but-not-stopping smile as we made our way out.

I must have been trying to get outside too fast because Judy said, 'Ma'am,' which meant that I was ahead of her when she'd prefer I not be. I slowed down.

'I'll call Angie,' Patrick said. 'She'll know just the right place.'

'Tell her to meet us there.'

Patrick nodded.

But just when we made it out to the street I stopped in my tracks. Judy, a step ahead of me, sensed it and spun. 'Ma'am?' It was her favorite word.

Patrick was right in my line of vision and he looked concerned. 'What is it?'

'That last man who nodded at you on the way out,' I said.

'It happens all the time, Sandy. You know that.'

'He was one of the guys who threw Angie and me into the van,' I said. My voice sounded dry. My voice wanted Judy's Diet Coke but the staff had probably cleared it already.

'Tell me what he was wearing,' Judy said. 'You two are going to stay here and I will go back inside.'

'Red T-shirt and jeans,' I said. 'No hat. Blond hair.'

Judy nodded and pulled the door open, once again insisting, 'Stay here.'

So we did. There was no chance either of us wanted to go meet the kidnapper, whether he was on duty or off. But I was searching the street for the dark-haired one and had not spotted him yet. Suddenly I was uneasy whenever Judy wasn't within my sight.

'It'll be OK,' Patrick said, and put his arm around my shoulder.

I called Angie while we waited at Patrick's suggestion. I got the impression he was trying to keep me distracted and that was a good move on his part. I told her where we were and what kind of place we'd like to be in and she said she'd text me an address in a minute. I did not mention that our blond abductor was maybe twenty feet from where I stood.

The only thing left to do was think about the case. It was the only thing I had control over right now. But my prospects there weren't fabulous either. After a moment I looked at Patrick and said, 'Do you know James Drake's wife?'

Judy chose that moment to walk out of OK and her expression . . . well, Judy doesn't actually have expressions. Or tones of voice. She is all bodyguard. 'He's not in there anymore,' she said.

I didn't ask if she was sure. Judy is always sure. 'Do you think he could have left through a back door?' I said.

'If he did it's too late for us to find him,' she answered. 'My best advice is to get back to the car as quickly as possible.'

Having learned from previous experience, I followed Judy's advice. I would have followed her advice if she'd told me to dress up like a crow and try to flap my way into the sky. Judy just engenders confidence. Even Patrick, who always wants to be my protector and defender, said nothing as we made our way into his car, Judy in back despite my knowing she would have felt more comfortable in the passenger's seat up front because it allowed her to have a more comprehensive view.

No one tried to get in our way. But my nerves were already shaken. 'Is anyone following us?' I asked once we were underway to the address Angie had given Patrick.

'No, ma'am.'

'Jim Drake's wife?' Patrick asked as he drove, following the directions his phone was giving him over the car's audio system. It sounded great, like the woman telling us to make a right turn in five hundred feet were right there in the vehicle with us, directing the trip in warm but insistent tones.

Jim Drake's . . . oh yeah. 'Yes. Have you ever met her? Do you know her well?' If the rumor Burke Henderson had told me about, that Drake and his wife were separating, perhaps because he was getting a little too friendly with the alleged Tracy Reeves, Drake's wife could be someone worth talking to, and maybe calling to testify.

'I don't know her *well*,' Patrick said, following the mellow tones of our pixelated tour guide, 'but we have met once or twice. Her name's Marnie? Martha? No. Marta. That's it. Why?'

'I think she's going to be my next stop,' I said.

'After dinner.' Patrick would not let me out of his sight tonight.

'After today,' I corrected.

Angie had chosen exactly the right place for me because she has known me since I wore undershirts and, more spectacularly, so did she. Pasta Fazool (no exclamation point) was two steps above a pizza parlor and two under a $200-an-entrée Northern Italian bastion of pretentiousness that people in actual Northern Italy would find hilarious or appalling. Patrick grinned when he saw the neon sign out front, because Angie is his executive assistant and knows him really well too.

By the time my chicken carbonara, Patrick's shrimp scampi, Angie's pear and gorgonzola salad and Judy's another diet soda had arrived, Angie had been brought up to speed on the state of the Reeves case, our elusive kidnapper, Robert Reeves's many marriages and Patrick's day of shooting on *Torn* because he is, after all, her boss. She asked the right questions and listened to all the details, but mostly seemed to be finding the whole situation, including spotting the blond felon, moderately amusing.

'Isn't it possible that guy was just there getting a burger?' she asked when the conversation circled back to our recent assailant.

'It is possible but it's a mistake to count on coincidences like that,' Judy volunteered. Judy's sense of humor is like her body fat – invisible. 'We should operate under the assumption that he was intending to do you harm and then adjust to any other facts we can gather.'

'Thanks for cheering me up,' I told her.

Judy looked surprised. 'I was explaining the proper strategy,' she said.

'Yes, and thank you, Judy.' That was Patrick, ever the healer of wounds. Then he faced toward me and, peripherally, Angie. 'With Judy here to help we need to create a plan.'

I think I closed my eyes and made a clicking noise in my throat. 'Patrick. Judy *is* the plan. And yes, thank you, Judy. You're making my life much more secure.'

'I hope so, ma'am.' Ever the ray of sunshine.

'So we don't need a plan beyond that, Patrick,' I continued. 'You can't help me strategize for the trial because you're involved in it. But I do wish you could figure out how you show up on that video of the accident so I can defend against my boyfriend being at the scene of the crime while insisting he's not.'

'It doesn't make sense,' Patrick said, as if that was news.

The carbonara, which used turkey bacon, was wonderful anyway, but my enthusiasm was somewhat muted. It had been a long day and I was not in a better position – now that it was almost over – than I had been when I'd rolled out of bed this morning.

We ate, we made small talk, and then we headed cautiously out the door to Patrick's car, which we had parked on the street nearby due to incredible luck finding a space. Normally Patrick uses the restaurant's valet service, but Angie had chosen Pasta Fazool and it wasn't ritzy enough to have that amenity.

As always Judy ran an inspection of the car before we got in. Patrick, Angie (who had parked two blocks away where there was no meter) and I stood and watched her with some detachment, not from a lack of concern but because we'd seen her do this many times before.

'I want a copy of that video,' Patrick told me. 'Can you provide it?'

'To a potential witness? I don't think so.'

'There must be some way. I need to study it.'

I thought about that. 'Let me check with Holly. She might have an idea.'

'It's me on the video,' Patrick started to protest.

'Ma'am.' Judy's normally serious tone was downright chilling.

We all looked at her.

'There is a device under the car's chassis,' she said.

I looked at her, not wanting to understand. 'A device?'

'A bomb,' Angie said.

TWENTY-FIVE

You shouldn't expect a homicide detective to show up when there has been no homicide. That seems straightforward enough. But the homicide division of the LAPD also investigates attempted homicides, and I would have bet money that having a bomb show up in your car's undercarriage would have fallen into that category. In addition, I'd become accustomed to Lieutenant Trench showing up whenever one of these weird threats happened to me, so I was looking around as the cruisers showed up to see his unmarked car.

But it didn't arrive. This time he didn't even send Sergeant Roberts. I guessed Trench didn't love me anymore.

They asked the usual questions (we didn't know anything except to mention that we'd been at the OK restaurant and seen one of the men who had recently been arrested and released for kidnapping Angie and me), and kept everyone well cordoned off from Patrick's car until the bomb squad showed up in enough armor to defend good King Richard against his evil brother Prince John and show off for a fair maiden at the same time. We all kept very quiet while one of the men approached the car with the sophisticated device of a mirror on a stick to look under the car and determine what we were dealing with.

A long moment passed while he dropped to the ground and actually positioned himself under the car. The vehicles that had been parked on either side and indeed anywhere up the street had been removed, either by their owners or the LAPD, to provide an open space for the intrepid man underneath the Tesla.

I caught myself holding my breath.

'The car's not going to blow up this time,' Patrick said quietly, holding my hand. 'They know what they're doing.'

'So did James Drake,' I said.

The man under the car pulled himself out and stood up slowly, all the while looking at the Tesla like it was an artifact from another planet, which was entirely possible. I had met Elon Musk at one of Patrick's premieres. Going to Mars might have been a homecoming for him.

The cop used his mirror-sicle again and turned toward the other bomb squad members standing around the car, because I guess their philosophy was that if one of them blew up, they'd better all blow up. He took a deep breath.

'It's a fake,' he said.

The spectators – that is, Patrick, Angie, Judy and me, as well as a few stragglers who'd been asked to move their cars while they dined at Pasta Fazool – stared at each other. The bomb squad members, who I guessed were used to such things, didn't even shrug their shoulders as they turned and walked away. Our hero, still standing next to the Tesla, ducked down one more time to look under the car, perhaps wondering who was going to take the silly thing out and throw it away. Judy walked over to him and seemed to strike up a conversation. Judy is ex-military and used to be a cop. She speaks the language, which is good because casual English seems to be beyond her grasp.

When I was capable of speech again, I said, 'A fake?' to no one in particular. 'Who goes to the trouble to put a phony bomb underneath a car just on the off chance that you might look?'

Angie, returning the glance of a bomb squad member who was no longer concerned with bombs, nodded at him and said to me, 'The same person who sends two guys to kidnap somebody and them strand them in the middle of nowhere without doing anything.'

'It's like someone's daft idea of a prank,' Patrick said.

'It's not funny,' I pointed out.

Judy walked over from her torrid assignation (for her) with the bomb squad cop and stood with her back to the Tesla.

Even when it was clear the car wouldn't explode, it was Judy's instinct to stay between me and the potential danger. I started to wonder if it was appropriate to tip a bodyguard.

'It's a relatively convincing device but it's made largely of plastic,' Judy reported. 'It's possible that much of what is under that car was created using a 3D printer.'

'Isn't technology grand,' Patrick said.

'Had the officer seen anything like it before?' I asked Judy.

'He said he'd seen things like it when he worked on security for film or TV shoots in the area,' she answered. 'It looks very much like a movie prop.'

The cop she'd been talking to was now jacking up the front of Patrick's car, presumably to make it easier to remove the stupid joke and have it analyzed by the Division of Phony Bombs in the LAPD's police lab. He kept looking at the thing, which was barely visible from where I stood (particularly with Judy between us) and wearing a befuddled smirk, like he'd seen something ridiculous in a YouTube video of a tortoise playing with a golden retriever.

Because Patrick is my liaison to the movie business, I looked toward him. He was looking at me because he does that a lot. 'Who do you know who could make something like that?' I asked.

'Probably any prop maker in town,' he answered. 'I doubt it's terribly sophisticated.'

'Officer DuBois said it was unusually detailed and had clearly been designed for maximum authenticity,' Judy told him.

Patrick looked away, which is unusual. 'OK,' he said.

'Who does that sound like?' I said, noting the look in his eye.

'A lot of people.'

That spoke to me because it's not in Patrick's nature to be evasive. He's very head-on, probably too much so, and when he decides to duck a question it's usually because he thinks I'm not going to like the answer. 'You have someone in mind,' I told him.

'I don't want to say anything,' Patrick said. 'I'm not supposed to interfere in your case, remember?'

So I turned toward Angie, who knows everything Patrick knows but in alphabetical order. 'Who does he think it is?' I asked.

She hesitated only to glance at Patrick, who made no sign. 'Burke Henderson,' she said.

Huh? 'I thought he was a stunt coordinator,' I said.

Patrick, the fount of information on the film business, tilted his head to indicate he understood the confusion, said, 'His background is in properties. But with so much being done digitally now, Burke has had to branch out into stunt work, which he's been doing for ten years.'

'Isn't most of *that* being done with computers these days?'

'Not as much. Between the two, an outside contractor like Burke can make a very considerable living.'

I wanted to sit. The bomb squad cop Judy had identified as Office DuBois had removed the cute little instrument of disaster from under Patrick's car and lowered it (the car) to the ground after taking many pictures with a tablet computer he carried. I looked over at Judy. 'Do you think we can get back in the car now?'

'I will ask,' Judy said, turning toward the car. Then she turned, and just to make sure that I knew I was the idiot in the conversation, she said, 'Stay here.' She walked over to DuBois and talked to him for a bit.

I leaned against a lamppost, hoping not to look like I was trying to get lucky for the night. Patrick walked over, ever attentive, and put his hand on my shoulder. 'Nobody was trying to blow us up, Sandy,' he said.

'That's the part that bothers me. If they wanted to kill us, I could guard against that. But whoever it is seems just to want to annoy us or scare us, and that doesn't make any sense to me. Patrick, do you think Burke Henderson is behind this, really?'

Patrick's face became impassive. 'I really don't know him that well, but I can't understand why he would want to. Even if he actually cut the cables himself, and there's no evidence I know of that he did, that would be a balmy plan. Making dangerous-looking props would only draw attention to him when he'd want it to be anywhere else. And how would

Burke find two men to kidnap you and Angie? I don't think it was him.'

Angie was watching from about twenty feet away. She knows when to stand back and doesn't mind it. She says. But her face showed concern and I couldn't tell if it was because we'd just found a fake bomb under Patrick's car, or if she was worried about the state of my romantic relationship with him. Angie puts on a good show but she cares about Patrick and me.

'Those are good questions,' I told Patrick. 'And even if I knew the answers, which I don't . . .'

'You couldn't tell me.' Patrick let out a long breath to show his frustration with the legal system in general and me in particular. 'I understand.'

'You don't, but I appreciate you trying,' I said.

He half-smiled. 'You've probably noticed I haven't mentioned moving in with me lately.' A clever tactic, moving the conversation away from something professional about me he found frustrating to something personal about me he found frustrating. And the half-smile actually made it charming. Patrick was a man of many talents.

'I appreciate that,' I said, then realized how it sounded. 'I mean, I haven't made any decision yet.' I looked toward Judy, who was still talking to DuBois.

He nodded even though he probably thought I was being obstinate for no reason. 'How about the premiere? Should I see if Cynthia' (Sutton, his half-sister) 'is going to be back from Vancouver and invite her?'

'That depends. How important is it to you that I go with you?'

It was Patrick's turn to look out toward the car. 'Here comes Judy,' he said, effectively evading the question. We seemed to be doing a lot more of that lately.

But at least he was being accurate: Judy did walk over and report that her new friend DuBois said we could have Patrick's car back. No further forensic evidence would be taken from it, he said, given that fingerprints underneath the chassis would probably have been visible even with the naked eye because they would have been made in grease.

DuBois said there were no such signs and, besides, the car hadn't actually blown up, which placed this somehow lower on the LAPD's priority list.

Recalling how I'd felt when the 'device' was first discovered, I thought the LAPD should have reconsidered its priorities.

We settled into the seats, which was a relief, and Patrick started up the Tesla. Judy, watching from the back seat, kept her head swiveling as she looked for possible threats. Because it was apparently possible that one heart-stopping moment a night wasn't enough for some people.

'Did you get his number, Judy?' I asked.

'I always do,' Judy answered.

TWENTY-SIX

Stacy Reeves (née Rabinowitz) was not pleased to find me at her door. I wasn't expecting a jubilant reception and a plate of freshly baked cookies, but Stacy's dour expression would have put Droopy Dog to shame.

And it wasn't like she didn't know I was coming; I'd called three days before to set up an appointment, to which Stacy had (perhaps reluctantly) agreed. Still, this was my job and dammit, I was going to talk to Stacy about her husband, her husband's other wife, and anything else I could think of that might make her a good witness – even a character witness – for Robert Reeves's defense.

'Come in,' she said without any evidence of conviction, so I did, and sat when instructed on a tasteful but hardly fashionable sofa in a room dominated by a very large flat-screen TV, and a coffee table upon which a respectable game of rugby could have been played. This was a large room with large furniture, in a normal-sized house that didn't scream affluence at you, or for that matter even whisper it from the outside. Clearly walls had been removed to make this living room a place where you could invite a friend or fifty in to watch a movie. Maybe a Robert Reeves movie. Because the man was not devoid of ego. In fact, he could have donated some to this wife and his other wife (who didn't need it) and still had plenty to spare.

'I'm sure you know why I'm here,' I began. I was particularly sure since I'd told her on the phone exactly what to expect from our conversation. But it was an opening that Stacy did not comment upon. 'Now, I'm wondering if you would make a good witness for your husband's defense and I'd like to explore a few areas to see if I should call you to the stand when we go to trial.'

'Oh, please don't,' Stacy said. To be fair, she'd said that on the phone too, but I was banking on my mystical powers of persuasion to prevail on her husband's behalf.

'You don't have to testify,' I said. I'd ramp up the mystical powers later. 'But maybe you can shed some light on a few things for me that I'll be able to use to help Robert get acquitted.'

'I hope you can,' Stacy offered. That was at least a step in the right direction. 'I really don't want to testify, though.' That wasn't.

'Well, let's see.' I couldn't have been less committal if I'd started planning it at six this morning, when I was running back and forth to the local convenience store. Does it make sense to run for exercise to a place that sells Snickers bars? 'First of all, did you know James Drake?'

'No. Who is James Drake?'

It was possible this was going to take longer than I'd set aside. 'James Drake is the stunt performer who died on your husband's film set. So I'm guessing you didn't know him.'

'Oh no. I never met any of Robert's work friends.'

'But you haven't heard the name? I mean, your husband is about to go on trial for this man's murder.' There's out of touch and then there's hermitic.

'Well, of course I knew about that. I just didn't know his name. It's a shame, isn't it? Did he have children?'

An interesting question. 'Actually, no. He and his wife were separated and they hadn't had any children.' Maybe the mention of separation might spark something.

Maybe it did. Stacy fiddled with the three TV remotes on the coffee table and organized them differently, as if that mattered. Why were there three TV remotes anyway? Why did I care? Another good question. 'That's really too bad,' she said.

I nodded my agreement. 'Stacy, I need to ask you about some fairly personal things and I hope you don't think I'm rude for bringing them up. It's all meant to help your husband once the trial begins.'

Her gaze went from the remote directly into my face and her expression was unreadable. 'You're going to ask about Tracy,' she said.

'Yes, I'm afraid so.'

'Don't be afraid,' Stacy said. 'It's not like the subject has never come up before.'

'So you knew about Tracy.' I mean, she kind of had to, but did she?

'Of course. Robert explained the whole thing to me. You have to understand, Ms Moss.'

'Please call me Sandy.'

'Sandy,' Stacy seemed to roll my name around in her mouth to see how it tasted. 'Sandy, my husband is in a very visible, very youth-oriented business. If he'd pretended to have another wife because he wanted to get rid of me, or if he'd just had an affair with some actress, I'd have been very upset, and to tell you the truth I probably would have divorced him. But this was strictly a tactic to maintain his image, and he needs that image to be able to work in his business. I understand that. We actually discussed it before he cast Virginia in the role.'

'Did Robert ever say anything that would indicate to you he was jealous of Tracy? That she was involved with another man, with the man who died, and that upset your husband?' What the hell. If she wasn't going to testify, I could ask questions that might implicate my client. I didn't *think* he'd killed James Drake, but I wasn't a hundred percent certain.

Stacy scrunched up her face into a look of incredulity. 'Jealous of Tracy? He barely ever saw her when it wasn't a public event like a red carpet or something. She could have been sleeping with seven men and he wouldn't have cared. My husband loves me, Sandy.'

'One last thing. Is Robert handy around the house? Does he repair things when they break? Does he have a tool shed or anything so he can do renovations?' Maybe he was the one who'd knocked down the walls. Maybe he'd learned how to sever steel cables.

Stacy actually laughed. 'Oh Sandy, that made my day. When we were married, the hinge on the front door was squeaky and Robert hired a man to come and spray it with WD-40. He told me, "I don't fix things, Stacy. I write checks."'

I thanked her, didn't ask her to testify, despite the fact that she might have been of some small help, picked up Judy at the door and drove to Marta Drake's house. It was Talk-to-the-Wives Day.

Marta, whom I'd also warned of my impending visit, was sitting on her front porch drinking what appeared to be iced tea. It was a very nice, if unremarkable, house on a suburban block in Mission Viejo. Get rid of the mountains in the distance and the waterfront within viewing distance and it could have been any one of thirty towns I knew in New Jersey. So what if it cost twice as much to live here?

Clearly not pretending to play the grieving widow, Marta had her feet up on a pillowed footrest and wore a straw hat with a teal band around it. The lower half of her equally teal one-piece bathing suit was covered by a white skirt with a floral pattern, loose enough to be comfortable but still show off the figure Marta had not neglected. It was probably unsweetened iced tea, so I declined her offer of a glass.

'Jim and I were separated when he died,' she said. 'I was in the process of filing for divorce and I can give you my lawyer's info if you'd like.'

'I would appreciate that, but it can wait until I'm back in my office,' I said. It was getting warmer today and, even though the porch had a roof, the sun was doing its best to find me. 'Maybe I'll rethink that iced tea,' I said.

Marta, a lovely woman with dark hair to her jawline, smiled and poured me a glass with extra ice, which I downed (unsweetened though it was) in three gulps. 'I didn't think it was *that* warm a day,' she said with a laugh.

'I'm still from New Jersey,' I said. 'It's not supposed to be this hot until July. But if you don't mind me asking . . .'

'Why was I filing for divorce?' The smile faded and I nodded; yes, that was what I had been trying to ask. 'A lot of reasons, and some of them were even over thirty years old.'

'Your husband cheated?' There's no diplomatic way of asking that. I'd been a divorce lawyer for close to two years. If you can think of a less upsetting way to broach the subject, please email me at smoss@seatontaylor.com and pass it along.

'He would have said no,' Marta answered. 'Jim would have said it wasn't cheating; it was a hazard of the profession and that he'd warned me about it before we were married and he would have been right. But when you're twenty-two you think you can change the guy.' She looked up. 'You can't change the guy.'

'No, you can't,' I agreed. I didn't even know if I wanted to change the guy.

'Anyway, we were going to get a divorce. Jim wasn't happy but he understood.' Marta took another swig of iced tea. I knew it wasn't spiked because I'd had some myself, but she was definitely – let's call it – relaxed. 'So if you're asking, no, I didn't have any reason to kill him. I was going to get the house and half of the savings account anyway. Try and get insurance for a stuntman some time. There wasn't a ton of money there.'

'You knew about the rumors that your husband was having an affair with the director's wife?' I asked.

Marta chuckled. 'The director's wife. The director's wife's stunt double, if you want to know the truth. She shows up for the photo ops and the real wife lives in the suburbs somewhere.' She looked around at her porch. 'A nicer suburb than this, I bet.'

'So that wasn't a secret?' I thought the whole idea was that Tracy stood in for Stacy because she looked younger and therefore . . . well, you know the theory.

'Oh hell no,' Marta said, even more relaxed than before. I wondered if she'd been using anything else to calm her down, but I didn't smell anything in the air. 'Everybody knew about it.

It was kind of a universal joke, but hey, the girl's got to make a living somehow.' She smirked. 'She can't act, I hear.'

'Did you ever see them together?' I braced myself for the answer because when I'd asked it of other wives involved in divorces, I had gotten some very graphic stories.

Not this time. 'Yeah. I ran into them once in a restaurant that Jim and I used to go to. He thought it was OK to bring her there. I think that's the only time I've ever seen her. Personally, I think Reeves could have done better, if you're asking.' I wasn't. 'She liked chicken with pesto.'

Something else I hadn't known. 'Marta, who do you think killed your husband?'

She sat back and lost the smile. She seemed to closely examine the ceiling of her front porch. And she sighed the way a woman does when she loved a man who was not the man she should have loved and now he was dead, when she should have been indifferent but couldn't bring herself not to feel anything.

'Honestly, it could have been any one of a hundred girls,' she said, 'but it was probably that son of a bitch Bob Reeves.'

TWENTY-SEVEN

The next two months are a blur. With so little time to prepare for a major trial, all I can remember are documents, precedents, police reports and witness statements. There was some negotiating with professional expert witnesses about who would be available to testify on what aspects of the case, and there was digging through the prosecution's discovery statements to try and get a handle on what that jerk Renfro (who actually seemed like a nice guy) might be planning to use to destroy me.

And there was the whole issue of whether or not Robert Reeves had actually melted the cables on the crane holding James Drake aloft or, more to the point, not. I hadn't completely decided that for my own purposes, but I kept reminding myself that it didn't matter because I had to provide a defense for Reeves whether he'd done the crime or not.

But on the upside, there were no attempts to kill me, and no particularly spectacular attempts to intimidate me into dropping the case. I guess with time running out, whoever had been doing so had decided there just wasn't a point anymore. A shame, really, because my client had been doing his best to drive me away but I couldn't take the bait.

Robert Reeves had been evasive on a good day. On a bad one he was dismissive, insulting, condescending and arrogant, but then arrogant had been the default setting he'd had installed when he was born. So perhaps it was just dismissive, insulting and condescending because the other was sort of reflexive and therefore involuntary with Reeves.

The LAPD had investigated the 'bombing' of Patrick's car and come up with a very large amount of nothing. The man I recognized as one of the two who had abducted Angie and me had been found and questioned, but had an alibi that took him away not only from Pasta Fazool when the car would have been tampered with, but also from OKBurger at the time I was certain I'd seen him there. So let's just imagine that my belief in his alibi (a girlfriend who said they were at home 'snuggling' at the time) was perhaps a tiny bit shaky.

I had, with the help of Jon Irvin, taken statements from Burke Henderson (again), Mrs Stacy Reeves, seventeen members of the *Desert Siege* crew from prop masters to grips (who apparently were in charge of lighting), and craft services people who essentially put out tables of food.

We had *not* been able to re-question the alleged Mrs Tracy Reeves, who had suddenly left Los Angeles for her ancestral home in Dayton, Ohio, and was no doubt there incognito because nobody including the Dayton police (or her alleged not-so-much husband) could locate her. Reeves did seem somewhat peeved about that, indicating that he had dropped his lovely sort-of spouse from the company payroll, tax benefits or no.

On the plus side, nobody remembered seeing Patrick

there on the day of the accident. And no one could testify (as far as I could tell) to seeing Reeves bend over the cables right before the stunt was attempted.

But on the minus side, nobody had seen anyone else do anything suspicious either. Now, it's not necessary in court to prove that someone else did the crime of which your client is accused. The onus of proof is on the prosecution, who has to prove he *did* do it. There's the whole concept of reasonable doubt and the one about innocent until proven guilty.

The problem is, juries hear all that and think they're being very cautious about the rules, but when they see someone they think did the crime, they tend to convict that person, and when they decide the defendant is a nice enough human they tend to acquit. In other words, juries are completely and totally unpredictable. The fact that there are mountains of legal rules in place tends to be secondary to whether the defendant takes the stand, and if they seem to be, you know, likable.

Robert Reeves, in my humble estimation and that of virtually everyone who had ever met him (besides Penny) was not likable. Even Penny wouldn't say he *was* likable, but refused to offer an opinion even when asked.

The night before the trial was scheduled to begin was, as always for me, a hectic time. Patrick, however, saw it as a time when I should take my eyes away from the paperwork, try to take a break from the tension, and therefore – as had become his completely unrequested custom – he hosted a pre-trial dinner at his house.

Patrick is insane.

The group of us – me, Patrick, Angie, Patrick's sister Cynthia (in from Vancouver for the evening, because of course . . .), Nate (looking as uncomfortable as a man can look, but still gawking at Patrick's massive movie memorabilia collection), Jon and his wife Diane – around a table only slightly less lavish than that set by Henry VIII. I'm guessing. Maybe Charles Laughton overplayed it and Henry just sent out for roast pheasant from a take-out place. The butler Jason was seeing to the service and Luann, the cook, had prepared enough food for a reunion of the championship Dodgers team from whatever year it was recently when the Dodgers won the World Series. A lot of food, I'm saying.

Cynthia seemed especially surprised that Robert Reeves, whom she would have assumed was the guest of honor, was not in attendance. Patrick explained it was because he, Patrick, might be called as a witness – he knew I wasn't calling him and he wasn't on Renfro's list or I would have seen it – because that was better than saying nobody liked the man I was about to start defending and we couldn't actually be sure he hadn't intentionally caused a stuntman to die on his set.

Law is a funny business. From the outside.

'But you're not going to testify against Sandy,' Cynthia said. Cynthia has no British accent because she is in fact Patrick's half-sister and grew up in Pensacola, Florida, after their father had relocated there sans Patrick's mom and their children. 'Aren't there rules against that?'

'There are rules that say a *spouse* isn't obligated to testify against their wife or husband who stands accused and can refuse to do so,' I explained. 'There's nothing that says if you're dating someone they can't testify for one side or the other, if an attorney is involved. It might seem a conflict of interest, but in this case Patrick isn't going to testify either way, I'm pretty sure. He wasn't there when the incident occurred.' I looked at Patrick. 'But just to be safe, that's all I'm going to say about the case.'

'There exists a video that shows me there in the park when they were testing the stunt,' Patrick told Cynthia, despite my trying to communicate how he shouldn't. A kick under the table used to mean so much more. 'But I wasn't there and I can't figure it out.'

I tried chatting about things other than Robert Reeves and whether he'd killed a man for reasons that didn't make any sense (that lack of real motive was going to be a key part of my defense, particularly if we ever managed to find Tracy Reeves or whoever she was), like Patrick's premiere the following week, which got me a wry look from Patrick who was still waiting for an answer to his invitation.

Honestly, I'm *never* this indecisive about anything. I don't always make the right decisions, but I always make decisions.

And this nagging feeling that committing to the premiere meant I was agreeing to live with Patrick was complicating my mind in ways that were completely unfamiliar. I just didn't think this way.

Patrick's previous romantic history was certainly a stumbling block. He was a champion at falling head over heels for someone and pursuing her. But once she responded, he wasn't great at sustaining the relationship. His marriage to Patsy had been headed for divorce before she was murdered. His most recent engagement, to a real-estate agent named Emily, was official before Patrick could honestly remember the color of his fiancée's eyes, and broken off after a five-minute conversation with me. And the aftermath of that, for the record, didn't go great.

He'd asked me to marry him seconds after I realized I was in love with him, and it took months before he'd take no for an answer. If I agreed to take him up on his offer and live in this enormous house, would Patrick immediately decide the hunt had been the fun part and try to find a diplomatic way to move me back into the apartment with Angie? Would Angie be able to keep her job? I didn't think Patrick would be that petty, but it was certainly a concern.

But yes. The dinner party. Right.

'It's going to be a weird affair,' Patrick was saying about the *Desert Siege* premiere. 'I mean, a man died on set, the director is on trial for his murder and I'm in the middle of it. The press will undoubtedly be brutal.' He looked directly at me. 'I find myself dreading the red carpet. Does that make sense?'

'Of course it does,' said Cynthia. A veteran of films and prestige television, she could weigh in knowledgeably about the need to do difficult promotional tours for films, although as far as I knew, no one had ever died while making one of her movies. 'I get nervous before one of these things and that's without someone being murdered while the movie was being made.' She stopped, looked at Patrick and then at me. 'Oh. I'm sorry.'

I assured her there was no need to feel that way. 'I'm just the lawyer,' I said. I was thinking of excuses I could use to leave the party early, because my stomach was clenching just thinking about showing up in court the next day. That was an excuse, wasn't it? I should say that.

'I get nervous before court every time,' Jon said. Was he stealing my excuse? I looked at his face. Nah. The man was in earnest. 'I'm sure Sandy is really nervous, even if it's clear the evidence against her client is at best circumstantial.'

Nate coughed. It wasn't because he was sick. Still, he seemed surprised when everyone turned in his direction. He sat back as if being attacked and blinked a couple of times. In a conversation about being nervous, I realized I'd never seen Nate look at all anxious before.

'Sorry,' he said, although I'm not sure for what. 'It's just that the evidence isn't all circumstantial.' He made eye contact with me and I knew where he was going, but the subject was already out on the table. 'We have video of the accused going after those steel cables with something that *might* have been a bottle of acid. And if we have it, you can be pretty sure the prosecution is going to have it.'

People like stories about crimes and trials when they're not directly involved. Cynthia, who had been so traumatized by her accusation and the events that surrounded it that she hadn't worked for six months, now seemed absolutely enthralled. 'Really! So your client *did* kill the stuntman?' she asked.

'No, that's not what it means,' I told Cynthia. 'That video could show a lot of things. We don't know yet.'

A phone buzzed and Angie reached into her jacket pocket to pull out her phone, but the work one Patrick had given her and not her personal line. She looked at the screen and her eyebrows dropped to half-staff. She hit a button and said quietly, 'Patrick McNabb.' I knew she wasn't Patrick McNabb but that was how she answered that phone. She listened for a while. 'Hold on. I'll see if I can find him.'

'Whoever it is, tell them I'm not available,' Patrick said. 'The movies can wait.' He looked at me with a twinkle in his eye, which always worked.

'Apparently there's someone at the door who wants to see you,' Angie said.

'Tell them I'm not home,' he said. 'How did they get this address?'

Angie's face looked pained. 'It's Lieutenant Trench,' she said. 'I gather he has a subpoena for you.'

Patrick swiveled his head to look at me. I put up my hands. 'Let him in,' I said. 'Looks like you're going to be a witness.'

Naturally. For Patrick, Trench came himself.

TWENTY-EIGHT

I f Judge Walter Franklin's house was anything like his court-room, it would have been terrifying to be invited to one of his dinner parties. He was maniacal in his insistence on neatness and order. Lawyers appearing before the judge knew better than to scatter paperwork all over their respective tables. Custodial staff in the courthouse were advised to keep the floors and all wooden surfaces polished, to wash the windows inside and out daily, and to make sure there were wastepaper baskets near both tables and at the end of every aisle of seats for spectators. There had better be no used facial tissues on the floor or there would be hell to pay.

So naturally the first time I'd been in Franklin's court I had been attacked by a woman with a condom full of fake blood. It had not been neat. And I believed that the judge carried a grudge. Against me. For standing there while she threw it at me. He probably believed I should have known better.

Today I had put on my most professional attire, sprayed with a product that claimed to repel liquids. I had my hair pulled back in a bun. My purse was stocked with disinfectant wipes. I was wearing low heels with soles that would make it less likely for me to slip.

I was taking no chances because this case was anything but a sure thing and I needed every advantage I could get.

Jury selection had been fairly quick. No misogynistic tweets from Robert Reeves had ever surfaced. He hadn't been accused of being anything other than slightly difficult to work with (these are Hollywood standards, and as far as I knew he'd never thrown a stapler at an employee), and he didn't seem to discriminate based on gender, sexual identity, race, religion or political affiliation. So I hadn't had to worry too much about demographics when we were seating the jury.

I had disqualified one man who had seen a previous film of Reeves's, *Dead Even*, and considered it 'stupid'. The prosecution had asked to have two jurors excused, one because he had once dated a cousin of the defendant's (I would have done the same if it had come to me) and one because she thought artists 'live outside the law'. That one had to be escorted away by security. I had made sure to look for something under my table as she passed by.

None of the prospective jurors had ever worked on a film set, which was something of an anomaly in Los Angeles, so no one with a special affection for or bias against stunt performers, stunt coordinators or film directors had been called. We had a jury seated with two alternates by ten a.m.

The press coverage resembled something that would have fallen between the Summer Olympics and Carnival in Rio, but with enough ghoulish fascination with the death of a stunt performer trying to do his job that I resolved to never watch the news on television again. I like a newspaper, but I spotted reporters from the *Los Angeles Times*, the *Hollywood Reporter*, *Variety* and even the *New York Times* and the *Wall Street Journal*, so I'd just have to duck all possible news outlets in every medium until two weeks after this trial was finished. Sure. That'd be a snap.

And that was fewer than had covered either Patrick's or Cynthia's trials, I reminded myself. That just got me to shaking my head in wonderment, which got me some seriously puzzled looks from my crew. Angie, Jon, Nate, and of course Reeves himself, looking like a man pretending he wore a suit to work every day, were present. And there was Penny, waiting like a puppy for some affection from her boss.

I had banished Patrick from attending until he was required for testimony for my opposition, which apparently was not going to be the case on the first day of the trial. He had protested, but in the end understood the logic in my not wanting a prosecution witness sitting right behind me, and besides he had to go be three or four characters on the set of *Torn* every day for the next week.

'Who's testifying first?' Reeves asked me after we returned from the break following the jury being seated.

'I'm not privy to the order of the prosecution's case,' I said. 'We'll find out as soon as Renfro tells us, but don't worry. There's no such thing as a surprise witness. We know everyone he has on his list.'

So the first witness Renfro called was not included on his list. I immediately objected when he named Alice V. Mandrill. 'Your Honor, this witness is not included on the prosecution's list and I have not been able to prepare for her.'

But even before I had stood up to object, I'd noticed the look on Reeves's face when he'd heard the name. He even tried to grab for my sleeve and shook his head, but it was too late. Judge Franklin looked over at the prosecution's table. 'Mr Renfro?'

'My apologies, Your Honor. The witness is listed on our information under her assumed name, Tracy Reeves.'

Of course. Now I was the idiot. Nicely done, Renfro.

'Withdrawn, Your Honor.'

Franklin didn't roll his eyes but I knew he wanted to. 'I should think so.'

Tracy, who had been waiting outside the courtroom, entered when a security guard at the door opened it for her. She wasn't playing the bombshell today, but I did notice a good number of the men in the spectator area straighten up as she walked by them and approached the witness stand. She paid them no attention at all.

After being sworn in, she sat down primly and folded her hands in her lap. Her skirt was not short. Her makeup was not overly noticeable. Her hair was pulled back in a bun exactly like mine. She was *good*.

'What's she going to say that I don't want to hear?' I asked Reeves.

He shrugged. 'Her middle name is Virginia?'

Clearly my client wasn't going to be much help. And apparently Renfro had either tracked Tracy (Alice) down where she was hiding or had been keeping her under wraps since I (and her fake husband) had seen her last. That could only indicate that he considered her to be a very important witness, but I couldn't figure out why. The best she could testify to was that she actually wasn't married to Robert Reeves and so therefore he would have had no jealousy of her alleged affair with James Drake and no reason to kill him. How did that help *Renfro*'s case?

I guessed we were about to find out.

'Ms Mandrill,' Renfro began, after whoever this was had been sworn in, 'have you ever gone by another name?'

Yeah, Benedict Arnold, I thought.

'Yes,' Mandrill – I'm going to call her Mandrill – answered. 'For eight months I went by the name Tracy Reeves.'

'You were married to the defendant, Robert Reeves?' Renfro asked.

My client, the aforementioned defendant, looked completely baffled.

'Yes,' Mandrill said.

I stood up. 'Objection, Your Honor. To my knowledge there exists no record of such a marriage taking place.'

But Renfro was already reaching down into his folder for a document that couldn't possibly exist, and yet there it was. 'I have a valid marriage certificate in my hand, dated just a little less than one year ago,' he said.

'I'd like to examine that document if Mr Renfro intends to introduce it into evidence,' I told Franklin. 'The defense has done an extensive search and found no such marriage to have been recorded in the state of California.'

Renfro brought the paper to the bench for Franklin to examine it. 'For good reason,' he told the judge. 'The marriage was recorded in Tijuana, Mexico.'

And my client went absolutely pale.

Reeves looked at me but he wasn't seeing me. He spoke, but to himself, and yet it was audible to anyone within a reasonable distance in the courtroom.

'That thing was *real*?' he said.

TWENTY-NINE

As you might expect, the rest of Mandrill's testimony did not go favorably for my client. She confirmed that she and Robert had been married in Tijuana with a valid marriage license and a ceremony performed by a local judge, just in case Franklin wanted to feel some camaraderie with the presiding party. Then Renfro, in his aw-shucks boy-next-door style, asked her about her 'relationship' with the victim in the case, James Drake.

'Jimmy and I were . . . we had a physical relationship,' Mandrill said, no doubt stopping herself from using a word that she'd never seen in a TV courtroom drama. 'It started around the time shooting began on *Desert Siege*.'

'And when did it end?'

'When Jimmy died.' Aspiring actress Mandrill did not overplay her role and sniff back a tear at that point. She'd probably had lessons from someone who had once read a book by Konstantin Stanislavsky.

'Was your husband, Mr Reeves,' (in case the jury had forgotten who was on trial) 'aware of this sexual relation-ship?' Renfro wanted the jury thinking dirty thoughts, and 'physical' just wasn't a suggestive enough word to use. Damn, he was good.

'Yes he was. In fact, it was Robert who introduced me to Jimmy at a party before shooting started. He said we looked good together.' I had always assumed she'd been lying about that, but repeating it in court made me rethink that assumption. It's not that people don't ever lie under oath, but most people are afraid of the penalty that comes with perjury, and this seemed like a trivial point to risk jail time about.

I looked at Reeves. He appeared to be severely nauseated. His face was pale (which in tan-centric Los Angeles is not easy to achieve) and there were beads of perspiration across his hairline. He didn't look at me because he was staring at

Mandrill. And he didn't look angry. He looked incalculably disappointed.

'Did your husband, Mr Reeves, express any reaction about your relationship with Mr Drake after you and he had started seeing each other regularly?' Renfro asked.

'Yes.' Mandrill was responding to her pre-trial briefing, which had clearly included the instruction that she should never offer anything but a direct answer to the question. They'd had her for some time.

'How did he react?'

'He was angry.'

'Did he say anything in particular that indicated he was angry?' Renfro said.

'He said Jimmy wasn't good enough for me and told me to stop seeing him.'

I looked over at Nate and he was holding up his hands, as if showing me his palms were going to make this all go away. It was his way of telling me he didn't know how Renfro had gotten hold of the marriage license when Nate hadn't been able to find it himself.

'Was he angry because you were his wife and you were sleeping with another man?' the prosecutor asked.

Mandrill had to think about that one. 'No, because he had another wife stashed away in San Bernardino.'

That sent the expected shock wave through the room. People in the spectator area registered surprise and shook their heads, but I didn't care about them because they didn't hold my client's fate in their hands.

The jury did and they looked positively angry. At Reeves. Like he'd lied to *them*, and he hadn't even taken the stand yet. If he ever would, which I was thinking would be the Mount Rushmore of mistakes, unless you count Mount Rushmore, if you're an indigenous person in South Dakota, but that's another whole issue.

This was bad on so many levels. The worst part is that I wasn't prepared for it because I'd been assured that there was no marriage and there was no jealousy. But now bigamy was also on the table and that was going to complicate matters.

'Another wife?' Yeah, Renfro, like you didn't know.

'Yeah. Stacy.'

'Were you aware of that when you married him?' the prosecutor asked.

'Yes.' Then Mandrill violated her pre-trial instruction and went beyond answering the question. 'See, I was more like an employee than a wife.'

Now. You have to know that Renfro knew all about the business arrangement between Mandrill and Reeves. And he had to know that the Mexican marriage certificate was, at best, questionable. But if his goal was to paint my client as an arrogant, unfeeling user of people, well, how could I argue with that? It did not, however, make him a murderer. Renfro no doubt knew that, too.

I felt like in that gee-whiz assistant DA I had found my Moriarty. Except Moriarty was evil and Renfro was just good at his job, which was making me lose. That was kind of evil, wasn't it?

'How did that work?' he asked Mandrill.

'He wanted someone who looked like me to be his wife so people could see him with a young, hot woman.' Mandrill was nothing if not direct. She was not the person who had first shown up in my office under the guise of Tracy Reeves. Maybe she was a better actress than I'd given her credit for; I'd have to ask Patrick. 'So we agreed he'd pay my rent and expenses and I'd go around telling everybody we got married. And we did, in Tijuana, so I wouldn't be lying.'

'But Mr Reeves did not divorce his other wife.'

I stood up. 'Objection. That's not a question and I don't see how this is relevant to the death of James Drake.'

'Ms Moss is playing semantics, but I do agree on the relevancy,' Franklin told the ADA. 'This is more an issue for a family court or possibly an indictment on the charge of bigamy, but I'd like to see you get to the point regarding the case currently before the court.'

'Of course, Your Honor.' But I could see Moriarty – sorry, Renfro – wasn't pleased. He'd wanted to milk the more salacious part of the story before getting to that silly murder. 'Mrs Reeves—'

I rose again. 'Your Honor, I'd appreciate it if, until that

document can be verified by the defense, Mr Renfro would refer to the witness as Ms Mandrill.'

Franklin looked down – they build the benches up so judges can look down on people – at Renfro. 'When was the marriage certificate added to the prosecution's discovery materials?' he asked.

Renfro kept looking at the prosecution's table because he didn't want to make eye contact. 'Yesterday, Your Honor.'

'Ms Moss has a point. Until the document can be verified by the court, you should not operate on the assumption that the defendant and the witness are legally married. Proceed, please.' Then he gave me a look as if to say, *I gave you that one. Don't slow down my trial with these petty objections anymore.*

I repressed the urge to nod.

'*Ms Mandrill,*' Renfro began again. 'You testified that your . . . that the defendant had been angry when he discovered you and the victim were having a personal relationship.'

'We were having sex,' Mandrill said, just to be clear. One of the male jurors smiled just a little. People have their dreams.

'Yes. Now, if your arrangement was a business one, why would Mr Reeves be upset that you and the victim Mr Drake were being intimate?'

I couldn't adhere to the unspoken agreement I had with the judge. 'Objection, Your Honor. The prosecution is asking the witness to speak to another person's reasons for having a certain emotion when it hasn't even been established that the defendant was really feeling that way.'

'I hate to say it, but sustained,' Franklin said. 'Ms Mandrill may not testify to why the defendant might think or feel a certain way. She may testify only to facts, such as what the defendant might have said on the subject.'

Renfro, having taken his cue from the judge, nodded. 'Thank you, Your Honor. I'll rephrase. Ms Mandrill, did the defendant Mr Reeves say anything to you that indicated he was upset about your relationship with the victim?'

Mandrill nodded. 'He said my job was to be his arm candy and that everybody would laugh if they thought I was . . . intimate with someone else while I was being introduced as his wife.'

'So this was an objection on a level of personal pride and the way others viewed the defendant?' Before I could raise a hand, Renfro added, 'Based on what he told you.'

'It was a professional thing,' she said, looking directly at Reeves. 'He said if he wanted to keep making movies for young guys, he couldn't be seen as an old man, and people seeing his real wife would have made him look like one. An old man.'

Two of the women on the jury started chewing lightly on their lips and glaring just a little at Reeves. Renfro's plan might not have been perfect legal strategy, but it was making the jury dislike my client, which meant it was working.

'Did Mr Reeves ever say anything to you that indicated he might mean some harm to the victim, James Drake?' he asked Mandrill.

'Yes,' she said. 'He told me that he'd see to it that James Drake would never work on a movie set in Hollywood ever again.'

'Thank you, Ms Mandrill. No further questions.' Renfro did not strut back to the prosecution table and he did not smirk. He was way too humble and down-to-earth for that. He was formidable.

Franklin nodded in my direction so I stood up and approached Alice Mandrill. 'Those were his words?' I asked. 'Mr Reeves said James Drake would never work on a Hollywood set again because of your affair?'

'Yes. That's what he said.'

'That's not quite the same thing as telling you that he planned to cut the cables on the crane and cause Drake to fall to his death, is it?'

'Objection.' Renfro this time. 'Asking the witness to draw a conclusion.'

I didn't wait for Franklin to rule. 'I withdraw the question. Ms Mandrill, did Mr Reeves ever say that he wanted to kill Mr Drake, or that he would tamper with the equipment on which the stunt was to be performed so that Mr Drake would be injured or die?'

There was a short breathless moment (for me) because I hadn't been expecting to question Mandrill today, and so I couldn't have known the answer to the question I was asking. But in a weird way I trusted Renfro. If he had something that damning, he'd have used it.

'No,' Mandrill answered. 'He didn't say that.'

'Did he ever indicate to you that he wished Mr Drake any physical harm, other than saying he might try to negatively influence Mr Drake's career?'

'No.'

'In fact, have you ever seen Mr Reeves act violently toward anyone at all?' I asked.

'Yes.'

Oops. Now what? Go on with the questioning? It seemed the only thing to do. I stole a glance at my client, who looked, for all the world, to have checked out of life and become something akin to a pod person. He stared straight ahead. I couldn't tell if he was afraid, annoyed, or just remembering a great strawberry rhubarb pie he'd once had at a diner.

'In what way?' I asked Mandrill. Then I braced for the worst possible answer.

'He threw a bag of potato chips back at his assistant once because they weren't the sea salt and vinegar kind.'

Oddly, no one in the courtroom laughed, but I found myself breathing normally again, unaware that I hadn't been a moment ago. 'He threw a bag of potato chips?' I repeated.

'It was the *way* he threw them,' Mandrill said with a defiant look on her face.

'Now, Ms Mandrill, you suggested that Mr Reeves introduced you to Mr Drake and suggested you looked good together.'

'Yes.' I hadn't asked a question yet, but OK.

'Then you said when he heard that you and Mr Drake were intimate, he became upset and said Mr Drake wasn't good enough for you.' Before Mandrill could confirm that one as well, I added, 'Did he say why he'd changed his mind so drastically from one time to the next?'

'He didn't explain it to me. But I didn't ask him either. I figured he was just jealous.'

'But you don't know that for sure.'

Mandrill scowled. 'No.'

Having dodged a bullet, the smart player generally leaves the inside of the shooting gallery. 'No further questions now, Your Honor, but I reserve the right to recall this witness.'

Franklin nodded. And scanned the courtroom for errant paper bags.

THIRTY

'Did that help or hurt?' I asked Jon.

We were on a recess for lunch and sitting at an outdoor café two blocks from the courthouse. Unlike the other two murder trials I'd done in Los Angeles, the defendant was not a famous actor, so we could be out on the street without any danger of my client being accosted by fans, detractors or other civilians. Patrick wasn't with us – it was me, Judy, Angie, Jon, Nate and Reeves (with the ubiquitous Penny) – so we just looked like normal people sharing a business lunch.

We were planning ways to keep a man out of jail but hey, that's a business, isn't it?

Jon is a savant-level tactician in the courtroom and can plan seven steps ahead of almost any lawyer I've ever seen. Until fairly recently I'd thought he was less strong in the courtroom, but then he'd gotten me out of jail so that opinion was currently under review. It was always, though, a good idea to talk to him about strategy.

He wiped some salsa from the corner of his mouth with the paper napkins supplied, guaranteed to fly away at the slightest breeze if not held down by a soda. 'I think it cut both ways. The jury wasn't happy to hear that Robert is a bigamist, but there was no evidence that he was in a particular rage about James Drake and certainly nothing that indicated he'd be violent toward the man.'

'You know I'm right here, don't you?' Reeves said. He was dealing with my choice of a lunch spot when he was generally used to places that had cloth napkins and, you know, roofs.

'You've been holding back on us since you hired us,' I said to him. 'You told me that you weren't really married to Tracy.'

'I wasn't!' the defendant protested. Then his puffery lost some of its volume and he added, 'At least I didn't *think* I was.'

'So tell me about Mexico,' I said. 'And don't leave anything out or change anything to make yourself look better. I need all the facts.'

'Yeah.' Angie looked thrilled with the idea of hearing about Mexico because she, like the jury undoubtedly did, figured it was a really juicy, sexy story. I was hoping it was not.

Reeves scowled and flattened his lips out. He looked around the table for support and found only Judy, who was trying at an outdoor café not to have her back to either the street or the restaurant. Judy hadn't protested at my choice of venue; that's not her style. But her neck was on auto-swivel and would not ever stop turning her head to look for threats. She wasn't going to offer Reeves an especially sympathetic smile, or any other facial expression.

'We went down there after we reached our business agreement, and I swear that's all it was ever supposed to be,' he began.

'If you swear to that in *court*, it had better be true and you'd better be able to prove it,' I told him. I was finding that it was possible to defend a man against murder charges without liking him at all. I was still deciding whether that was worth knowing.

'It's true,' my client insisted. 'I'm not sure I can prove it because it was a verbal agreement.'

That seemed implausible. A guy like Reeves would never operate on a handshake deal. 'There was no written contract?' I asked.

'Not as such. We had a handshake deal on it and there was absolutely no mention of a real marriage.'

'Why did you go to Tijuana?' Jon was right back on point and acting very much like a prosecutor. Good for him; we needed to question Reeves with an almost adversarial tone if we wanted to get anything resembling facts from him.

'It was a celebration,' he said. There followed a fairly long pause while we stared at him. 'Virginia had just taken a job, I'd solved a problem, and it was only a few hours away.'

'Did your wife go with you?' Angie asked.

Reeves's mouth tightened a bit. 'Having Stacy there when the whole point was to celebrate Tracy would have been contradictory. It makes no sense.' I'm sure you'd think it was Reeves who said that but no, it was Penny. Because that was her job as Head Toady.

'I had to maintain the image,' was what Reeves chimed in. It wasn't better, but at least it was from the person who had been asked the question.

Remembering I was the lawyer, I decided to take the reins of the conversation. 'And you don't remember actually marrying Alice, or Virginia, or Tracy, or whoever?' I already had some attorneys with better experience in Mexican law (you'd be surprised how often it comes up in Southern California) at Seaton, Taylor looking over the scan of the document that the former fake Mrs Reeves had insisted made her the former real Mrs Reeves.

'I mean, I had been doing *some* drinking, but I wasn't that drunk.' Reeves looked like the damage to his dignity was worse than the damage to his case in court, which was not the, you know, case. 'I figured it was a silly souvenir thing that Virginia had bought at the gift shop because there's a gift shop everywhere in Tijuana, and it was all in Spanish. She said sign it and I assumed it was part of the gag.'

'So you signed it,' I said.

'So I signed it.' He looked miserable. Good. Not good that he signed it; I was holding out hope that the signature had been forged. You don't always get what you hope for in life. In case you were wondering.

Of course, as a woman with a very nice job in a big exciting city, dating a remarkably successful actor, I had very little to complain about. But my roots are deep, and we from the Garden State enjoy nothing as much as a good gripe. It's because we live between New York City and Philadelphia and we have middle-child syndrome.

But I digress.

'OK, well, there's nothing we can do about that,' I told my

client. 'When we get some indication of how authentic the document is, we'll have a plan to go forward. I'm getting ready for both possible outcomes. But what I need to know is if you had any access to a supply of hydrochloric acid.'

I specifically hadn't mentioned this to Reeves in any of our phone conversations because I wanted to see the look on his face when I did, and it wasn't just because I didn't like the guy. I needed to know whether he'd ever told me the truth for a full minute since we'd met.

His eyes narrowed and his mouth half-opened. It wasn't an expression of surprise, which I might have expected, or of dread if I'd caught him in a lie. It was more a look of confusion, like I'd just told him that the next thing we'd do in court was bring in a flock of doves.

'Hydro . . . what now?' he said.

He was very good at selling the disconnect, but I did notice that Penny gave her boss a very quick, almost imperceptible, look of something that appeared to be worry, like I'd touched a nerve that she was afraid would send him to jail.

'Come on,' I said to Reeves. 'You've heard of hydrochloric acid before.'

The director went back to his favorite attitude, which was condescension. 'I'm sure this will come as a shock to you, Sandy, but I was not a chemistry major in school. What does hydrochloric acid have to do with anything?'

'It's the tool that was used to wear down the cables so they'd snap at just the right moment,' I informed him on the odd chance that he didn't know. 'And I need an honest answer from you about whether or not you could have had access to some before Jim Drake fell off the crane.'

'I have no idea what you're talking about,' Reeves said.

But Penny was already tapping away furiously at her smartphone. 'Hydrochloric acid is readily available at hardware stores and many other retail outlets in the United States and abroad,' she (clearly) read. 'Anyone could have access to it for less than five dollars.' I'm pretty sure that last part was Penny editorializing.

I decided, diplomatically, to ignore her and turned back toward Reeves. 'OK. So who on the set would be able to get that close to those cables a number of times over the course of the twelve hours before James Drake fell?'

Reeves the Director took over. His brows dropped and met at the center and he put his hand to his chin. If he'd been directing himself, he would have said that the 'thinking' pose was too on-the-nose. Or maybe not. I had to ask Patrick how good he was at dealing with actors.

'If it wasn't for the twelve-hours thing it could be virtually anyone,' he began. 'But we were on set at six thirty a.m. and that would mean that whoever did this would have had to basically sleep in Griffith Park the night before. There's security on the set so that means it would probably have to be someone the security people knew. There might be records.'

I looked at Nate. 'I'm on it,' he said.

'OK.' I looked over my tuna sandwich and decided it could make a decent lunch tomorrow if I brought it home tonight after time in the courtroom break-area fridge. 'Let's get back to court.'

THIRTY-ONE

Subpoenas are funny things, although not for the people who receive them. It seemed that when Trench was delivering one to Patrick, he'd been having a busy day. And the thing about being subpoenaed is that it makes the witness either timid and intimidated, or pissed off and somewhat hostile. That was fine with me because these were witnesses for the prosecution.

They were expert witnesses (neither of whom was under a subpoena to testify) who were not Brady O'Toole, but were explaining the operation of the crane and the use of the camera equipment. That was interesting since no camera equipment was being used when Jim Drake was strapped into the crane or when the crime – which we were all admitting now had taken place and was not an accident – had occurred.

They didn't have that much to say that I found especially

damaging to Robert Reeves, because they weren't testifying that he'd had anything to do with the tampering that had been done and they weren't members of his crew, so they couldn't speak to the awful way he treated his employees. Those, no doubt, were to come.

But first there was Burke Henderson. If he didn't have an agenda on the stand, nobody would. Henderson clearly hated Reeves, for reasons that were at least understandable. Reeves had, in fact, been bad-mouthing Henderson all over the film industry, and when you make your living in the film industry, well, that can be a bad thing. There are those who say Los Angeles is a company town. Guess which company.

Henderson's gaze, once sworn in, rarely left my client, sitting immediately to my right, so I got a million-dollar view of the resentment and hostility coming from the witness. It was a wonder he'd had to be subpoenaed. You'd think he would have been lining up to testify at the DA's office as soon as the case was assigned to Renfro.

'You were the stunt coordinator on the set of *Desert Siege*,' the prosecutor began, not at all asking a question.

'Yes.' Sometimes people just answer.

'So you supervised the preparations for the sequence that was being rehearsed on the morning Jim Drake was killed,' Renfro went on. Again, not a question, but notice the language: He referred to the client as 'Jim', making him sound like just a regular guy the jury might know, and he said, 'was killed', making it an active, probably premeditated occurrence. It was not 'the morning James Drake died'; it was 'the morning Jim Drake was killed'. Renfro was paying attention to the details so I would have to do the same.

'Yes I did,' Henderson said. No inflection in his tone yet and the eyes never left Reeves. Certainly the jury was noticing.

'How long before Jim was strapped into the harness did you last check the cables to make sure they were safe?' Renfro asked. Now the victim was just 'Jim'. And Henderson was being given credibility in that he was the one who had to check the cables for safety. Given how that turned out it probably didn't score major points, but every tactic is worth trying.

'Maybe thirty-five or forty minutes,' was the answer.

'And when you checked, the cables were in working order?'

Henderson was not one of those subpoena recipients who was going to be resistant to answering questions. 'They most certainly were,' he answered.

'So sometime between your last inspection of the equipment and the time the stunt was being rehearsed, something happened to those cables. Can you speculate on what it might have been?'

I stood up. 'Clarification, Your Honor. Should the witness be allowed to speculate? He's not being presented as an expert witness but someone who was on the set.'

Franklin considered and then nodded. 'Please restrict your questions only to things the witness could have seen happen.'

Renfro changed his direction, thinking about approaching the bench but then seeing Franklin's demeanor, switching back toward the witness. 'I will, Your Honor. Mr Henderson, did the defendant Mr Reeves ever share his feelings about James Drake with you?'

Reeves closed his eyes briefly; I knew about this and it was not going to be good.

'Yes he did.' Henderson, wanting to continue working in the film business, was going to be reluctant to be seen hanging a prominent director out to dry, no matter how often that director had suggested he was not a competent stunt coordinator. He was going to answer the questions and give damning evidence, but Renfro was going to have to work for every piece of information he got from his witness.

'And what did he say?' he asked.

'Well, he said a number of things over a series of conversations,' Henderson said. 'We were working together pretty closely on a picture that was very action-oriented.'

Renfro gave up no irritation on his face, but I knew that if my witness was being this cagey with me, I'd have been a pit of burning lava inside. 'On one particular occasion, did Mr Reeves suggest that perhaps Mr Drake should not be employed by the production?'

'Yes.' This could take quite a while.

'What were the circumstances under which he made that suggestion, and what were his exact words, if you can remember them, please?' Renfro was looking at Reeves, and therefore in my direction, and not at his witness as he asked this question.

Or questions.

'Well, he said that a few times,' Henderson said. Perhaps noting that Renfro turned to face him (and also perhaps seeing his expression, since I couldn't), he added, 'but there was one time in particular when he said I should fire Jimmy and replace him with a sack of potting soil.'

There was a light titter from the gathered. Even a couple of jurors chuckled at that one, then remembered where they were and why they were there, and stopped themselves.

Renfro chose to ignore the witty comment supposedly made by my client and pressed on. 'As the director of the movie, wouldn't it have been Mr Reeves's responsibility to fire the stunt performer and not yours?' he asked.

'Yes,' Henderson agreed. 'It would. I mean, the fact is that I hired the stunt performers for my team and they were just approved by the director, but if he really had wanted to fire somebody, he could have gone over my head and done it, but he didn't.'

'Why not?'

I was back up on my feet. 'Speculation again, Your Honor, and this time on the decision-making process of my client.'

Franklin did a move I'd only ever seen in movies before, and that was to actually pick up his gavel and point it at Renfro. 'She's right, Mr Renfro, and you knew that before you asked the question. I won't warn you again.'

Reeves took his hands away from his eyes, where they had (against my expressed advice) been situated. Because that had only made him look like the most guilty man on earth. Now he only looked like the second most guilty.

'Apologies, Your Honor.' Renfro wasn't the least bit sorry and had asked the question only to get my objection. 'Won't happen again.'

'You'd better believe it,' Franklin said quietly.

'Did Mr Reeves ever mention why he was so opposed to employing the victim, Mr Drake?' Renfro said.

'He said that he thought Jimmy was a bad stuntman, but

that was clearly untrue. He'd worked with Jimmy on four other movies, and as far as I've heard never complained about him before.' Henderson had given up the monosyllabic answers and decided to vent his dislike for Reeves, whether word got around that he'd savaged a director or not. Maybe he had a pension to fall back on or something.

'Well, I won't ask why he'd say that if he didn't think it was true,' Renfro began.

'That's right,' the judge broke in. 'You won't.'

'Exactly, Your Honor. I won't and never intended to. Mr Henderson, did Mr Reeves mention any other reasons he didn't like Mr Drake?'

'Well, the fact that Jimmy was banging his wife probably wasn't really popular with Bobby,' Henderson said.

There was, not surprisingly, a decent amount of commotion around the courtroom at that point. Franklin used the gavel for its other purpose, creating a loud noise that would cause the spectators and others in the room to quiet down, which they did fairly soon.

I had already stood and waited for the noise to subside. With a weary tone I said, 'Your Honor. Need I point out that this was once again speculation on the part of the witness, even if Mr Renfro didn't actually ask for him to do so?'

When judges talk to witnesses or jurors, they are more polite and less stern than with, say, lawyers. Franklin was clearly not pleased with what Henderson had said but didn't want to scold him. 'Mr Henderson, kindly restrict your answers only to things you know to be facts. If the defendant did not say anything about his wife and Mr Drake to you specifically, you may not mention it. Is that clear?'

'Yes sir.' Henderson was not used to being reprimanded, even lightly. His eyes didn't show anger as much as surprise.

'Please proceed, Mr Renfro.' Franklin looked a lot like he wished we'd never come back from lunch.

Renfro nodded. 'Mr Henderson, *did* the defendant Mr Reeves ever say anything to you about his wife Tracy Reeves and her alleged affair' – he looked at me when he said the word *alleged* just to stave off any possible objection – 'with the victim Jim Drake?'

Henderson, glad to be back on the judge's good side, put on an especially serious expression, like he was trying to figure out a really complicated math problem in his head. 'Yes he did. He told me that if he ever found out it was true, he'd kill Jimmy.'

One of the jurors coughed. Nobody else made a sound.

Reeves reached over and wrote on the pad between us: *Putting up a front.* I wasn't sure I knew what that meant but it didn't matter at the moment.

Renfro, well aware of the impact he'd just made, turned away from the witness. 'No further questions,' he said, and walked back to the prosecution table. *Your turn, Moss.*

I stood up before Franklin would feel the need to summon me, and approached Henderson the way one approaches an unfamiliar beagle: wary but not afraid. 'Mr Henderson, did you see Robert Reeves tamper with the cables that held James Drake?'

'No.' Seeing me as hostile, Henderson was back to using as few letters as possible.

'Now, as you have testified, you inspected the cables before the rehearsal that took James Drake's life.' I didn't ask a question and Henderson didn't offer an answer. 'Were there any marks from a saw or a grinder on them?'

'No.'

It occurred to me that just for sport I might see if I could get Henderson to say nothing but *no* the whole time I was questioning him, but then I figured it was probably more to my advantage if I could get Robert Reeves acquitted. Sometimes you just want to pad your stats and sometimes you play for the team. I was playing for the team.

'Were there any marks from any kind of metal tool?'

'No.'

Time to stop playing the game. 'Was there a strong smell?'

That took Henderson by surprise, and even Renfro stayed in his seat, not knowing whether there was any basis for an objection, or even if he wanted one. 'A smell? What kind of smell?'

'I don't want to influence your testimony, Mr Henderson. Did you notice a smell when you examined the cables on the morning in question?'

Instead of trying to be combative, it was clear that Henderson was sincerely trying to remember. 'It's possible,' he said quietly.

'The court couldn't hear you,' Franklin told him, and Henderson looked up.

'I said I might remember a smell off the cables. But my sense of smell is somewhat diminished because I had the Covid virus.' That was still true for many people. 'I don't really have it all the way back yet, and this was months ago.'

'Can you describe the smell, Mr Henderson?' That was me, not Franklin. It's not the judge's job to send the witness off on a tangent. That was for the defense attorney to do.

'Not really. Like I said, I can't smell much now, and it was worse then. But I remember people complaining about a smell near the crane and I remember thinking it was kind of like burning.'

That was consistent with the use of acid. But I didn't want to drop that particular piece of information yet so I pivoted. 'You testified that Mr Reeves told you if he discovered his wife was having an affair with Mr Drake that he, Mr Reeves, would kill Mr Drake. Is that a direct quote?'

Henderson took on that adorable gee-little-lady expression he'd used in his workshop when Angie and I were busy stifling our impulses to pummel him with our purses just to show him it could be done. It was not quite a smirk, but it wanted to be one when it grew up. 'Well, I wasn't recording the conversation but I believe that is what he said.'

'Did he say it in a way that indicated he meant what he said literally?' I asked.

Renfro rose to his feet. Which doesn't make any sense. He rose and his feet stayed on the floor where they were, but an expression is an expression. 'Now who's asking the witness to draw a conclusion?' he asked Franklin.

'I am,' I told the judge. 'But the only two people in this conversation were Mr Henderson and Mr Reeves and I'd like to hear the witness's perspective on the comment. I think the court would appreciate it as well.' It never hurts to play up to a judge. If you don't think they're all about ego, you clearly have never had dinner with one.

'Objection overruled,' Franklin said. 'I think the question is relevant even if Ms Moss is being a wiseacre about it.' *Wiseacre*. Honestly.

I didn't wait for Henderson to ask for the question to be repeated. 'Did you have the impression that the defendant meant he would literally kill James Drake if the rumors about his affair with Mr Reeves's wife turned out to be true?' I asked again.

'Yes, I believed that was what he meant.' Henderson must have really hated Robert Reeves.

'And this conversation took place how long before Mr Drake died?' I asked.

Henderson hesitated but it was honest recollection and not grandstanding. 'I'd say about two weeks.'

'Why didn't you call the police?' I said.

'What?'

'Why didn't you call the police? Alert studio security? Contact the FBI?' (The FBI wouldn't have wanted to hear about it, but it sounded good.) 'If you believed that the director of the film you were working on was posing a serious threat to the life of one of *your* stunt performers, why didn't you notify the authorities and report the threat?'

'Objection.' Guess who. 'Counsel is badgering the witness and trying to place the responsibility for the victim's death on Burke Henderson when absolutely no one believes he committed the murder.' I didn't know whether anyone believed that or not, but it wasn't the point.

'That's not at all what the defense is attempting to do,' I told Franklin. 'The defense is not aware of any physical evidence tying Mr Henderson to the crime. If we were, *we* would have called the police. What we're trying to do, Your Honor, goes to the claim that Mr Henderson made, which the jury just heard, that he thought the defendant was sincere in his threat to kill James Drake.'

Franklin thought it over. 'I'll allow it.' I was having a good day with objections. No idea if that was carrying over anywhere else.

I looked back at Henderson. 'Why didn't you call the police?' I asked again.

'Well, he hadn't actually hurt anyone at that point,' he answered. You'd think with all that time to consider it, he would have come back with a better answer.

'Do you think it's better to alert the authorities only after someone is dead, or should a person try to prevent something like that from happening?' I said.

'Your Honor,' Renfro complained. 'Are we asking for moral judgments from the witness now?'

'Withdrawn,' I said, eliminating the need for a ruling that would have broken my winning streak. 'Mr Henderson, is it possible you didn't call the police because you thought Mr Reeves might have been speaking figuratively? That he said, "I'd kill him", meaning he'd be very angry, and not that he would violently end James Drake's life? Is that possible?'

'I don't know.' Really, it was a miracle this guy hadn't made a living in improv theater. Without rehearsal and a script, he wasn't exactly wowing the crowd.

'You don't know if it's possible or you don't know whether you thought that?' Either way I was in good shape. Legally. I still needed to exercise more. Everybody in LA looks like they're headed to the gym or just got out of the gym. I occasionally run a half a mile in the morning. As a result I don't look like them.

'I'm not sure whether I thought he meant it or not,' Henderson said, teeth clenched.

'No more questions.' I sat down.

Franklin looked over at Renfro. 'Redirect?'

Renfro stood up, which I guessed meant yes. He approached the witness box. 'Mr Henderson, at the time he said it, did you think Mr Reeves meant that he would do violence to James Drake if he discovered there was a physical relationship between him and Mr Reeves's wife?'

'Yes.' Henderson had hesitated, but that was probably to absorb the question, which had been wordy.

'No more questions.'

Henderson was excused from the witness stand and gave me a grumpy look on the way out. Had he expected me *not* to try and make his accusations sound less legitimate? People get awfully testy in courtrooms.

Renfro did not affect a triumphant smile, largely because he hadn't triumphed all that much, but he did look pleased with himself. 'The state calls Detective Lieutenant K.C. Trench,' he said.

This was going to be interesting.

THIRTY-TWO

rench took the stand with the air of a man who wasn't exactly above it all but was maybe one riser up on the stairs. He did not change expression – I wouldn't want him to violate his sworn oath to the Stoics – and he sat without unbuttoning the coat of his blue suit. Other cops are cops. Trench is an officer of the Los Angeles Police Department.

Suffice it to say that Renfro spent some time questioning Trench about his record, which culminated with him appearing whenever the Trench Signal was shined in the sky over LA. He had an impressive résumé. I wasn't about to dispute that.

At that moment, however, I was planning on asking him why he had stopped talking to me when I got to question him on cross. Petty? Yes, you can say I'm petty. But first it was Renfro's turn.

'Lieutenant, you were the chief investigating officer in the death of James Drake; is that correct?'

'Yes.' If Trench could have just said, 'Y,' he probably would have been happier. More efficient.

'Why would a homicide detective be assigned to a death that at the time appeared to be nothing more than a terrible accident?'

'When a death occurs and the cause is not medical or obvious, an investigation is opened,' the lieutenant said. 'Even in automobile accidents that result in a fatality, such elements as the vehicle's brakes might be inspected. In this case, a man had fallen to his death in the course of filming a dangerous scene for a film. I was assigned to investigate and report. There were no suspects at the time of the incident.'

'So you weren't there to make an arrest.' Renfro liked to make statements and pretend they were questions.

'Not immediately,' Trench answered. 'Until evidence became clear that the death was not accidental, there was no presumption that anyone in particular might have deliberately caused it. But it was also possible that negligence or malpractice might have been involved, which could have resulted in charges of involuntary manslaughter if the district attorney had made that determination.'

'So you don't charge people?' I was sure the least experienced juror in the box knew that.

'No. I arrest people and send my findings to the district attorney, who might convene a grand jury or might charge the individual or individuals involved, depending on the circumstances.' I wondered if people invited Trench to parties for his scintillating repartee.

'In the case of Jim Drake's death, what were your findings concerning responsibility or culpability?' Renfro used two words that mean the same thing.

'After examination of the cables holding the man up on the crane, I determined with the help of some of the experts you have questioned that they had been tampered with and that had caused them to snap, sending Mr Drake to his death.'

The tabloids had sensationalized the case to the point that I believed Robert Reeves had been hacking away at the cables with an axe while James Drake pleaded with him to stop. Trench was the anti-tabloids. He made everything sound like a plumbing manual.

'Did you determine what had caused the cables to deteriorate to that point?' Renfro asked.

'Some of the tests were inconclusive, but recently it has become widely accepted that some sort of chemical agent, likely an acid, had been applied to the cables and that had worn them to the point that Mr Drake's weight had caused them to snap.'

'An acid. So it did not require a long time sawing away at the metal when people could have seen it happen.'

Again, no question. 'No,' Trench said anyway.

'Any idea what kind of acid?'

'Probably hydrochloric acid, according to the forensic lab.'

'Who would have access to that kind of acid?' Renfro asked.

'Virtually anyone. It's available at Home Depot, Lowe's and any neighborhood hardware store and is very inexpensive.'

Renfro walked forward and leaned in like he was about to ask Trench a question only those in his most intimate circles might venture. Trench didn't exactly recoil in horror, but he clearly wasn't pleased, and besides, the assistant DA wanted the jury to hear his question so he couldn't whisper.

'Lieutenant, what led you to arrest the defendant Robert Reeves for the murder of Jim Drake?'

'There had been rumors about the director's wife and the victim on the set of the film,' Trench began. 'That's not enough to justify an arrest, certainly, but there was also Mr Reeves's insistence that he had been in the video village at the time of the fall and couldn't have been involved. We knew that he'd been near the cables in the spot where the deterioration had taken place, not long before the stunt was performed.'

'And how did you know that, Lieutenant?'

'We had video that showed him there not long before the rehearsal began,' Trench said.

Of course they did. I had never expected for a moment that the as-yet-unnamed person who had given the iPhone video to Nate would have kept it from the prosecution. The video at the very least showed Reeves talking to James Drake about the stunt minutes before Drake died. Neither side was paying for information, but LA is a town that's all about being recognized, and having some acknowledgement from the district attorney's office would not be a bad thing. (Some people also act out of a sense of community responsibility, but it's usually a better bet to assume they didn't.)

'Your Honor,' I said from my seat, 'the defense has not been made aware of this video. If the prosecution wishes to enter it into evidence, we should be allowed to review it ourselves.' If for no other reason than to confirm that it was the same footage. Believe it or not, there can be more than one person with a cell phone on a movie set.

'That is only reasonable, Mr Renfro.' Franklin knew it was also required but he wanted to see if the DA had any objections to sharing his video with us, or if he just wanted to post it on TikTok and be done with it.

'It would be, Your Honor, but the prosecution has no intention of entering the video into evidence at this time.' Renfro, I swear, was looking at me the whole time he said that.

Huh? Why wouldn't Renfro want to show Robert Reeves bending over the essential cables looking like the villain in, well, a Robert Reeves movie? What possible logic was there in that? I looked over at Jon, who was wearing a very serious expression and writing furiously on his legal pad.

'In that case, Your Honor,' I said, 'I move that the mention of the video be stricken from the record and the jury advised not to consider it because we don't know exactly what is in that footage.'

Franklin didn't wait for any argument from the prosecution. 'So ordered,' he said. 'Ladies and gentlemen of the jury, please do not consider any mention of video footage in your deliberations. We are not going to see that video and therefore we don't know what it might contain, no matter how much description we are given. You should not consider it and, frankly, the prosecution should have advised Lieutenant Trench not to mention it.'

That did not go unnoticed by Renfro, who made a point to be looking at his notes and nodded noncommittally. 'Lieutenant,' he said, doing his best not to look like he'd just pulled a cheap trick to plant an image in the jurors' minds, 'what other evidence did you gather that implicated Mr Reeves to the point that you considered an arrest to be justified?'

Trench, doing his best Vulcan, glanced in my direction, and I wondered if that was a signal. 'The evidence that had been revealed, including the rumors, eyewitness accounts and . . .' – he didn't want to mention the video – 'other data indicated to me that Mr Reeves should be brought in for questioning.'

'Thank you, Lieutenant.'

Wait. Had I just heard what I'd heard? I stood up for my cross-examination. 'Lieutenant Trench, thank you for coming in today.'

'It is a requirement of my job.' Which is true.

'Yes, sir. Lieutenant, I have seen your report on the incident in question and I've looked over all the records from the LAPD regarding James Drake's death. Can you verify that you were the arresting officer in this case?'

'I am listed as the arresting officer.'

I was right! Trench was being deliberately coy. He was looking me in the eye but communicating nothing other than the answer to my question, but now I understood his silent treatment for the past few weeks. He was demonstrating his respect for me by disapproving of what he saw as my reckless approach to Reeves's defense (he was wrong, but I knew that was how he saw it, especially after the kidnapping incident when I'd told him I didn't care that much about Reeves). And there was a reason that bothered him so much.

'But after sifting through the evidence you had, you brought Mr Reeves in for questioning. He was not officially arrested or charged right away, was he?'

The very slightest glimmer in Trench's eye. I'd hit the right nerve. 'No. He was not charged until four days later.'

'What were you doing regarding this case for those four days?' I asked.

'I was questioning more witnesses and visiting the scene of the incident three more times to gather physical evidence,' Trench answered.

'Was there anything in that additional questioning and examination that made it more clear the defendant was guilty of deliberately degrading the cables holding up Mr Drake and causing him to fall to his death?'

Renfro stood up. That was when I knew I had him. 'Does the timing of the evidence matter here, Your Honor?' he said. 'The key fact is that Lieutenant Trench decided to charge the defendant Mr Reeves with first-degree murder.'

'I'll let Ms Moss go on a bit more,' Franklin said. Then he turned to face me. 'Just a bit.'

'Thank you, Your Honor. Lieutenant Trench, *did* you decide to charge Mr Reeves, or did someone else in the department make that determination?'

'My name appears on the records as the arresting officer,' Trench repeated.

'That's not what I asked.'

'Objection.' No doubt Renfro was trying to justify an objection even as he rose to his feet.

Franklin waited. 'On what grounds?'

Hesitation. 'Badgering the witness.'

'Sit down, Mr Renfro.' He did.

'Lieutenant Trench,' I said, knowing I was out of line, 'in your professional judgment as a homicide detective, do you believe Robert Reeves actually killed James Drake?'

Renfro wanted to object. Truly, he did. But it was at worst a rude and misleading question, not an inappropriate one. So he bit his lip and watched his key witness consider what I'd asked.

'It is my opinion that the evidence is inconclusive,' Trench said.

'Those are all my questions, Lieutenant,' I said. 'Thank you very much.'

'Redirect,' Renfro said, and approached Trench even while Franklin was nodding his agreement. 'Lieutenant Trench, are you saying that Robert Reeves did *not* tamper with the cables?'

'No.' Damn Trench and his monosyllabic answers. Renfro sat down and Trench was dismissed.

'How did that go?' Reeves whispered to me.

'It went,' I said.

THIRTY-THREE

I shook that day off, had Patrick over to the apartment for Chinese takeout with Angie (and what's with the red-box thing on the west coast?) and did my best to relax. I wasn't sure which witness Renfro would be calling first the next day, but he'd been clear he wasn't going to admit the video and that meant I needed to look at it again and figure out what he didn't want the jury to see.

I watched that thing eleven more times and couldn't identify a single frame (if digital video had frames) that would prove

Robert Reeves innocent. On the other hand, I didn't see anything that definitively proved him guilty, either. That last look at him hunched over the base of the crane, seeming to be touching the cables in some way, wasn't a great look for my case. Why Renfro didn't want to show it to the jury was a mystery. So, as I always do when I have a mystery, I called Nate while Patrick and Angie watched *Torn* in the living room. (Patrick is not one of those actors who can't bear to see himself on screen. He's very serious about it and seems to be taking mental notes but it doesn't make him suffer.)

'You've got to tell me who gave you that video,' I told Nate when he answered his phone.

'Why?'

'*Why?* You don't think it's relevant to the case? I need to know the source so I can figure out how likely it is to have been sent by someone who wants to prove to me that my client is guilty, like for example the people who have kidnapped me and pretended to blow up a car I was riding in because they wanted me to drop the case.'

Nate made a sort of gargling noise in his throat to the point that I wondered if I should hang up on him so I could call 911 and report a man drowning in his own house. Assuming Nate was in his house. Finally he stopped doing that, as I guessed it was his thinking sound, and said, 'You realize I'm trying to protect the source.'

'Not from me. You don't protect the source of valuable information from the client who's paying you,' I pointed out.

There was no gargling this time but a low hum. I began to fear that Nate had become a white-noise machine, or dropped his phone next to one. 'Let me call the source and ask permission,' he said. 'I'll call you right back.'

'And then you'll tell me either way, right?' But Nate had already hung up.

I hadn't gotten all the way through the video again when he called back. 'I didn't get permission,' Nate said. 'But I figure I'm not the lawyer and I don't have client confidentiality to worry about.'

'All good things to figure,' I agreed.

'The source is an assistant to one of the producers, a woman named Margaret Houlihan. She was on set, doing her job and minding her own business. She got the video later from a third party.' Nate stopped, and for a second I thought that was all I was going to get from him. 'She doesn't want to testify in court because she thinks it'll screw up her job. Like she's being disloyal to her boss or something.'

'Can you set up a meeting with me?' I asked. 'Maybe I can convince her.'

'Look, she didn't even want me to tell you her name,' Nate reminded me. 'But let's say I can find out where she'll be for lunch tomorrow if you just happen to stop by.'

'I'll be in court tomorrow.'

'Jon can sit there and watch Renfro question people just as well as you can,' Nate said. 'Isn't that why you asked for a second chair?'

He had a point. 'Find out about lunch and text me,' I said, and hung up.

Nate and I have a very affectionate relationship.

I can't say I slept great that night because I had a nagging feeling there was something I was missing, something I should have been anticipating for the next day in court. But when I got to the courtroom the next morning and saw the regular crowd – Angie, Jon and Reeves and Penny on my side, Renfro and his second assistant, a woman named Leona Arozarena, at his table – I relaxed a little. But just a little.

The morning wasn't especially notable. Renfro asked one of the craft services people from the set whether Reeves was a testy director (spoiler alert: he was) and I didn't bother to cross. Yeah, he was a grump. I had checked the California penal code that morning and it still wasn't a crime. But after that exchange I noticed Renfro with a tight smirk on his face. This wasn't going to be good, and I was willing to bet I knew what it was.

Renfro cleared his throat. 'The state calls Patrick McNabb,' he said.

Patrick was ushered in from the corridor, where the next witnesses to testify are usually asked to sit. There was some commotion around the courtroom because an actual TV star was entering, bringing him stares from both women and men, possibly for different reasons in many cases. Or not.

He looked at me on his way in and appeared somewhat sheepish. It wasn't as if I hadn't known he'd be testifying. I just didn't know it was going to happen today. But I had prepared for him despite my having no idea why Renfro thought Patrick was in any way a useful witness for the case against Robert Reeves.

Patrick was sworn in and took the stand looking confident and relaxed. I knew he was neither; he was very concerned that something he did or said would cause me trouble. Patrick, despite having done so almost constantly since we met, hates to cause me trouble.

After the usual recitation of Patrick's résumé and the appreciative stares from the jury box, Renfro began in a way I really hadn't seen coming because it was something it would never have occurred to me to do in his place. 'Mr McNabb,' he asked, 'are you romantically involved with anyone in the courtroom?'

I was on my feet in a nanosecond. 'Your Honor, where is the relevance in Mr McNabb's private life?'

Renfro was prepared. 'Sidebar, Your Honor?'

Franklin, looking puzzled, nodded and waved Renfro and me to the bench, where the microphone was turned off so our conversation would not be part of the record and would not be heard by the jury. 'I'm tending to wonder what Ms Moss is wondering, Mr Renfro,' he said. 'What does the witness's love life have to do with the case against Mr Reeves?'

'Ms Moss knows perfectly well why I'm asking,' Renfro told him. 'She and the witness have been romantically involved for some months.'

The judge did his best not to look surprised and didn't give any indication that he was wondering why Patrick McNabb would date so far below his station. He did look at me for a moment and then shook his head. 'I'm still not seeing the relevance. Clearly you knew that before you called Mr McNabb to the stand. Why is it necessary for the jury to have that information?'

Renfro tilted his head slightly to the right, not conceding the point but allowing that Franklin might ask the question. 'I want it to be understood by the jury that Mr McNabb might . . . color his answers based on his bias toward the defense in this case,' he said.

I felt molten lava rising up from my shoes to my brain. Renfro had seemed like such a nice guy when I'd first met him. 'Are you suggesting that the witness might commit perjury because we are dating?' I'm afraid my voice might not have maintained the level of calm I might have preferred.

A look passed between Renfro and Franklin and I didn't like it at all.

'I am suggesting nothing of the sort, but I think there might be, let's say *nuance* in Mr McNabb's testimony, and if the jury is not aware of the situation they might not notice it and process it fairly.'

That was another way of saying yes, he thought Patrick might commit perjury because we were dating. But more polite.

'Step back,' Franklin ordered, and I saw my options narrowing. Renfro and I retreated to our designated tables. Microphone restored, he said, 'I'll allow the question.'

'Yes,' Patrick said without asking to hear the question again. He wasn't happy. Patrick protects me even when I don't need it, or have I mentioned that before?

'Would you tell us with whom you've been involved who has a role in this trial?' Renfro asked because he knew Patrick wasn't volunteering anything.

Patrick turned toward Franklin. 'Am I required to answer, Judge?' I was pleased he didn't say, 'M'lud.'

'I'm afraid so, Mr McNabb.'

Patrick smiled. I recognized it as an acting smile, but the jury wouldn't have any idea it was anything but pure joy. 'I am very pleased to be in a relationship with the lead defense counsel,' he said.

A few of the male jurors looked at me and seemed disappointed. A couple of the female jurors looked at me and seemed angry. You can't please all of the people pretty much any of the time.

'Good for you both.' How magnanimous Renfro could be, allowing Patrick and me to date. 'I wanted to make that clear so we could continue without any concern about prejudice for the jury.'

I had started standing at the word *concern*. 'Objection!' I didn't think I needed to explain myself any further.

'Sustained. Mr Renfro, you are a sentence away from being held in contempt. Unless it's pertinent to the facts of this case, you will make no further references to the romantic life of the defense attorney or the witness. Is that clear?'

'Absolutely, Your Honor.' Renfro didn't even bother to smirk. The damage had been done.

But I wasn't. Done. 'Your Honor, I'd like to add Mr Renfro's wife to the list of defense witnesses.'

'Knock it off, Ms Moss.' You can't win them all.

Renfro approached Patrick as if nothing unusual had happened. 'Mr McNabb, you were in the cast of the film in question, *Desert Siege;* is that correct?'

'Yes I was.' A lot of actors would have been put out to be described as 'in the cast' when they were playing the lead in the movie, but Patrick did not correct Renfro to mention that he was the star. Patrick is by no means without ego, but he's considerably more down-to-earth (in his own extravagant way) than many of the actors I have met since I've known him.

'In fact you are the star of that film, aren't you?' I wasn't clear on what Renfro was going for, if it was anything other than to show that he thought Patrick was a cool guy.

'I am one in the cast.' Patrick was mad at the prosecutor and wouldn't have agreed with him if he'd said that Patrick deserved an Oscar for his performance in Reeves's movie.

'And you appear in virtually every scene in the film, is that correct?'

I stood up. 'Your Honor, Mr McNabb is in one of the leading roles in the film. That's not in dispute. Does the prosecutor have a point that relates in some way to this trial?'

Renfro shook his head, assumedly in disgust over my lack of imagination, or something. 'Judge, if you give me a *minute* you will certainly see the relevance.'

'Go ahead, Mr Renfro. But no more than a minute.' Franklin

was nothing if not fair. He was equally irritated with Renfro and me.

The prosecutor turned his attention back to Patrick. 'Now, Mr McNabb. You do appear in most of the scenes in *Desert Siege*; is that correct?'

'Unless there's been a major edit that I'm not aware of, yes.' Patrick wasn't looking at me because he knew that wouldn't help. He was eyeing Renfro as he would have the blond guy who put Angie and me in the back of that catering van.

'So it's logical to assume that you were present on the set the morning that James Drake was murdered.'

This was a difficult question for Patrick and I figured Renfro knew that. If he'd seen the same video footage I had, he'd have been unable to miss the shot of Patrick on the set that day. But Patrick was still insisting he had absolutely no recollection of being there. Patrick had seen the video. Should he answer that he was there because he'd seen himself there, or that he wasn't because he truly didn't think he had been?

'Is it?' he replied. Improv training. Never say no. Ask a question back if you can.

Renfro raised an eyebrow. 'I'll be more direct, then. Mr McNabb, were you present on the set in Griffith Park on the morning that James Drake was killed?' Renfro never used a phrase like, 'fell to his death' or 'fell from the crane' because neither of those would be damning enough toward Reeves. He knew how to use language effectively.

'I don't recall being there, no.' Patrick answered as honestly as he could. If Renfro was about to pull the video footage out of his jacket pocket, I'd be able to ask for time to review it (largely because Renfro didn't know I had it already) and that would stop Patrick from having to explain why he didn't know he was included in those scenes. It would buy us time, anyway.

'Why would you not have been there?'

'Because I wasn't required for the scene. The stunt performer was the only cast member who had to be present, and he wasn't even doubling for me, so there was no reason for me to show up. I was filming a television series at the time.' Patrick looked serious so the jury wouldn't think he had taken Drake's death lightly. 'It was a terrible thing that happened. I spent the day talking to members of the cast and crew about Jim and how awful it was he was gone.'

Oddly, that seemed to be the very thing that Renfro had been hoping to hear, and he didn't bring up the video footage at all. 'And what did you hear from the people you spoke to?' he asked.

'Mostly that everyone was very sorry Jim was gone and what we as a company could do for his wife.' Patrick looked a bit bewildered by Renfro's questioning.

'Yes. Mr Drake's wife Marta.' Renfro said *Marta* as if it were a tasty chocolate cookie. 'Did the members of the *Desert Siege* company mention that she and the victim were in the middle of divorcing?'

Patrick's face looked more like he was drinking lemon juice straight. 'Oddly that didn't seem to come up on the day the man died such an unexpected death,' he said.

'Had you heard rumors before the murder that James Drake and Robert Reeves's wife were having an affair?' Now I guessed we were finally getting to the point of Renfro's subpoena for Patrick.

The corner of Patrick's mouth twisted up with a tiny scintilla of scorn. 'I heard rumors that everyone was sleeping with everyone else on every film set I've ever been on,' he said. 'About a third of them are true.' But *third* had come out *fird*, which meant Patrick's Cockney roots were showing. He was agitated.

'What about the ones about Tracy Reeves and Jim Drake?' Renfro asked. 'Were those rumors accurate or not?'

'Objection.' It was becoming my favorite word. 'How could the witness know that?'

'I'll withdraw the question.' Renfro wasn't really interested in asking Patrick about the alleged liaisons between the fake wife and the separated stuntman anyway. He'd already covered that ground with Mandrill (Tracy). So what *was* he getting at? 'Mr McNabb, did you ever hear the defendant Robert Reeves express hostility toward Jim Drake?'

Patrick looked slightly startled. 'Hostility?'

'Yes. Did Mr Reeves ever say, for example, that he would have liked to make James Drake suffer?'

I saw Patrick's face just tighten; I can't explain it better than that. He looked relaxed if annoyed one second, and completely tense the next. Renfro was onto something and that wasn't a surprise. The fact that it was my boyfriend who would deliver the bad news was something of a twist, for sure.

'Sometimes things are said on movie sets that—' Patrick began.

'Did he say that or not?' Renfro wanted his point and he wanted it made without any editorializing.

Patrick chewed on his bottom lip for a short moment. 'Yes.'

'Did he say it in context of the stunt that eventually killed Jim Drake?'

He inhaled and exhaled. 'Yes.'

'How long before the murder did the defendant Robert Reeves say he liked to make James Drake suffer?'

'I don't remember exactly,' Patrick said. He knew from his years playing an attorney and from being with me that he absolutely could not lie on the witness stand, so I believed he was not. Patrick would call it 'acting,' but that was a joke and we both knew it.

'Was it the day before?'

'Definitely not,' Patrick answered. 'I was not on the set at all that week. I had completed my scenes and was not required for anything being filmed.'

'The week before?'

There was the slightest twitch in Patrick's left eye. 'Possibly.'

'If not the week before, then when?' Renfro asked.

'It was probably the week before the accident,' Patrick admitted.

'That was no accident, Mr McNabb.'

I uttered my favorite word again and Franklin agreed with me. 'Keep your comments to yourself, Mr Renfro, and don't make me remind you again.'

'Yes, Your Honor. Thank you, Mr McNabb.' Renfro walked back to his table looking infuriatingly pleased with himself.

'Ms Moss,' Franklin said.

I stood, and in the walk from the defense table to the witness stand changed my strategy entirely after I asked one question: 'Mr McNabb, did Robert Reeves ever say in your presence that he wanted to kill James Drake?'

'*No.*'

'All right, then. Mr McNabb, I'd like to remind you that you are under oath. Do you *really* want me to move in with you?'

Angie couldn't hide the laugh that exploded from her mouth. The rest of the spectator gallery was, in a word, abuzz. Renfro leapt to his feet. I'm not exaggerating. He leapt.

'Objection, Your Honor! What possible relevance does this have to the case?'

I looked at the judge and did my best to pretend that butter would in fact not melt in my mouth. 'The prosecution opened the door on this line of questioning himself when he asked about the defendant's relationship status. I'm following up.'

Franklin was way too serious a judge to admit that he found this amusing, but he probably did want to see where I was going. 'Overruled.' That was it.

I looked at Patrick. 'Do you need the question read back to you?' I asked.

Patrick looked bewildered but somehow pleased. 'No. I remember the question and yes, I definitely meant it when I made that invitation.'

'Will you lose interest in me when I stop trying to slow the relationship?' He was under oath. I'd never have such a custom-made platform again. 'You won't be embarrassed to have me at your side at premieres?'

'I will not,' Patrick said. Four reporters from online services were already hard at work on their phones. 'Does this mean you're agreeing to move in?'

'I'm asking the questions, Mr McNabb.'

THIRTY-FOUR

'Why didn't you ask him any case stuff?' Angie demanded.

Angie and I were walking toward my 'impromptu' meeting with Margaret Houlihan, the woman who had supplied

Nate with the iPhone video of the Griffith Park set. But the topic was still what I'd done in the courtroom with Patrick (who had been told not to come along and for once agreed) and Angie would not be denied.

'Renfro had gotten Patrick to say Robert Reeves' (who was lunching with Penny because I *really* didn't want him anywhere near Margaret Houlihan and therefore hadn't told him about the meeting) 'had made a comment about wanting James Drake to suffer,' I explained. 'I couldn't get him to say that wasn't true. Maybe I could get context, but it really didn't matter what the context was. The jury wouldn't care; they'd heard that the defendant said something about the victim suffering and they won't forget that. So I got done with it as quickly as possible.'

Nate had texted me with the proper name and address of the outdoor café where Margaret would be having lunch. We were about half a block away and I could already see it. The ruse would be that Nate would approach her to say hello and then I'd *happen* to just be in the neighborhood (after an Uber and a three-block walk to cover the fact that I'd taken an Uber) and Nate would do the introductions. Then I'd see what I could get out of the videographer.

'And you made Patrick say he loved you right out in open court.' Angie hears what Angie wants to hear and there's no point in telling her she didn't hear it, so I didn't try.

'If I'm going to decide about moving in with Patrick, I need to know that he really means what he says about me and it's not just him having fun with the pursuit,' I told her. 'I figured the threat of perjury wouldn't hurt my chances of getting that honest answer.'

Sure enough, Nate stood within thirty yards. Before we got close enough for him to hear Angie said, 'So are you going to move in with Patrick?'

'Don't ask a question you don't know the answer to.'

'Then how am I going to learn anything?' She had a point. But I didn't answer her question.

Margaret Houlihan, it turned out, was a woman about forty, slim (it's LA) and attractive (see previous parenthetical expression), seated at an outdoor table under an umbrella. Nate was standing next to the table, hands at his side, non-threatening. Angie and I approached and Nate looked over at us, then did the worst job of feigning surprise that I could imagine. This comes from dating an actor.

'Sandy!' he shouted so people six blocks away could hear. 'What are you doing here?'

'I'm here to meet Ms Houlihan, Nate,' I said. 'Remember, we talked about this yesterday.' I pivoted to avoid seeing his eyes pop out of their sockets and to face the woman. 'Nice to meet you, Ms Houlihan. I'm Sandy Moss and this is Angie.' Nate hadn't recovered well enough to acknowledge his alleged protégée yet. More like unpaid intern, really.

Margaret's eyes narrowed a bit at the mention of my name and got narrower as I brazenly gave up the ruse of the coincidental meeting, so now they were barely slits. 'I told Nate I didn't want you to know my name, Ms Moss, and that was for a reason. I don't want to be part of your court case and I won't testify if I'm not subpoenaed.' Margaret was not naïve.

'I don't blame you, Margaret. May I call you Margaret?'

She thought it over. 'All right.'

I sat down at one of the empty chairs, since Angie had already helped herself and was now appraising the menu that had been left on the table. 'Margaret, I have no desire to force you into court but I need to know what you know. An innocent man could go to prison for life and I'm trying to stop that from happening.'

Margaret sneered. Honest. 'Innocent man. Bob Reeves? The man's as innocent as Charlie Manson.'

Angie didn't look up from the menu. 'You think he killed James Drake?' she said.

Margaret waved a hand to dismiss the notion. 'Nah. But he's a jerk. Got mad at me one time because the spread for craft services didn't have any garlic bagels, and that's not even my job. Threw cream cheese at his assistant. I'm asking you.'

The one thing I didn't need at the moment was a recitation of Robert Reeves's failings as a human being. I needed evidence that he wasn't a murderer and time was getting short. 'But you took that video of him the day the stunt was being rehearsed and Mr Drake fell,' I said. 'Why did you happen to be shooting video with your phone right then?'

Margaret held up her hands from the table, palms out, like she was telling someone very short to stop. 'I didn't take the video,' she said. 'A friend of mine took it and sent it to me, and I sent it to this guy when he started asking all the crew members if they saw anything.' She pointed at Nate, who was still standing and looked worried, like he'd done something wrong and didn't know what. 'I didn't even watch it before I handed it over. I figured it wouldn't have much on it that mattered.'

'Who's your friend?' I said.

'What?'

'Your friend, the one who took the video and sent it to you. What's their name?'

Margaret's eyes, no longer slits, were not warm and welcoming either. 'There's no way I'm telling you that,' she said.

'Why not?'

'Because then you'll get *her* all caught up in your case, and she'll blame me. I'm not doing that.' So Margaret's friend was a woman. That narrowed it down. Not by much, but I'd take what I could get.

'OK. You don't have to,' I said.

'I know.'

'Did *you* see anything happen that day before the stunt? Did you see someone tampering with the cables holding up the stuntman?' I asked even as Nate shook his head; he'd clearly asked Margaret this question before.

'Nah. I was nowhere near there. I was all the way at the other end of the set, maybe a hundred yards away. I wouldn't have been able to see someone at ground level look at the cables, not even with binoculars.'

'Did you give the video to the DA?' I asked Margaret. 'Or did your friend do that?'

'The DA?' Margaret looked stumped.

'The district attorney,' I explained. I hadn't figured that term would need definition.

Margaret sneered again. She was good at it. 'I *know* what "DA" means,' she said. 'Why would you think I sent the video to the DA? I gave it to this guy and that was it.' Again a thumb pointed in Nate's direction.

'So your friend gave it to them?' I asked.

A shake of the head. 'I'd be real surprised. She hates the cops. She shared it on the Facebook group but I don't think she'd go to the DA. But I don't know for sure; nobody mentioned it to me except her.'

Something was starting to make sense to me, but I couldn't exactly pinpoint what it was yet. I stood up. 'Thank you, Margaret. I won't bother you again. But I do have one last question: was anyone else on set taking video that day?'

Margaret chuckled with condescension. 'Honey, it's a movie set. Half the people there were taking video. I'm amazed it hasn't shown up on *Entertainment Tonight*. Everybody thinks they're a director.'

'Not everybody,' I said half to myself.

Angie looked up at me. 'We're not staying for lunch?' she said, sounding disappointed. 'The buffalo wings look amazing.'

'They are,' Margaret told her. 'But don't get the hot sauce. You won't be able to kiss for a week.'

THIRTY-FIVE

'I don't understand what's happening,' Robert Reeves said. Sitting in a courthouse conference room with Penny, who appeared to have been Velcro-ed to his side, Reeves was shaking his head in, well, disbelief. I'd made one suggestion based on my extremely rudimentary knowledge of filmmaking (gained through osmosis) and Reeves, the director of at least eleven feature films (according to IMDb) was floored.

'It's something about the iPhone video,' I told him/them. 'We know Patrick wasn't in Griffith Park that morning because the studio records show him to be on the set of *Torn*, and you're certain that you didn't spill hydrochloric acid on the steel cables regularly for a period of twelve hours. And

yet there both of you are, right in pixels, doing things we
know you didn't do.'

Angie had gone off to assist Patrick in his actual day, now
having dispatched his duties as a witness (well, I thought).
We'd gotten back to the courtroom just in time for Jon to
report that Renfro had asked Brady O'Toole about the
possibility of hydrochloric acid eating through the cables,
established that there was some in a trailer on the set for use
in maintaining some of the machinery, then inexplicably rested
his case. Franklin had then declared yet another recess before
I was to start calling witnesses, none of whom I had slept
with, the next morning. Judge Franklin liked his calendar as
tidy as his courtroom.

So it was me, my client, his appendage, and Jon seated around
the conference table trying hard to make sense of what was
going on, including the information Margaret Houlihan had
grudgingly supplied. I wouldn't be calling Margaret to the stand
either, because I'd promised not to, and her source wouldn't be
an asset either because Margaret had refused to give her (we
knew it was a woman based on Margaret's comments) up.

'I don't understand why the DA didn't want to introduce
that video into evidence,' I said. 'I mean, even if we're that
lucky and Renfro never intended to show the video in court
. . . why wouldn't he show the video in court?'

Jon was in his thinking position, hands steepled with
the fingertips up to his lips, looking down at the municipal
wooden conference table, as if its empty surface must hold
the answer to all life's questions. 'There's a theory that fits the
facts,' he said quietly.

I looked over at him. 'Amazing, Holmes! What might
that be?'

Jon didn't react outwardly. I'm sure on the inside he had
found my remark hilarious. It's how I get through life.

'I think the only way it makes sense is if the video that the
DA has isn't the same as the one we have,' he said.

Everyone in the room, even Penny, looked stumped. It
didn't even occur to her to ask if Reeves (not anyone else,
mind you, just her boss) wanted something to drink. Because
I'd seen it happen more than once: Reeves would mention

wanting a Diet Coke and seeing Penny walk directly by a perfectly functional vending machine in the courthouse that would have dispensed one, gone out to a local drugstore a block away to buy one she could choose herself, then come back into the courthouse through the metal detectors, all because Reeves believed that you shouldn't buy the sodas in vending machines because 'you don't know where they've been'.

'How does that work?' I said. 'The video was taken on someone's phone. She passed it along, I assume through Dropbox or something, to Margaret Houlihan and a few other close friends.' (*Note to self: get Nate to find out who Margaret's close friends were.*) 'Somehow a copy of it found its way into Renfro's hard drive. How does that work, and why would it have anything other than what we saw on it?'

'You told me yourself,' Jon said. 'Margaret said there were a lot of people on the set taking video on their phones. One of them probably thought they were doing a civic duty or maybe searching for a weird kind of spotlight and got the video to Renfro.'

'But it's not the same as the one we have. If it was the one we have and I were the prosecutor, I would have opened with that video and not bothered to call any witnesses. The thing is damning.'

There was another fairly long silence. Penny pursed her lips at one point as if she were about to speak, but it turned out she had merely had a burrito with extra beans in it for lunch.

Finally Reeves, the last person I'd expect to come up with something constructive, said, 'I need to see that video again, but I need to see it in my office.'

'Why?' I asked.

'You'll see. Or, more to the point, I will.' He was already standing and heading to the door.

When Jon and I followed (after Penny had already followed because she was Penny), he looked somewhat askance at me. 'Are you coming?'

'I'm your lawyer. You don't get within driving distance of that video without me.'

Reeves stopped, thought, and shrugged. 'Come along then,' he said.

Jon and I followed him in my car. For months while he was recovering from a gunshot wound, Jon had been unable to drive, and now he was just used to me taking the wheel when we went anywhere, but he drove himself to work in the morning and home at night. It took about forty minutes to get to Reeves's office at Majestic Pictures, which in LA traffic means it was about three blocks away (I'm exaggerating; a little). Reeves seemed more energized than I'd ever seen him before, walking at the same pace as your average thoroughbred racehorse and standing straight up, shoulders back like he was on a mission. And now maybe he was.

He strode – because there is no other word for it – through a door marked 'Spectacular Productions', which was Reeves's company because of course it was. Penny was by his side but always seemingly a step behind him, deferring to his authority and amazing brilliance (or something). Jon and I struggled to keep pace. I knew it was difficult for Jon still as he'd only given up walking with a cane two months previously. Speed wasn't going to be his thing – probably for the rest of his life, but certainly not now.

We were able to follow him through corridors only because they weren't that long, and we couldn't actually lose sight of Penny as she barreled on through. Eventually we reached an unmarked door which had been left open when Penny had followed her boss inside. This was the alternative entrance to Reeves's office, which I had not noticed when Angie and I had visited here earlier.

By the time we got inside, Reeves had shed his jacket, which was being draped lovingly over the back of his chair by Penny. He was sitting behind his desk and leaning into it, seeming like he wanted to become one with his computer monitor. He was furiously clacking the keys and watching with the attention a trained Rottweiler has when a piece of bacon is being held in front of his eyes but he's been told to stay.

'I said you shouldn't watch that video until I was in the room,' I said when I could catch my breath.

'Well, now you're in the room, aren't you?' Jon and I

positioned ourselves behind him, essentially looking over his shoulders because why put chairs behind your desk? 'I can't believe I didn't realize this sooner.'

'Realize what?' Jon asked.

Reeves was running the iPhone footage we'd seen so many times before I was starting to think I had shot it and leaked it to myself. I knew every leaf on every tree, every cable leading to every portable generator and every light pointed upward at the spot where James Drake would think he was performing a stunt and was actually being murdered. But I didn't see anything new this time.

'It's done so well that even a trained eye like mine wouldn't notice it. Honestly. The person who did this is a master, an artist.' Reeves's forehead was sweating and his eyes were wide. He looked like he'd just made the first small step in his mad scheme to take over the world. But of course he'd done that years ago.

Penny, who to the naked eye looked like she was watching her dad explain how to cross the street, crossed her arms over her chest with the hands up, almost clutching her own shoulders. She was absolutely enraptured. She didn't speak, but then that wasn't really unusual for Penny.

'What are you talking about?' I asked Reeves. 'It's an iPhone video.'

He pointed at the screen as if specifying the key function in a long equation that I would never be able to understand. 'Precisely. That's what makes it so astonishing. I've never seen it done so well.'

I grabbed the arms of his executive chair and swiveled him to face me and not the computer screen. 'What?' I sort of shouted. '*What* have you never seen done so well?'

'CG,' he said.

I immediately assumed he was speaking in tongues. 'CG?' Maybe if I said it I would get an idea of the definition.

'Computer generated,' Penny said. 'It's CGI, computer-generated imagery. Someone must have tampered with the original footage from the phone.'

Reeves pointed at Penny and jabbed his finger back and forth. 'What she said.'

'So the images we saw weren't real,' Jon said, I think largely to himself. 'Patrick really never was at the set that morning.'

'And you never tampered with those cables,' I said to Reeves.

He looked insulted. 'Of course not,' he said. 'Did you ever doubt that?'

'I saw it with my own eyes.'

Jon shook his head in wonder. 'Apparently not.'

I took my hands off the arms of Reeves's chair. 'How can you tell?'

He swiveled back to point at the screen and used his mouse to manipulate the footage backward and forward in time at one critical point, when we had assumed we were seeing him bend over the cables wielding an unknown object. 'Like I said, it's really artfully done, but when you know what you're looking for, you can see it. Focus your attention on whatever that is that's supposed to be in my hand. And watch my right thumb.'

'On your mouse?' OK, so I was in a little over my head.

'On the *screen*.' Penny. How dare anyone question the wizard!

Reeves, obviously feeling that Penny had expressed the necessary despair at my lack of technological prowess, did not comment. He got the image onto the very frame he wanted and then repeated, 'Watch the right thumb.'

He kept the speed slow so the moment could be seen clearly. The Reeves on the screen was bent over the cables and his right hand seemed to hold some small black object which I assumed was meant to be mistaken for a bottle of hydrochloric acid. He extended his hand and bent his elbow up parallel to the ground as he seemed to pour something onto the cables.

'The thumb,' he reiterated, as if we hadn't heard him the first two times.

It was barely visible at first, but his right hand did come into view when 'Reeves' moved his shoulder just so. It appeared to be grasping that object, whatever it was, which meant his right thumb was wrapped around the small black thing.

And then, as he was supposed to be pouring acid on the

cables, the thumb disappeared, just for a split second, then reappeared right where it had been a moment before.

'Wait, what?' I said. 'What just happened?'

'Whatever footage of Mr Reeves they used to make this video must have lost sight of his thumb at some point, obscured it behind something maybe, and when it was spliced into the iPhone video, which most likely was just footage of the crane by itself, the thumb flickered out of sight just for that split second,' Penny explained.

Reeves was still shaking his head in disbelief. 'Amazing,' he said. 'They did it without a green screen or motion capture.'

'But Lieutenant Trench testified that they had footage of you seeming to tamper with the cables,' Jon said to Reeves. 'If their version is different from ours, why would he say that?'

'He *didn't* say that,' I corrected Jon. 'He said they had footage of Reeves there by the crane, but he didn't go so far as to say he was tampering with anything. It could have been when you were talking to Drake about the stunt, Robert. And then Judge Franklin struck mention of the video from the record. So I think Trench was sending *us* a signal, knowing that I'd object. He doesn't like their video for some reason.'

'That's a huge assumption,' Jon said, grinning. 'But I think you're right.'

'The person who edited this video and put in that extra footage was sending a message, too.' I was thinking out loud. 'They wanted us to know that they could produce images of you looking like you were killing James Drake. And they added footage of Patrick on the set when he wasn't really there because they wanted to get my attention. They were clearly saying they could frame you, Robert, anytime they wanted, and that they could implicate Patrick too if that was the goal.'

Jon got a slightly wide-eyed look. 'So what you're saying is, the person who edited that video . . .'

'. . . is a genius,' Reeves said.

'. . . is probably the real killer,' I said.

'I'd hire them in a minute,' Reeves added.

THIRTY-SIX

After a very pleasant night at Patrick's house, where we assiduously avoided the subject of cohabitation, the defense (that's me) began the morning in court – after a one-mile run that had become my go-to activity on the morning of an appearance before the bench – by calling Michael Armbruster, the security chief who had been working on the Griffith Park set, to the stand. After establishing his credentials as a man who had been doing such things for location filming since I was a teenager, I asked Armbruster how he kept track of the comings and goings of people and equipment on a set that had to be built up and taken down quickly in accordance with the agreement the production company had with the city. Because Los Angeles owns the park.

'We have personnel at every entrance and security cameras elsewhere, and everyone who comes to the set is required to have a credential that can be scanned against a list of people the production company gives us of those who are allowed on set at any given time.' Armbruster, a man with an exceptionally long and wide neck, was not the crew-cut, biceps-heavy type you might expect in the security profession (mostly based on images from popular culture and not real life). He looked like a very competent landscape architect, which as it turned out was something he'd done professionally before getting into the security business. He was not an ex-cop or a military veteran. He was a graduate of Oberlin College with a degree in botany.

He was perfect for the film business.

'Who at the production company compiles the list of people who can be present?' I asked.

'The production company submits a list of necessary crew based on the needs of each department head, but they don't send it directly to us. The studio vets everyone who is on the crew before shooting begins, but there are always requests made for guests, friends of the actors and people like that,' Armbruster said.

'Do people have to have their security passes scanned when they leave the set as well as when they enter?'

'Yes.' Good. That was going to be important.

I turned and scanned the jury just to see how bored they were; it didn't seem too bad yet. I'd have to keep this quick to avoid overload. 'When did you begin giving out security passes and making checks on people in regards to the incident we're discussing here today?' I asked.

'Weeks before.'

'And when was the section of Griffith Park that had been leased for the stunt closed off?'

Armbruster could have referred to notes if he wanted to, but he didn't. 'Two days prior,' he said. 'That's a very short period of time for a shoot like this, but the city didn't want to close off that much of the park for a long time.'

'In the twelve hours before the stunt was attempted and James Drake died, were you monitoring the set?' I said. 'That would be starting the evening before, maybe even the late afternoon of the day before.'

'Of course we were,' he said.

'Of course you were,' I repeated, hopefully sounding respectful, which was my aim. 'Do you have a list of the people who were present beginning, let's say, twelve hours before the attempted stunt, and a list of those who left that night before returning early the next morning?'

'I do,' Armbruster answered. 'May I access my tablet computer?'

I looked over at Franklin, who looked at Renfro. 'Objection?'

'None, Your Honor.'

Franklin nodded in my direction and I told Armbruster he could look up the list on his iPad.

'How many people were there for those twelve hours, continuously?' I asked.

'For the whole night, very few,' he said. 'Some technical crew had to work through the night to set up the cameras and other types of equipment. The stunt coordinator was not there the whole time, but scanned in and out on four separate occasions. Other people came and went during the period.'

'Was Robert Reeves there?' I asked.

'For some of the time,' Armbruster said. 'But after midnight he didn't come back until five thirty.'

Just to drive the point home to the jury: 'So there was a five-and-a-half-hour period when Mr Reeves was not present on the set at all?'

'That's right,' Armbruster said.

'Thank you.' I walked back to my table as Renfro rose from his.

'Has anyone ever snuck onto a movie set?' he asked.

'Ever?' Armbruster seemed nonplussed by the question.

'Let's make it more specific,' the DA agreed. 'Has anyone ever snuck onto a movie set that you were in charge of securing?'

'Once in a while.' Armbruster's jaw was closed pretty tightly. It was hard to know how he got the words out audibly.

'How often?' Renfro asked.

'There's really no way to know but it doesn't happen often.' Armbruster's eyes, if it had been possible, would have been clenched as well.

'So it is possible that Robert Reeves could have snuck onto the set multiple times in those five-plus hours and approached the crane?'

'It's highly unlikely. That was the most secure area of the set.'

Renfro folded his arms in an attempt to seem more condescending. 'But it is possible,' he said.

'Yes. I suppose it is possible.'

'That's all, Mr Ambruster.'

I spent the rest of the morning talking to people who had been on the set when James Drake died. They all were clearly traumatized by the event, and they all reported not having seen Reeves approach the crane at the ground level or anywhere else, except when he was accompanied by Drake or Burke Henderson. He had never been spotted there alone and certainly not with a bottle of acid. Renfro had asked each one if they were watching the crane the whole time they were on set and each had to admit they were, you know, doing their jobs and therefore not in constant surveillance mode.

Just when the judge had ordered us in recess for lunch, Nate, who had not been present in court that morning, came in looking even more intense than he usually does and made a beeline for the defense table. He was actually breathing a little heavily.

'You OK?' I asked him when he had reached Reeves, Penny, Jon and me. (Reeves and Penny were definitely not paying him any attention.)

'Yeah. But I've got something for you. I've done some contact tracing on our friend Margaret Houlihan and I think I've figured out who was distributing that doctored video of the set.'

OK, my interest level had risen considerably, to the point that I was no longer very concerned about Nate's health. 'Who?' I asked.

'I don't think you're gonna like it,' he said.

THIRTY-SEVEN

I t was an action-packed lunch and I didn't eat a bite. I called Angie and saw to it that she and Patrick would be in court for the afternoon, just to be my support group in case things went wrong. And things could go very wrong. Or very right. There was no way of knowing.

Then I sent a message to Judge Franklin saying I planned to recall Alice Mandrill, so he would issue an order for her to be present in court when the recess was finished. I also told the judge, although it was not required, that I planned to change the order of my witnesses and would be calling my computer imagery expert Mason Gross first. Then I asked the judge's team leader, Mabel Tompkins, if I could have some audio-visual equipment ready for the afternoon session.

Jon was busy doing some research on tracing video effects to their origins, and Nate rushed himself back out to see if he could give a ride to Marta Drake so we'd know she'd be in court on time.

Except for Nate and Marta, they basically all arrived at once, Alice annoyed at being summoned on such short notice, Mason having already expected to testify but not necessarily today, Angie and Patrick looking eager and taking their seats in the courtroom just as Franklin was about to come back in.

If the lunch had been hectic, I knew the afternoon would be at least as lively, and probably critical to Reeves's case.

He, for the record, was looking nervous, and I hadn't even told him the whole breadth of what I planned to do, largely because there wasn't time. Reeves and Penny had headed out for lunch at some exclusive restaurant or another, unaware of the efforts being made on his behalf.

I didn't like Robert Reeves personally and I'd only seen the one film of his, which I considered, well, beneath Patrick. But I don't like to see an innocent person get convicted and I knew that under his many layers of pomposity, Reeves was scared. He just thought it would be bad for his career to show it.

The job now was to prove he hadn't done it. Proving who had was outside my purview and someone else's job – like, for example, Trench, whom I noticed in the back of the courtroom. How he knew what I was planning was as hard to figure as everything else about Trench.

Franklin sat down behind the bench and told everyone to sit down. Half the spectators already were in seats but it's the gesture that matters. 'Your Honor,' I began. 'Before I call the next witness, I'd like to introduce an exhibit into evidence. This is referred to as Exhibit Defense Eight.'

Usually when you enter something into evidence, you need to tie it to a witness to prove it is legitimate and to trace its origins. In other words, to prove it's not fake. But Margaret Houlihan had adamantly refused to testify, and I wasn't going to have her subpoenaed if I didn't have to.

'This is a cell-phone video, Ms Moss?' Franklin asked.

'Yes, Your Honor.'

'Is the person who took the video present in court?'

I sighed inwardly because this was going to be a hard sell. 'No, Judge, but that's sort of the point.'

Franklin sighed outwardly because he was a judge. 'Ms Moss . . .' he began.

But Renfro was already on his feet. 'Your Honor, where is the witness?'

The judge, not being accustomed to having his speech interrupted, scowled down at the prosecutor, which I thought was a positive sign for me. 'Mr Renfro, the bench has not yet ruled on the admission of the defense's evidence. Please sit down.'

Renfro, wisely, sat down.

'Can you explain yourself, Counselor?' the judge asked me.

'Thank you, Your Honor. The video footage we have obtained purports to depict events leading to the tragic attempt to rehearse the stunt in which Mr Drake lost his life. We believe that this footage can have a major impact on the facts in this case.'

'So you believe the footage to be genuine, but you can't produce the person who supplied it to you?' Franklin was sincerely trying to understand.

'No, Your Honor. We believe the footage is *not* genuine, and that the person who shot it very likely had motivation to make the defendant seem guilty. The person who supplied it to us did so with an agreement that they would not be called upon to testify in court and the defense is honoring that agreement.' I thought that was as close to clear as I could get without betraying Margaret Houlihan's trust.

'Then who will you be questioning about the video?' the judge wanted to know.

'Once the jury has seen the footage, we will call Mr Mason Gross, a film technician and expert on digital imagery who, you'll notice, already appeared on our witness list.'

'I'd prefer you call your witness now and, once he has explained the theory you are putting forward, I can rule on the admission of the video.'

There's no arguing with judges, despite the fact that lawyers do it all the time. So I called Mason to the stand and he was sworn in. I established his credentials, including a master's degree in digital imagery, one he had created for himself, from Drexel University in Philadelphia, and fifteen years' experience working in the film industry, with virtually every director except Robert Reeves.

'Mr Gross,' I began after the preliminaries were out of the way, 'is it possible to tell the difference between a live image, that is, one taken of a person doing something, and a computer generated or altered image?'

Mason, a very relaxed techy kind of guy, was wearing a suit and tie and was clearly not happy about it. He didn't pull at his collar like Rodney Dangerfield did, but he did move his neck around trying to find the sweet spot, which clearly wasn't making itself obvious.

'Absolutely,' he said. 'There are a number of ways to detect computer-generated images, but in a lot of cases, when the contrast is too high, the average person can see the difference.'

'What about when the computer imagery is created by someone who really knows how to do it?' I asked.

'The average civilian might not be able to see it, but those of us who work in that area will either spot it without testing, or we can run it through various software to determine the origin of the footage.' Mason was getting a little more comfortable, although I'm sure he would have preferred to be wearing a T-shirt bearing a slogan like, 'Your password was too short so I changed it.'

'I sent you an unaltered copy of the video I'm hoping to show the jury,' I said. 'Have you been able to review it?'

'Yes.'

I turned toward the judge. 'Defense requests admission of the video into evidence,' I said.

'I assume you're going to object, Mr Renfro. May I ask on what grounds?' This was not Franklin's first trial. Or his thousandth.

'You are correct, Your Honor, and we object on the grounds that there is no way to authenticate this video footage without the videographer at least being deposed and signing a sworn statement as to its authenticity.'

'I have such a statement signed and notarized,' I told Franklin, 'but the defense will not submit it unless the court agrees to keep the witness's identity secret.'

'Do you have an objection to *that*, Mr Renfro?'

'I do but you'll overrule it, Your Honor.'

'You've got that right. Ms Moss, please submit your document.'

The usual protocols were followed so in a few minutes the prosecutor and the judge had seen the notarized letter I'd convinced Margaret Houlihan to sign. Franklin read it and did not comment. 'Proceed,' was all he said.

Renfro read the letter and looked stymied. How did I get video that wasn't from the same source as his? Why would I be introducing evidence that actually made my client look guilty?

Good questions.

With the help of the courtroom's video equipment, I called up the file and showed the jury, without any editorializing, the video Nate had first shown me in his office. When they reached the moment where Reeves seemed to be tampering with the essential cables, some jurors gasped and others were visibly shaken. I hit the pause button at that instant.

'Mr Gross,' I said to my witness, 'please tell the jury whether the image they're observing right now is, in your expert opinion, genuine.'

'No, it's not,' Mason said. 'And it's not just my opinion. It's a fact.'

Renfro objected, as I would have, and there followed a great deal of technical testimony as to how the software he'd used to examine the footage was the same as was used by military intelligence agencies and how the accuracy rate was over ninety-eight percent. Strikingly, Franklin allowed the answer to stand.

'Now I *am* asking for your opinion as an expert, Mr Gross. How could that footage have been faked to make it appear that Mr Reeves was tampering with the cables?'

Mason leaned forward. This was his professional comfort zone. 'It's actually fairly easy, but I will admit that it's done extremely well here, and on first glance I would have thought the footage was organic. But what has been done is that someone has taken footage of Mr Reeves, probably taken from the same phone or one just like it, isolated his image from the background he would have been in when that was taken, and transplanted it onto this footage of what was probably a shot of the crane with no one in front of it, making it look like he was there doing something he was not.'

'Like Photoshop,' I said.

'Yes, but considerably more sophisticated.' Never tell a tech geek that the average person can do something he can do much, much better.

'Just to be clear: What we're seeing here is *not* Robert Reeves pouring hydrochloric acid on the steel cables of the crane. Is that correct?'

'Yes. That's not what it is at all. It's footage taken of him at another time and in another place, although the lighting has been expertly manipulated to make it look like he's in the park. My best guess is that he's pouring cream into his coffee.' The spectators chuckled.

I thanked Mason and let Renfro have his turn, which consisted of asking if the things Mason had stated as fact were actually opinions (and being told no) and whether the lack of video footage of Reeves sabotaging the cables was proof that he hadn't at some other time, to which I objected because Mason wasn't an expert on *that* subject, and Franklin agreed with me.

Nate and Marta arrived while Renfro was questioning Mason, which worked out perfectly for me. I called Marta to the stand and she was sworn in without objection from Renfro, which was refreshing.

'Mrs Drake,' which was what Marta had asked to be called, 'were you in the process of divorcing the victim, Mr Drake, when he died?'

'Yes. I had filed the papers about three weeks before.'

'Why were you and your husband planning to divorce?'

Marta and I had already been through this conversation but not in front of a jury. 'He was seeing other women and I was getting tired of it,' she answered.

'Was there one woman in particular who was the impetus of your filing for divorce?'

Marta sat back in the witness chair, much as she had relaxed into the cushion of her seat on her porch when we'd spoken last. 'Not really,' she said after a moment. 'There had been a lot. You're told that's going to happen when you marry a stuntman. You don't believe it when you're young but then it happens. A lot.'

'So the rumors about Mr Drake having an affair with Robert Reeves's wife Tracy were not the reason, in particular. Is that right?'

'It wasn't a rumor. I saw them together. But no, that's not why. I mean, it *was*, but not just because of her. If it had just been her, I would have made Jim go into couples therapy or something. It was the number of them over the years. I'm not even sure she was the only one he was . . . seeing at the time.'

I took a deep breath and it wasn't just because I wanted to be certain I could be heard. This was going to be the real moment of truth for my case and I needed to get it right. I also needed to ask a question to which I *thought* I knew the answer, but I couldn't be sure. It was a dangerous ploy, but I figured Reeves wasn't looking especially innocent and the trial was getting close to an end. I had to take the chance.

'Mrs Drake, you said you had seen your husband with the woman he was seeing when you filed for divorce.'

'Yes. Tracy Reeves.' Marta looked like she was wondering why I was asking her this question again.

'Where?'

'In a restaurant we used to go to called Italia!,' she said. You could hear the exclamation point in her voice. 'Jim and I went there pretty often when we were first married. I went there for dinner one night and he was there with her. I hadn't filed for divorce yet so it came as a bit of a surprise, I'll say.'

'Did he introduce her to you?'

Marta's face contorted into a mask of disbelief. 'Of *course* not!' she said. 'I got out of there as fast as I could, went home and ordered a pizza. And then I ate it myself, with two frozen daquiris.'

I nodded, as if I cared what she'd been drinking almost a year before. There was no more build-up; this was it. 'Mrs Drake, do you see the woman your husband was with at that restaurant in the courtroom today?'

Marta pretended she hadn't been looking right at her the whole time she'd been on the stand, and made a point of scanning the courtroom, looking from the right side to the left. She looked right past Alice Mandrill and focused her gaze back on the row right behind the defense table. 'Yes,' she said.

'Would you point her out to the court, please?'

Marta raised her right hand and pointed straight behind my table in the courtroom, as I'd expected. '*Her*,' she said.

'Your Honor,' I said, 'may the record show that the witness is pointing at Penny Kanter.'

THIRTY-EIGHT

Renfro did his best to discredit Marta's testimony. After all, he was still basing his prosecution on the idea that Robert Reeves had killed James Drake because Drake was having an affair with one of Reeves's wives. The idea that he *hadn't* cared when he found out Drake was sleeping with his wife but *did* when it turned out he was also *shtupping* Penny meant Reeves would have to be jealous of a man having an affair with his assistant, which quite frankly wasn't that compelling.

'You said you'd only seen the woman you thought was Mrs Reeves once,' he asked Marta. 'That was why you thought Ms Kanter was in fact Mrs Reeves? You never even saw a picture of her in the newspapers after your husband had been murdered?'

'I didn't watch any of the coverage,' Marta said. 'I knew it would be upsetting to me and probably distorted. I did love Jim once, you know.'

'Wasn't it possible that your husband was just having a friendly dinner with Ms Kanter when you saw them in the restaurant and was still involved in an intimate relationship with Mrs Reeves?'

'Possible, sure,' Marta said. 'I mean, I don't think he'd ever had something going with two women at a time before, but anything's possible. Except they weren't having a "friendly dinner" when I saw them. They could barely keep their hands off each other.'

Reeves had been staring at Penny in shock since Marta had pointed her out from the stand. He hadn't looked anywhere near this upset when there had been testimony about his supposed wife Alice Mandrill (Tracy) sleeping with the stuntman. I hoped Renfro wouldn't notice and start shifting his case toward the theory that Reeves killed Drake because he couldn't stand the thought of the guy with his assistant.

Penny, for her part, looked very much like she wanted to bolt for the door but couldn't.

'And you're certain it wasn't Mrs Reeves you saw with your husband?' Now Renfro was grasping at straws; the two women didn't resemble each other at all. He pointed at Mandrill.

Marta acknowledged this by making a raspberry sound with her lips that was probably involuntary. 'I'd never seen that woman in my life before I walked into court today,' she said. 'And no, there's no way I'd mistake that one' (Penny) 'for *that* one' (Mandrill).

'No further questions,' Renfro said. Why get himself in more trouble?

Angie, whose jaw had dropped a couple of feet when Marta outed Penny, was now grinning because she thinks I'm the same kind of lawyer Patrick used to play on *Legality*, a theatrical, flamboyant attorney who manipulates the true culprit into confessing on the witness stand. I figured I was about to prove her wrong and hoped it didn't diminish me in her eyes.

Patrick, for his part, was watching me, not the witnesses or Reeves, with an expression that indicated nothing could diminish me in *his* eyes. That felt like an awesome responsibility, but it couldn't be my focus now. I had a couple more pieces to fit into the jigsaw puzzle.

'The defense recalls Alice Mandrill,' I said.

The ostensible Mrs Reeves, who looked less stunned than everybody else, probably because she hadn't figured out what was going on yet, walked to the witness stand swinging her hips a little more than was necessary, given that no hip-swinging was called for. Once reminded that she'd taken an oath to tell the truth, she took on a look of solemnity and nodded with great conviction. She folded her hands in her lap like a good schoolgirl and looked at me.

'Ms Mandrill,' I began.

'Mrs Reeves,' Mandrill corrected me.

I looked at Nate and he shook his head. 'I don't think so,' I said. 'We have information indicating that the so-called marriage license you signed in Tijuana is not a legal document there or in the United States.'

Nate smiled with satisfaction. That was what he'd meant.

'Yeah it is,' Mandrill said just as Renfro, predictably, objected.

'Can you produce this documentation, Ms Moss?' Franklin asked.

Nate stood up and handed me a piece of paper that had obviously been printed out from an email. The address of the sender was (in Spanish, which I don't speak) the office of the mayor of Tijuana, indicating, with the help of the court's Spanish translator, that the establishment handing out such 'licenses' was a roadside gift shop not imbued with the authority to perform legal marriages. Renfro tried to object but Franklin apparently *did* speak Spanish, agreed to the authenticity of the document that had been scanned, and overruled him.

'Ms Mandrill,' I began again. She did not offer an argument. 'Did you actually have a physical relationship with James Drake? Remember that you are under oath and a conviction on a charge of perjury can result in a sentence of up to four years in prison.'

Mandrill had the nerve to look insulted. 'Of course I did. Jimmy and I did it a bunch of times.'

Marta, sitting in the third row, rolled her eyes a little. Just a little.

'And were you aware when this relationship was happening that Mr Drake was also involved sexually with Penny Kanter?'

Mandrill thought about that. 'No. But I wouldn't have cared. It was just fun.'

'And you didn't care that he was married?'

'That was his problem, not mine. Besides, he was getting divorced.'

'Did you think he was going to marry you once he divorced?' I asked.

Mandrill actually laughed out loud and I thought it was genuine. 'No! I didn't want to marry that guy. Besides, I was already . . .' She wisely didn't finish that sentence.

'Do you know if Mr Drake told Penny Kanter about the relationship he had with you?'

'I didn't know about her so how would I know if she knew about me?' Mandrill said. And she had a decent point.

Renfro had nothing to ask Mandrill so now it was time for the main event.

'The defense calls Penny Kanter.'

I had looked it up, by the way, and the name on her birth certificate was indeed 'Penny Kanter'. Not Penelope. A name like Penny makes you realize how much you are valued by your parents, I'm guessing.

She stood up from behind her boss wearing an expression that resembled the love child of Lieutenant Trench and Droopy Dog. If a two-by-four could walk and sit in a chair, it could very well have been Penny Kanter. She was sworn in and agreed to tell the truth with an intonation giving the impression that she was being asked her favorite breakfast cereal by an auditor for the IRS.

I walked over to her but did not lean in. I didn't want to appear too friendly. They get dangerous when they're cornered.

'Ms Kanter, what do you do for a living?' I knew and you knew but the jury didn't know.

'I am the executive assistant to Mr Robert Reeves.' Still the proud employee protecting her mentor. I knew better.

'And in that capacity, you were present with Mr Reeves on the film sets where he was directing, is that correct?'

'Yes. Mr Reeves hardly ever went anywhere without me because I was in charge of his scheduling, his meetings and his budget.' She didn't make him breakfast in the morning but I'm not sure didn't want to.

'So you were a fixture on the set of *Desert Siege*?' Penny didn't see it coming yet but she *had* to know her nice-little-functionary act wasn't going to cut it much longer.

'I was there whenever Mr Reeves was there.' She didn't want to admit to being there when Reeves wasn't present. There was time for that.

'Is that where you met James Drake?' I asked.

'I met Burke Henderson and all of the stunt performers,' Penny answered.

'There has been testimony heard in this court that you and Mr Drake were having a romantic relationship,' I said. 'Did that start when you met him on the set?'

When did you stop beating your wife, Senator?

The real question here was whether Penny would admit to the affair or commit perjury. She was an intelligent woman and chose the former. 'We began dating about a month before shooting began,' she said through tight lips. 'Mr Reeves had met with the stunt crew because it was such an action-heavy picture, and Jim asked me out right at that meeting.'

'How long did the relationship last?'

'Until Jim died.' It was too many months later for her to sob uncontrollably at the thought, so Penny just looked upset. For her.

'Did Jim tell you that he was also seeing the woman he thought of as Tracy Reeves?' I asked. 'You were obviously aware that Alice Mandrill was playing that role.' Renfro started to raise a hand, thought better of it, and scratched himself behind the ear like a cocker spaniel.

The two-by-four regained its expressionless manner. 'No. He didn't tell me he was seeing anyone else.'

'But since you were a fixture on the set surely you had heard the rumors. We've heard testimony that everyone in the company knew about Jim Drake and Tracy Reeves.'

At the defense table, Robert Reeves was probably more agitated than I'd ever seen him, even when people were claiming from the witness stand that he had deliberately murdered a stunt performer on a film he was directing. He couldn't hold still and was looking all around the courtroom, anywhere but where I was standing and Penny was sitting. He crossed and re-crossed his legs three times as I waited for Penny's reply.

She pursed her lips but kept her tone neutral. 'You hear all sorts of rumors about everybody on a movie set,' she said. 'For example, I heard a rumor that Patrick McNabb was going to marry his real-estate broker. I guess that one was wrong.'

It actually wasn't at the time but I wasn't getting into the cat box with Penny. 'So you didn't believe the rumors that you heard about Jim Drake and Tracy Reeves?' I said, equally businesslike.

Renfro had been itching to object, so here it came. 'Your Honor, I'm not aware of any charges having been filed against Ms Kanter. Is she on trial here?'

'I think this goes to reasonable doubt, Judge.' The ground I was standing on was shaky but it wasn't going to cave in. 'I'm not charging anyone with anything.'

'A good thing, since you do not have that authority,' Franklin said by way of warning. 'I'm going to allow this line of questioning, but only so far, Ms Moss.'

'Understood, Your Honor.' I turned back toward Penny. 'Did you believe the rumors about Jim Drake having a relationship with someone other than you?' I asked again.

'Well, he was still married, but I didn't pay any attention to the stuff about Mr Reeves's wife because I knew she wasn't really Mr Reeves's wife.'

That didn't make a ton of sense but I didn't want to beat it into the ground. 'So you weren't jealous of Alice Mandrill,' I said. 'Is that correct?'

'No. I mean yes, it's correct. I wasn't jealous.'

Switch gears and get to the nuts and bolts. Almost literally. 'Ms Kanter, the night before the stunt in question was to be rehearsed, the night before Jim Drake died falling from that crane, where were you?'

Renfro was on his feet again. 'Your Honor,' was all he said.

I spoke before Franklin could tell me we weren't trying Penny Kanter, as if I didn't know that. But Trench was taking notes on his tablet at the back of the room. 'Your Honor, as Mr Reeves's executive assistant, Ms Kanter would surely know if he was present on the set at the time in question and whether he could have sabotaged the cables. I think that's relevant to this case, don't you?'

Franklin hadn't been anticipating that, so it took him a moment to think. 'Yes I do,' he said. 'Proceed, Ms Moss, but only try *this* case.' Renfro sat down without shoving his arms up into the air in frustration and that was probably his biggest accomplishment of the day.

'Where were you the night before James Drake died?' I asked again.

'I was on the set with Mr Reeves, seeing to details and making sure all the plans were set,' Penny said. 'If you're going to ask, I didn't have any conversations with Jim that night at all.'

'I wasn't going to ask,' I said. I actually *had* been planning to go in that direction but I can be flexible. 'Were you with Robert Reeves the whole night?'

Penny flashed her eyes at me with something approximating anger. 'Not the *whole* night,' she said.

'My apologies; I meant no insinuation. Were you there the whole time he was on the set?'

'Of course.'

'Did you ever see him approach the cables and pour something that smelled really bad on them?'

'No.'

'So the video we showed here in court was false?'

'I can only guess.'

'And did you leave when Mr Reeves left, just around midnight?' I asked.

'Yes.'

I had two areas to get to and this was one of them. 'Ms Kanter, we've obtained records from the security supervisor, Mr Armbruster, about the comings and goings of personnel on the set that night and they're very accurate. So please answer this question carefully: Did you return to the Griffith Park set that night between midnight and five thirty a.m.?'

Penny's eyes bulged so slightly that I think I was the only one close enough to see it happen. To be honest, Armbruster's records had not indicated that Penny had come back but I figured she'd somehow gotten around it, possibly by swiping someone else's card to regain entry. But she didn't know that.

'Um . . . yes. I went back around three to check on preparations for the camera equipment because Mr Reeves had forgotten to do that before he left.'

'Had he asked you to drop in at three in the morning?' I added a touch of incredulity to my voice, intimating that Penny must have had a very unreasonable boss.

'No. I took it upon myself to do that. I knew everyone would be back in less than four hours and wanted to be sure everything was set.'

'Very conscientious of you. When you started in the entertainment business, you didn't set out to be an executive assistant, did you?' I asked.

'No.'

'In fact, your goal was to work in digital effects, wasn't it?'

'That's right.' Penny wasn't going to volunteer anything.

'You had studied computer-generated graphics and other effects in college, hadn't you?'

Penny nodded and Franklin made her say, 'Yes,' for the record.

'Ms Kanter, how is Mr Reeves to work for?'

She looked confused. 'I'm sorry?'

'As a boss. Is he kind? Does he understand when you have to take a day off to visit an ailing relative?'

Penny shifted in the chair. 'He understood.'

'But he didn't let you go, did he?'

'It was a shooting day and he needed me there,' Penny said. 'It wasn't a big deal.'

'Didn't your mother pass away the next morning without your being there to see her one last time?' I said. You can get people in a production company to tell you anything as long as it's not about them.

'She was unconscious,' Penny answered. 'She wouldn't have known I was there.'

'Has Mr Reeves ever thrown anything at you?' I said.

Renfro didn't object. Making Reeves look bad, I'm sure he thought, would only help his case.

'Thrown something?' Penny knew exactly what I was referencing and didn't want to answer me.

'Yes. I'm told he threw a full can of diet soda at you because you'd gotten the wrong brand from the vending machine. Is that true?'

'It didn't hit me,' she said quietly.

'But he did throw it.'

'Tossed,' Penny said. 'He tossed it. So I could exchange it for a Pepsi Zero.'

'And you weren't angry at him?

'No.'

'Never? Not that you might want to make it look like he'd done something wrong? So he'd get the blame?'

'Objection!' Renfro was no idiot.

'Sustained. Ms Moss!'

'Apologies, Your Honor. Ms Kanter,' I continued, 'do you belong to an online group called EACH, for the Executive Assistants Cocktail Hour?'

That might have been when Penny saw the trap spring around her but it was too late and she wasn't going to let it show. Her gaze met my eyes and it wasn't a pretty sight: She looked like she wanted me up on that crane with some deteriorating cables.

At the same time, I saw Angie write down the words I'd just said because it sounded like a group she might like to join.

'Yes I do. It's a fun way to talk to other people who have the same job as me in the entertainment industry and might understand what it's like.'

I tried not to look at Reeves. 'You get to let off a little steam about your boss without naming names and everybody can commiserate, right?'

'I don't complain about Mr Reeves, but there are other issues that people in my job might want to talk about, and some of the other assistants do tell stories about their bosses, yes.'

'Of course,' I said. I reminded myself that I couldn't mention Margaret Houlihan's name. 'And people in the group occasionally share files, like pictures and documents or memes that the others might appreciate. Do you ever do that?'

'Sometimes.' Could she know where this was going?

'Ms Kanter, did you share the video I showed here in court with EACH?'

Renfro was on his feet. 'Your Honor, how is this relevant? According to Ms Moss that video isn't even real!'

'I'll withdraw the question, Your Honor, and will refrain from asking Ms Kanter if she had added the computer-generated effects we saw that implicated the defendant.'

'Objection!'

'We're striking that from the record,' Franklin said. 'If you have anything else that's actually relevant to the case against *Mr Reeves*, please proceed.'

'Your Honor, the defense rests.'

And as I walked back to my chair, I swear I saw Trench at the back of the room nod toward me as he walked out.

THIRTY-NINE

Closing statements are always a problem for me. I don't like to write them out and memorize them because I don't want to sound like I'm reading or reciting. I tend to outline some very basic points I want to hit, try to remember *that*, and essentially wing it from there. Sometimes I do well and other times . . . well, it's how I do it and that's not going to change anytime soon.

Renfro had questioned Penny only about what she'd seen and heard on the set of *Desert Siege* and, frankly, it wasn't as scintillating as my questioning of the witness. In fact the only interesting moment came when, in what I could only assume was a moment of desperation, he asked Penny if she would have poured acid on the cables if her boss had ordered her to do so. Penny, publicly loyal to the end, said no.

For my part, I hadn't proved that she'd gotten hold of hydrochloric acid and spent time overnight pouring it on the steel cables to make James Drake fall and die. I hadn't proved that she was jealous of Drake's affairs with Mandrill and who knows how many other women. I hadn't even proved that she'd tried to frame Robert Reeves with the doctored video, which ironically had impressed her boss so much it might have gotten her hired as a computer-generated imagery technician on Reeves's next film.

But I didn't have to do any of that. All I had to establish was reasonable doubt. For the first time since I'd taken this case, I felt confident that my client was not guilty. Now all I had to do was convince twelve total strangers.

Try it sometime.

I don't like to open with, 'Ladies and gentlemen of the jury.' That sounds so Perry Mason. I just dive in.

'This case is about perception,' I began. 'People heard rumors and that created a perception about the accused that was considerably less complicated than the truth, we've discovered. Even in my office, we saw a video of the crime scene and almost believed what we saw until experts showed us how it could be – no, *was* – faked.

'The idea that Robert Reeves killed James Drake out of jealous rage is ridiculous. Mr Reeves is not married to the woman who was pretending to be his wife, and they had no personal relationship. He had no reason to be jealous.

'The perception that Mr Reeves poured hydrochloric acid on the steel cables that were to hold James Drake in place comes from more falsehoods. The video was faked, as we heard. We might know who performed that technical wizardry, and we might not.' I saw Renfro think about objecting and decide against when I said that last part. 'But we know that he didn't come back every two hours to keep the deterioration of the cables from being detected because we have the records of the security personnel in charge of the Griffith Park set. Robert Reeves wasn't there for close to six hours before the incident occurred and Mr Drake died. He couldn't have performed the sabotage.

'Remember that the system under which our laws operate contains the concept of reasonable doubt. I'm sure Judge Franklin will explain that very clearly in his charge when you're ready to deliberate. But it is just what it sounds like. If you have any doubt in your mind that Robert Reeves deliberately killed James Drake, and that doubt is not unreasonable, or in other words, you don't have to rationalize major parts of your thinking to make it work, then your choice is clear. You must vote for acquittal.'

Reeves was sitting quietly in his gray suit, blue dress shirt and black tie, the most conservative, uninteresting clothing I could convince him to wear. I'd given him no instructions on how to behave at this moment because, frankly, I had no delusion that he would listen to me. So far he'd simply sat there, looking mostly at the legal pad in front of him and not writing anything.

The trick for me was to make each juror feel like I'd looked directly into their eyes without seeming like I was trying to do that because it's kind of creepy. I didn't smile warmly. I wanted the jurors to know this was serious business. Some lawyers want to be the jurors' friend. I want to be their conscience.

'I can't tell you who poured that acid, more than ten times, on the cables, because we don't have definitive proof. Many people might have had motives, including witnesses you've seen testify here in court. Some of them might have had access. Anyone can get hydrochloric acid, readily and cheaply. No. I'm not going to provide you with the actual culprit and you have to remember that's not your job here.

'Your task is a difficult one, but it doesn't include finding the murderer. What you have to do is consider all the evidence you've seen and heard, and then determine in your own mind whether there's reasonable doubt of the claim that Robert Reeves was the person responsible for James Drake's death. I think we've all seen enough to have that reasonable doubt, and more. I think you should vote to acquit. And I thank you for your attention today and throughout the trial. You've all done great work. Keep that going in the jury room.'

(In fact I had seen at least three jurors nod off during some of the testimony. One was definitely flirting with the juror to her left, who might have been interested. Another had snuck one air pod into his left ear, away from the bench, and for all I know was listening to a podcast about this trial during the trial.)

I sat down and patted Reeves on the hand. He did not move.

'Now comes the waiting. That's the hard part,' I whispered to him.

He picked up the pen in front of him and wrote on the legal pad.

This was the easy part?

FORTY

'Is it good or bad that they only deliberated for two hours?' Angie asked.

'In my experience it's usually bad for the defendant,' I answered.

I was lying. The fact of the matter is that no attorney has the vaguest idea of what a short, or for that matter long, deliberation by a random jury could mean for a case. Everybody's seen *12 Angry Men* and thought it was a documentary. But if I told Angie I didn't know, she'd think I was lying, so I lied to make her think I was telling the truth.

'You're lying,' she said. Angie can always tell. There's never any point. She has powers.

'Well, the truth is I have no idea.'

'You're still lying.' You can't win for losing. Whatever that means.

We'd been sitting there for ten minutes since Marty the bailiff had informed us that the jury had reached a verdict and we'd be needed back in court. It was admittedly something of a surprise they'd decided so quickly but, as I said, it wasn't indicative of anything in particular.

Robert Reeves, sitting immediately to my right, was visibly nervous. He leaned over and whispered to me, despite the fact that court wasn't yet in session. 'What kind of sentence could I get?' he asked.

This was the first time the question had crossed his mind. 'It's a murder case, Robert.'

He paled. 'You mean it could be execution?' I thought he might pass out at the table, which would thrill the small battalion of news photographers and videographers in the room.

'No, Robert. They haven't executed anyone in California in sixteen years and counting. But it's still possible to get life imprisonment.' I probably shouldn't have said that but, seriously, this is when he chose to ask?

'Oh.' He sat back and stared straight ahead. Just as well.

Patrick caused a minor scene by walking into the courtroom carrying a fairly large box that I assumed had made it through the metal detectors at the entrance but still looked very odd. But I didn't get a chance to ask him about it because Franklin was entering the room and we all had to stand up. I've tried rising when they say 'rise', but this is as high off the ground as I can get.

Across the aisle from me Renfro looked very businesslike. *He* didn't have a client who could go to jail for life, so his heart probably wasn't attempting to beat its way through his chest wall. But I was just guessing.

Franklin didn't waste any time after we'd all settled back into our seats. 'Ladies and gentlemen of the jury, I am informed that you have reached a verdict. Is that correct?'

The jury's foreperson, Juror #7, stood up. She was a woman of around fifty and was actually wearing pearls. 'Yes it is, Your Honor.' She'd probably been rehearsing that for an hour, and delivered it well.

'Please hand your verdict to the bailiff.' Juror #7 did as instructed and Marty walked the small piece of paper, folded over, to Franklin, who took it from his hand and unfolded it. He glanced at it then folded it back over again.

Now, for the record, there is no reason at all aside from theatrics that the verdict has to be read first by the judge. It's a perk for the court that they get to know before everyone else. The judge can't change the jury's verdict. They can set one aside if they think something completely outside the rule of law has been done, but that is extremely rare and almost certainly grounds for an appeal, and knowing the verdict for an extra thirty seconds before the rest of the assemblage probably wouldn't add all that much to the deliberation process.

Franklin handed the paper back to Marty who brought it directly back to Juror #7, just to underline the absolute lack of necessity in the whole ritual. 'Madame Foreperson, what is the verdict of this jury?'

Reeves took in a deep breath through an O-shaped mouth. Patrick fingered the lid of the box he was carrying. Angie was sitting with her elbows resting on the rail between us, chin propped up on her hands.

Penny was not present, oddly having been dismissed from her employment with Reeves before the jury began its deliberation. And he told me he was sorry to let her go as she'd been the best assistant he'd ever had.

I'm asking you.

Nate was sitting near the back of the room. He likes to be there when the trial ends and this was our first jury verdict together. He looked exactly like Nate.

Juror #7 stood proudly and read what she already knew from the scrap of paper. 'The jury finds the defendant Robert Reeves not guilty of all charges.'

There wasn't the 'spontaneous' outburst of applause that you're used to from the movies. Instead there was chatter, like a large group of people mumbling, and the sound of cameras taking pictures. Alice Mandrill aka Tracy Reeves stood up from her spectator's seat and left the courtroom. I never saw her again.

The real Mrs Reeves, Stacy, was nowhere to be found. She was off somewhere not looking young enough, one supposed.

Her husband smiled but did not speak. I don't shake hands anymore but extended my elbow for bumping. He looked at it for a moment and then stuck his own out and we touched elbows. It was the closest Robert Reeves would ever come to thanking me for keeping him out of jail.

Franklin thanked the jury for their time and effort, ordered the officer of the court to release Reeves (who hadn't been in custody but they say that) and raised his gavel to declare the business of the court completed.

When he pounded it on the surface of the bench, at that very moment, there came a loud BANG from somewhere behind me, in the general vicinity of Patrick. My heart stopped beating. I'd heard gunshots before.

But that's not what this was.

I forced myself to look back. Patrick had lifted the lid on the box he'd carried in and it had somehow caused an explosion of sorts: Confetti was *everywhere*, some even floating down on me from fifteen feet away. And the box held a sign that read, 'Congratulations!'

He looked at me and beamed. 'Sandy!'

I could not answer fast enough. Franklin, the notorious neat freak, was looking over the paper-covered remains of his courtroom and somehow still managed to croak out, 'Ms Moss . . .'

FORTY-ONE

Angie made me buy a dress.

I thought I could go to the 'official' premiere of *Desert Siege* wearing a business suit like the ones I wore in court all the time, but she informed me that, 'slinky is definitely the rule of the day.' I didn't think I could pull off *slinky*, but Angie made me buy a shiny dress anyway. So, feeling conspicuous and constricted, I showed up on Patrick's arm at the red carpet, which smelled exactly as I'd remembered, only this time it wasn't a daydream.

After the interchange we'd had in court about living together, there had been a spate of press about Patrick and me in which I had assiduously refused to participate, first saying it would make me seen less professional during a murder trial, and afterwards using the excuse that I just really didn't want to. Patrick had been fine with it, Reeves had been a little prissy because I wasn't helping to promote his movie, and I got to not be asked what Patrick might be like in 'intimate moments', all of which was good.

In the previous week, no arrest had been made in the murder of James Drake, but I knew that Trench was gathering evidence and word was that he was focusing (surprise!) on Penny Kanter. He had told me the police were watching her pretty continu-ously, which meant I did not need to fear her and so I'd had a tearful goodbye with Judy, who had nodded at me without moving a facial muscle and sent a bill to my law firm.

Maybe 'tearful' was overstating it.

Interview requests had been constant at first, but I'd avoided all I could and only done those that focused on the case. That was relevant. Patrick and me, well, that wasn't.

Tonight, however, we were fair game.

'Sandra!' (Some of the press had only read my name in articles from others in the press.) 'Mrs McNabb!' (Others were just uninformed.) 'Hey you!' (That was more like it; I almost stopped to let that guy take my picture.)

'Just keep walking and look for friendly faces,' Patrick said, holding my left hand and making sure I didn't pause. Ever.

There were friendly faces in the crowd because Patrick had arranged for passes to the premiere and made sure virtually everyone I knew in Los Angeles was there, which admittedly was still a fairly small but congenial group. Nate Garrigan, in the company of a woman I had not met but who was, refreshingly, age-appropriate for him, stood by looking like he was in line for a Disneyland ride that was either going to be awesome or embarrassing. He held up a hand in the Nate version of a wave.

Angie was, of course, working the event as Patrick's assistant, eyes down at her iPad and legs appearing in the slits of her skirt as she walked. Angie does not let an opportunity go by if she might meet a man she might find interesting. And she found all of show business interesting.

I didn't, for the most part, but pretended to because I did find Patrick interesting. He had seen to it that any press requests for him also included Robert Reeves, who might have become a pariah in town despite his acquittal. He let Reeves do much of the talking, and tonight the director was, of course, present at the premiere of his film but also enjoying a little more of the spotlight than his lead actor, who didn't seem to mind that at all.

Patrick did have to submit to the red carpet 'interviews', which were akin to a press gaggle for a corrupt politician (or is that redundant?). He was periodically surrounded by four or five reporters, TV light suddenly coming to life, microphones appearing seemingly from out of the sky but strangely attached to the arms of people I couldn't really see for the lights. Luckily Patrick answered the questions directed at me too because he knew I was averse to that sort of thing. I didn't want to be on the covers of tabloids as Patrick McNabb's girlfriend. To be honest, I didn't want to be on the covers of tabloids at all.

'We wanted it to be a fun ride for the audience,' Patrick was saying in one of the patented responses I'd heard him practice three other times. 'We have that message about global warming but this is not at all an issue movie. It's all about the action, really.'

'What about the guy who died?' Reporters can be so sensitive. 'Was making the movie worth that happening?'

As a layperson, my response to such a rude question would normally be to ask Angie to hit that person for me. But Patrick was used to the game and his face took on a somber quality. 'Of course not,' he said. 'That was a bloody tragedy but we couldn't have foreseen it. Would I erase this movie to get Jim Drake back? Of course I would. But that's sadly not at all possible. OK, that's all.' He moved on from the spot.

The promised land, which in this case was the inside of the huge auditorium where the film would once again be shown, was only about twenty yards away, and I was starting to feel the relief that would come once we were inside in its air-conditioned, completely controlled atmosphere. No press in there until after the movie, and then Patrick would be onstage and I'd be in the wings letting him handle this stuff because it was his job and not mine.

A few steps later I heard a shrill, angry voice scream, 'Sandra Moss!' with such vehemence that even having heard Patrick's advice I felt compelled to turn and look. 'You ruined my life!'

It was just like the daydream, but this time I knew the person yelling at me. It was a voice I'd heard only once but one that had stuck with me because of the circumstances. I hadn't called her to the witness stand, but Stacy Reeves was a memorable woman. I'd thought I knew why but obviously I had been mistaken.

Because right now she was ten feet away from me and holding a carving knife. Since there was no food at the event and there-fore nothing to carve, the message was stomach-droppingly clear.

Stacy wanted to kill me.

'What did you *do*?' she wailed as people noticed the scene and a few screamed. There was much running. 'You got him *off*!'

Robert Reeves, fifty feet from me, looked over and seemed to vaguely recognize the woman with the deadly weapon advancing on me. He did nothing.

Patrick, on the other hand, placed himself between me and Stacy, causing her to weave back and forth trying to find an open lane to fillet me through. She clearly didn't want to kill Patrick.

'Isn't that what you wanted?' I said. And out of the corner of my eye I saw the blond-haired man who had helped kidnap Angie and me. Things were happening too fast. I needed a moment to absorb it all. But I didn't seem to have that long.

'No! He was supposed to get convicted and then I could have all the money without having to be married to him!'

'That's what divorce is for,' Patrick said. He's so helpful.

'I signed a *pre-nup*! I was getting *nothing*! But if he was in jail I could have had it all!' Stacy looked at me around Patrick's head. 'What did you *do*?'

My job, I wanted to say, but that wasn't going to get me anywhere. 'I thought you were happy with Robert,' I tried. Maybe I could convince her there was no reason to off the lawyer, especially after the trial was over.

Deranged angry people, however, are notoriously hard to convince verbally. 'He made me hide in that house because I was too old!' she moaned. 'And I'm three years *younger* than him!'

'I agree, the emphasis on youth and beauty is ridiculous in this business,' I said. 'Why don't we figure out a way to sue him for . . .'

But Stacy suddenly faked to the left and Patrick was caught off guard. She saw the opening and leapt forward. I raised my fists, as if that was going to stop what I was sure was a very sharp, very efficient knife. If I was going down, I wasn't going down quietly. I yelled.

In my peripheral vision I saw security making their way toward me but they were swimming upstream against the tide of partygoers running away in hysterics. They weren't going to get there in time. I told myself that – no matter what – I was going to keep my eyes open. Stacy's face filled my vision. I reached my right fist back and wound up.

The punch never landed. In fact, it was never thrown. Over my right shoulder I heard Angie yell, 'Sandy, *duck!*' and I always do what Angie says. But I kept my eyes open. So I saw a hole open up in Stacy's arm and I saw the knife drop to the ground. I lunged at it and picked it up as the security officer arrived.

'What happened?' he asked.

'I'm her security officer,' Angie said, and she walked into my line of sight. In her hand was literally a smoking gun. I'd forgotten she had it. 'Chekhov's gun,' I said to her.

Angie looked at me, not understanding. 'Chekhov carried a phaser.' She turned the handgun around so the barrel was facing toward her and gave it to the security guy, who was almost immediately joined by a uniformed LAPD officer. Stacy, still standing but with a bleeding arm, was already being restrained by another.

'What were you aiming for?' I asked Angie.

'Her head. You can't fool around with this stuff.'

FORTY-TWO

Lieutenant Trench showed up at the premiere maybe five minutes after all the excitement and no, I don't mean the movie. In his impeccably pressed suit and perfectly complementary tie he questioned the cops at the scene and then walked over to Patrick, Angie and me.

'We really must stop meeting like this,' he said.

'I wouldn't mind,' I told him.

'Apparently Mrs Reeves is a trifle irritated with you for successfully defending her husband in court,' the lieutenant went on. 'She had hoped to scare you off with faux kidnappings and artificial bombs made by her husband's prop department for what they thought was a surprise birthday party.' Trench's tone was one not of skepticism but of disappointment in what human beings might do or think. He believed in order. Stacy Reeves apparently had put her trust in chaos.

'Where did she find the men who kidnapped Sandy and me?' Angie asked.

'Believe it or not, Central Casting. They thought they were auditioning for Mr Reeves's next film as a gang of thugs.'

'They were very convincing,' I said. 'I hope they get work.'

'I'm very grateful to you, Lieutenant,' Patrick said. 'And I'm grateful to Angie for not letting Mrs Reeves kill Sandy.'

'There will be an investigation, but I doubt charges will be brought,' Trench said, looking at Angie. 'The gun was licensed and you were registered as a security officer.' He kept looking at her face, something many men have trouble doing. 'Clearly you were here in an undercover capacity.'

'I was invited,' Angie said.

'Of course.'

'Is Penny Kanter going to be arrested for killing Jim Drake?' Patrick asked.

'Mr McNabb, it is against LAPD policy for me to speculate on who *might* be arrested for any crime,' Trench said. Then he turned toward me. 'But if your phone rings and Ms Kanter is on the other end, it might be a business call.'

I gestured to Trench to step away. 'Lieutenant, may I have a word?' I thought he'd like it if I said it in as formal a manner as possible.

He tilted his head. 'Ms Moss.'

Patrick and Angie backed off as Trench and I found a safe haven behind the temporary police tape, beyond which I could see Robert Reeves actually getting into the ambulance to accompany his wife to the emergency room and then, presumably, jail.

'Lieutenant,' I said, 'I had a feeling during this case that you . . . disapproved of me.'

Trench's eyes, never exactly huge, narrowed a bit. 'Is there a question in there, Counselor?'

'I respect you and don't want you to disapprove,' I said carefully. 'I wanted to know why you stopped talking to me.'

'Ms Moss,' the cop said, 'I believe your estimation of the time I spend thinking about you might be a trifle inflated.'

'Come on, Trench. You practically threw me out of your office and then you sent Sergeant Roberts with messages. You wanted me to know you thought I was doing something wrong. I'd like to know what.'

Trench looked up at the night sky, or what can be seen of it in a town this well-lit. He breathed in what had, in 1878, been fresh air. 'Ms Moss, it is possible that in our early conversations about this case you were less than completely serious about the circumstances surrounding a man's death and the person accused of causing it. It is possible that I thought you were not putting all your best effort into it and anything less than total professionalism tends to rankle me just a bit. Is that what you meant?'

I let him stand there without an answer for a few seconds then folded my arms. 'Is it also possible that you had been pressured into charging Robert Reeves when you didn't think he was guilty and you were concerned that my lack of *total professionalism* might end up with an innocent man *you arrested* going to jail for a long time? Is that possible?'

'This is LA, Ms Moss. *Everything* is possible.'

FORTY-THREE

The movie was shown that night but I don't remember any of it. I'd seen it before anyway and only watched Patrick because he's Patrick. We said our goodbyes to our friends at a brief party afterward (which we attended so Patrick could make the rounds and perhaps make a connection for a more serious role next time) and left for Patrick's house, where the 'staff' of two people had been given the night off.

Conglomerate Pictures, the studio behind *Desert Siege*, had sent over a bottle of very good champagne, so Patrick and I were on the sofa in front of a fire we didn't need for warmth, drinking the wine and not saying much. We kissed for a while recreationally. I felt very comfortable in his arms and liked the way he brushed my hair out of my eyes.

'So what do you think?' he asked out of nowhere.

I knew what he meant. 'What do I think about what?'

'You know perfectly well what. I've asked you again and again. This is the last time I'll ask. What do you think about moving in here with me? You have me under oath swearing I won't suddenly stop being interested in you, so this is it. Will you move in here or not?'

I closed my eyes for a moment. It wasn't like I hadn't been thinking about it. 'No,' I said.

Patrick sat back on the sofa and a little champagne spilled on his shirt. 'No,' he repeated. 'I wasn't expecting that.'

'I won't move in here, Patrick. The place is cavernous, it's intimidating and it's all yours. I think we should have a place that's *ours.*'

Patrick blinked three times. 'So you will move in, but not here?' he asked.

'That's what I just said, isn't it?'

He leaned forward and took me into his arms again, but tighter. I didn't mind that at all. After a while he laughed lightly. 'You know, you stage-managed that moment beautifully. That was as Hollywood a thing as I've ever seen you do.'

'I know.' I pulled him in a little closer. 'I think I'm starting to get the hang of this.'

CAST OF CHARACTERS

Sandy Moss: A lawyer in Los Angeles transplanted from New Jersey

Angie: Sandy's best friend from Jersey, who came out to LA to visit and stayed

Patrick McNabb: Famous TV actor whom Sandy defended successfully in a murder trial

Detective Lieutenant K.C. Trench: LAPD homicide detective

Nate Garrigan: An investigator sometimes employed by Sandy's law firm

Holiday Wentworth: Sandy's immediate superior at the firm

Cynthia Sutton: Patrick's sister, also an actor

Judge Walter Franklin: Judge, duh

Judge Crater: Mysterious figure of the 1930s, not appearing in this book

Jon Irvin: Sandy's associate

Robert Reeves: Sandy's client, film director and egomaniac

Herbert Bronson: Reeves's former attorney

Jim Drake: Dead stuntman

Burke Henderson: Stunt coordinator

Penny Kanter: Reeves's assistant

Justin Renfro: Assistant DA prosecuting Reeves

Patricia ('Tracy') Reeves, née Alice Virginia Mandrill: Robert Reeves's fourth wife

Dr Sidney Chao: Psychiatric expert witness

Stacy Reeves: Robert Reeves's other wife

Marta Drake: The victim's (estranged) wife

Brady O'Toole: Construction equipment expert

Samuel J. Cogley: (Alleged) mob attorney

Janine McKenzie: Seaton, Taylor receptionist

Margaret Houlihan: Craft services worker and videographer

Michael Armbruster: Security chief

AUTHOR'S NOTES

Sandy Moss came about because of a number of people, not the least of whom is my wife the ex-prosecutor who is, to be honest, nothing like Sandy at all, but is a wonderful role model.

First among the people I must thank is Penny Isaac, the copy editor who makes sure all my typos, misspellings and idiot mistakes are corrected before you get to see them. Sorry about the joke on your name, Penny. Sandy gets a little snarky and forgets briefly who her friends are.

Of course thank you to all at Severn House, particularly Rachel Slatter, Natasha Bell and for the last time Kate Lyall Grant, for believing in Sandy and Patrick and wanting to know what happens next. If only I knew.

My agent and friend Josh Getzler and the team at HG Literary are without question to blame for you reading about Sandy and her posse because I would have given up on the first book in this series long ago but he just wouldn't. It didn't hurt that it was my wife's favorite of everything I've ever written.

I don't claim to be an expert on film production, construction cranes, hydrochloric acid or anything else technical that happens in this book. So please assume that whatever I said about those things is wrong, and what are you doing trying to find out how to drop a man from the top of a crane, anyway?

These past couple of years have been rough on everybody. There have been sacrifices we've all had to make and we haven't been able to spend as much time together as we wish we could. For a writer, being stuck at home is nothing new; we work by ourselves in little rooms pretty much all the time. But this has been different and it's been scary and frustrating and has in some cases brought out the best and the worst in those we know. Keep in mind that some of 'the worst' is because everybody else is scared and frustrated too. But we'll get through it because we really just don't have another choice.

Thank goodness, then, for email and texting and my writer friends who help me get through not just the process of making a (hopefully) coherent mystery novel but also life as it happens. I'm not going to name people here because I'll leave someone out by accident and feel horrible about it every time I see this page for the rest of my life. But you guys know who you are, and you are valued and loved. If you just read this and thought, 'I wonder if he's talking about me,' yes I am.

To the librarians: Since we spoke last my son has joined your ranks, having earned his master's degree in information library science and gotten his first job in the field. I've always appreciated librarians and now it's possible I appreciate them just a little more.

Readers. Ah, readers. Please know that you are constantly being thought and worried about as these books are being created, because you are the people I'm hoping to reach. If this is your first book of mine, welcome and thank you. If it's the 28th, wow it's been some ride, hasn't it? And we're far from done.

E.J. Copperman
Deepest New Jersey
October, 2021